The Primitive

Stephen Amidon was born in Chicago in 1959, and now lives in London with his wife and two children. He is a regular contributor to the *Sunday Times* and *Esquire*. He is also the author of *Splitting the Atom*, *Subdivision* and *Thirst*.

BY THE SAME AUTHOR

Splitting the Atom
Subdivision
Thirst

STEPHEN AMIDON

The Primitive

INDIGO

First published in Great Britain 1995
by Victor Gollancz

This Indigo edition published 1996
Indigo is an imprint of the Cassell Group
Wellington House, 125 Strand, London WC2R 0BB

A catalogue record for this book is
available from the British Library.

ISBN 0 575 40017 X

Printed and bound in Great Britain by
Guernsey Press Co. Ltd,
Guernsey, Channel Isles

96 97 98 99   10 9 8 7 6 5 4 3 2 1

PART ONE

1

David Webster raced down the mountain, roaring past cautious trucks and lumbering Winnebagos, swaying through bends like a downhill skier. He'd slotted the gear stick into neutral several miles back, content to let gravity fuel his descent. It felt good to move so fast, on the brink of being out of control. The pickup that had been on his tail at the summit had long since disappeared from the rearview mirror; the billboards were passing too quickly now to read. He savored the speed, knowing this plummet down the six-mile gradient would be the only good thing about his trip to Elk Run.

His ears popped around the halfway point, though the hush of passing air and the occasional keen of his tires were the only sounds to fill the void. He passed a truck escape lane whose sand wall was dark with recent rain, as uninviting a cushion as the striated granite lining the road. Redwine once claimed that the truckers knew they wouldn't survive these runoffs, that they were only there to keep them from crashing into others. For an instant David pictured himself in that position, brakeless and forced to choose. He wondered about such selflessness, wondered who wouldn't rather take his chances with the slope.

He checked the speedometer. Eighty-eight. Too fast. He pumped the brakes, annoyed at the minuscule delay that meant. It had been a long day and now all he wanted was to get home, crack open a brew and hunker down on his porch until dinner. Watch a video after that, or maybe just go to bed. He'd certainly earned a rest. He'd been up before dawn to attend a long, boring breakfast meeting with Team Elk, the twenty splenetic salesmen who would be selling the resort's golfdominiums and A-frames. After the congealed eggs and lukewarm coffee a motivational counsellor with a dancing Adam's apple had given them an hour-long pep talk, a dizzying succession of bromides, high fives and triumphant whoops. The idea seemed to be that if your value system didn't bring you success then you should trade it in for another. Make the paradigm switch, he kept on saying. Whatever that meant. At one stage he had ten of the salesmen form a human pyramid to illustrate a point about teamwork. David tried to maintain his usual detachment throughout the presentation. After all, he wasn't like these guys. But the atmosphere was infectious, and by the end he was chanting along with everyone else. And hating himself for it.

After that he wandered the resort, passing aimlessly through the dozed foundations and earth-movers and piles of green lumber, a tape recorder held before his mouth like a consumptive's handkerchief as he searched for words that never came. It rained sometime around midmorning, forcing him to retreat to the clubhouse, where Team Elk had been replaced by a squad of rehearsing waitresses. They enlisted David in their charade, putting plates of plastic meats and vegetables in front of him only to snatch them away, time after time, as if he were a character in some obscure myth.

When the weather cleared he continued his stroll, wondering if he was going to have to roam all twelve hundred acres before coming up with those incantatory phrases his boss was after. He stopped to get his raincoat from the car – though it was an unusually warm April day, the brief shower had charged the air with the possibility of greater storms. His meander took him past the golf course, the nascent golfdominiums and unadorned A-frames, the amphitheater that looked like some great dental mold. The site was busy with work and noise, exhaust from back hoes mixing with the pockets of mist tumbling over the mountain. He stopped to watch a machine pull a big stump from the ground, wet clay dripping from its roots like butterscotch from a spoon. He took a breather when he reached the resort's highest point. From here you could see along the deep valley until it curved to the east twenty miles away. David sat there for a long time, transfixed as a gang of thunderheads shouldered through a distant gap in the mountains. They were small yet mean-looking, vivid with light, spluttering with weather.

He became increasingly weary as the morning dragged on, his pessimism about this job deepening with every step he took. Grand Opening was in just a few weeks, when Elk Run's electrified security gates would swing open to let in potential buyers and time sharers. The advertising campaign would be launched with a big insert that was going to impregnate local newspapers a week from Sunday. That was David's baby. Redwine was playing this one close, doing as little pre-selling as possible to jack up demand and prices. He knew he was going to make a killing.

The problem was, though David had the art squared away, he had yet to come up with the copy. He simply didn't have a clue what he was going to write. Redwine demanded something special, something that would make people want to buy in the Carolina mountains instead of the more obvious choices of Florida or Arizona. He'd made his request in such a way that David realized this was it, the pay-off, why he'd been hired. The usual scribbling he did to promote wet T-shirt contests and efficiency apartments wouldn't cut it this time. But as hard as he tried the words just wouldn't come. At two o'clock he decided to call it quits, erasing the few minutes of nonsense he'd consigned to tape, wondering if now, after four years, the shallow well he'd been dipping into was finally running dry. Maybe he really would come up with nothing and Redwine would fire him. As he drove down the mountain, David couldn't bring himself to see that as being such a bad thing.

The road bottomed out and his car reared back, like a swimmer emerging after a long glide. He relaxed his grip on the padded steering wheel, the imitation leather slowly expanding beneath his fingers. The highway was two lanes now, crumbling at the edges, lined by fading billboards that spelled out mile-long sentences for the patient. Smoke Kool Menthols. Relax in Your New Double Wide. Watch Newscenter Twelve. Protect the Unborn. Try Jesus. Head for the Mountains. Dense pine gave way to a continuous scroll of weedy meadow, stoic brick churches and shabby ranch houses. There were barns and mobile homes and, more and more these days, high-tech bunkers housing companies with names full of Zs and Xs. Most of the tobacco fields he passed had gone to seed. Roadkill appeared with the dull regularity of mileage markers, small assemblages of bleached meat, mammal suggested only in flashes of hoof or fur or eye.

Bored with the flatlands, David punched on WBRR. There was only static for a few miles, a strangely entrancing ocean of noise. Then he began to hear the faint echo of his wife's voice. It took him a few seconds of fine tuning to be sure it was her, several more to realize that she was reading a storm warning. The reception was weak so he could only make out the odd word. 'Severe'. 'Three County Area.' 'Force.' He bent forward to check the sky, remembering the squall line he'd seen earlier. The clouds were high and puffy white, nothing like what Mary Beth was describing. She finished the warning and introduced 'The Dream of Gerontius'. He hit the seek button, which landed him on Z93, Kickass Rock. The deejay shouted something about Two for Tuesday. David settled back into his seat. A farmer perched in a tractor waved him by with a weary, pontifical gesture. The mountain suddenly seemed a long way away. He'd be home in less than an hour.

Ten minutes later he rolled to a stop on the shoulder behind a row of parked cars. He stared down the road, shaking his head in frustration. The bridge crossing the Mud River had washed out. A ten-foot section of asphalt was missing, leaving a tangle of bent rods. There was a small knot of people gathered just short of the pulsing brown water. I don't need this, David thought. I really don't. He got out and walked down, surveying the crowd as he approached. There were two state policemen and a dozen citizens, local men with sagging faces, broke-brimmed caps and cheeks distended by wads of tobacco. They nodded. David nodded back. Then everybody looked at the water.

'They say they got four inches in lessen an hour up near Boone,' one said.

'Shee. You don't get four inches in an hour under the ocean.'

'They're sandbagging in Wilkesboro,' the original speaker said defensively.

'Those boys'd sandbag if there's dew,' replied the skeptic, a man with a Shakespeare hat and a glass eye that seemed more receptive than his real one.

Someone spat.

'Anybody hurt?'

'Don't know about hurt but I heard a few got kilt.'

This silenced everyone for a moment. Water continued to pound by.

'Ya'll hear the one about the old fella in the flood?' one of the policemen asked.

Nobody answered.

'Ho boy,' said the second cop. 'Here we go.'

Hats were adjusted and arms crossed; feet shuffled and heads cocked. Then, stillness. The old men had adopted their joke-hearing positions.

'Well, there was this old coot lived alone in a big old house . . . ' the cop said.

'Nah, I heard that one,' said the man with the glass eye.

Without another word he walked to his pickup and drove off. When he was gone everybody turned back to the cop.

'And one day there was a flood,' he continued, undaunted. 'Worst in years. Well, folks started clearing out of town. Except for this particular old fella. He wasn't goin' nowhere. When the water nearly got up to his porch some people came along in a rowboat and said, "Hey old timer, you better git." Well, he just set there in his rocking chair and shook his head. "Nope," he said. "I'm putting my faith in the Lord." So they headed off. Well, the waters rose and rose until the old guy had to go up to the second floor. And another boat came along, one of those power boat deals they got out at Lake Norman. Well, the old guy still wouldn't budge. "No, you go on now, I'm putting my faith in the Lord." Well, the waters rose even higher until he had to go up on the roof. And wouldn't you know it but a helicopter comes along. And they got on the horn and said, "Come on, you old such and such, let us winch you up." But he wouldn't go up. "No, sir," he said. "I'm putting my faith in the Lord."'

The cop paused for effect.

'Well, the water rose even higher and drowned that old timer.' He snapped. 'Just like that. Dead as a doorknob.'

'Nail,' the second cop said.

'That too. And so the old fella's spirit is called unto the Lord and when he gets there he just can't help himself. He gotta ask. "Lord," he says, "why did you forsake me when I put my faith in you above all else?"'

He paused again. The second cop was already smiling.

'"Forsake ye heck," the Lord said. "I *sent* two boats and a helicopter."'

Everyone laughed. For some reason, David laughed the longest.

They all looked at him and he stopped laughing.

'I'm looking for another way back to Burleigh,' he said.

The cop who told the joke gave him directions, placing one hand on his shoulder, making chopping gestures with the other. David thanked him and was about to go when he heard something. Everyone else heard it as well. Coming downstream. A sharp, regular sound like some defective gong. They waited for it. Finally it made the bend. A dog, perched on a small section of corrugated metal. It glared at the unreflecting water, yelping with rhythmic fury. A few of the men whistled but the animal didn't notice. It passed quickly, its metronomic call dopplered by the swift current. A few seconds later it had disappeared downstream.

'You know what that is,' the second cop said.

'What?' David asked when it was clear no one else was going to.

'That's a gone dog.'

The detour took him down a narrow road shaded by occasional arches of trees. It had rained here recently – the asphalt was slick with water that would catch the lowering sun in places, blinding him for an instant. After the first flash he reached for his sunglasses before remembering they'd been stolen a few days earlier as he walked from the office to Kwik Kopy. He'd made the mistake of taking a shortcut through one of the badlands of derelict buildings that now spotted downtown. A pack of kids had materialized, some barely in their teens, all intent on crime. They surrounded David, maneuvering him into an alleyway with their jaunts and shoves before he fully realized he was in danger. Gold teeth flashed; hands were formed into palsied configurations. David hesitated, having seen this so often on screen that he was unable to believe it was truly happening. But then knives were produced, followed by a pistol with a taped handle. It wasn't pointed at him, just displayed, like it were for sale. He'd left his wallet locked in his desk at the office so they stripped him of everything else – his watch, his wedding ring, his sunglasses, even the envelope filled with 8 × 10s of model homes. It was over before he had time to get scared.

Now, eyes unprotected, David tried to follow the detour. But for some reason he couldn't remember the cop's directions. He came to a few intersections, made some choices. The roads became more remote and before long he began to suspect that he was lost, heading north instead of east. He checked the digital clock on the dash. After four. He began to drive faster, as if speed were the issue and not judgment. A half mile later the road bent west, leaving the sun perched on the horizon directly before him. David realized he was doubling back. He began to look for a place to turn around when suddenly the road flared again, brighter than ever. He averted his eyes, taking one hand from the wheel to make shade just as he downshifted with the other. The unreined Mustang lurched wilfully toward the center of the road.

He grabbed the wheel and then he could see again. It took him a moment to understand there was another car now, coming right at him, moving fast, less than fifty feet away. Before David could react it began to fishtail hard to the left, rainbowed spume rising behind it. Instinct or luck caused him to swerve in the opposite direction. They passed so close their sideview mirrors collided.

And then the Mustang was spinning, a turn and a half that jerked him violently within his seat belt. He cut through the other car's suspended wake, skidding to a stop on the far shoulder, just inches from a steep slope. He sat still for a moment, his heart pounding, acid washing through his stomach and throat. Red lights appeared on his dash – he'd stalled out. He looked down the road. The other car was gone. For a moment he thought it might have simply driven on. Then he remembered how out of control it had been when they passed.

He restarted his motor and drove back, moving slowly, staying on the shoulder. He was almost parallel with the other car before he could see it at the bottom of the embankment. A small sedan concertinaed against a fractured oak. Its turn signal flashed meaninglessly. As he rolled to a stop David could make out someone in the front seat, silhouetted by blue radiator smoke. He put on his hazards and contemplated his next move. The slope was long and steep, a thirty-foot plummet. He looked around – there was nothing but an Adopt-a-Highway sign. North Burleigh Methodist Church pledging to keep this place clean and tidy. A thought strayed into David's mind. He could just drive on.

But the thought disappeared as quickly as it had come. Of course he couldn't do that. Whoever was down there was almost certainly hurt. Maybe badly. He checked the rearview mirror, hoping for an assist on this one. But there was no one coming and he knew in this neck of the woods there might not be for a long time.

'Great. Just fucking great.'

When he got out of the car he was immediately struck by the utter silence, so eerily incongruous with the mangle below. He set off down the hill, following the fresh ruts, slipping and sliding on the slick, impenetrable surface of the rained-on clay. He lost control halfway down and was forced to run the last few steps. When he hit the bottom he fell on his ass, the moisture soaking straight through to his skin. He stood quickly, for some reason embarrassed, and walked toward the car.

The driver was a woman. His age, maybe younger. Her head had fallen back against the seat. Her eyes were closed, her mouth half-open. The pale skin on her face and neck was mottled; a blood-moistened welt sprouted on her forehead. For a moment David wondered if she were dead, but then he saw the gentle heave of her chest.

The turn signal was clicking and clicking.

'Hey,' he said.

She didn't move. He touched her shoulder, shaking her as softly as he could. She gasped and sat up, her eyes falling open. She looked straight forward, studying the tree for a moment. Then she turned to David. Her expression was strangely calm.

'What?' she asked.

'Are you all right?'

She closed her eyes and took a quick, constricted breath.

'I was until some jerk ran me off the road.'

David looked back up at his Mustang.

'That would be me,' he confessed.

'Oh. Why were you driving in my lane?'

'I was blinded by the sun. Look, I'm really sorry.'

Her sudden movement had squeezed a single drop of blood from the wound on her forehead. It skirted her eye and disappeared into the matted hair on her temple. David patted his pockets for something to daub it with but realized he had nothing.

'Are you hurt?'

She thought about this for a moment, then looked down at her

14

lap. Her breathing became shallow and fast.

'I think I broke my hands,' she said.

David looked. Her left hand lay twisted awkwardly across her thighs, a knuckle of fractured bone stretching the wrist's skin. Burst capillaries surrounded it like a scene from a satellite photograph. He took an instinctive step backwards, nausea swelling up into the back of his throat.

'Yeah, it's wrecked,' she said, covering it with her stiff right hand. She twisted her torso experimentally. 'I fucked up my ribs, too.'

'I'd better go for some help,' David said.

She looked up at him.

'Help?'

'There's bound to be somewhere nearby that has a phone,' he explained.

She looked down at her hands.

'Maybe I should go back to Will's place first.'

'To where?'

'No, just . . . '

She closed her eyes as her head fell back on the rest. She took another of those strangled breaths. David touched her shoulder again.

'Hey now, don't pass out on me here.'

'No, I'm all right,' she said. 'I'm just trying to think what to do.'

He wasn't liking this.

'Look, you're hurt. You shouldn't do anything. I'm going to call for help.'

'Could you get me out of the car first?'

'Maybe I'd better not move you.'

She opened her eyes and nodded tersely out the window.

'I'm not exactly thrilled about sitting under that tree.'

He looked. The oak bowed slightly forward, long green splinters sticking from its guts like picadors' lances. He doubted it would fall but then again he wasn't sitting beneath it. He looked closely at her eyes, wondering if she was in shock. She seemed so calm, too calm. But as far as he could tell she was lucid. It occurred to him that all he knew about emergencies were the usual clichés. Don't move people. Keep them warm. Stick something in their mouth if they're having a fit.

'Please?'

'All right,' he said finally.

He opened the door, propping it with a hip. Her hands were just lying there.

'OK. You ready to try this?'

She nodded slightly and even that seemed to hurt her. Her face was chalk white. The pain was coming now. A second drop of blood followed the first into her hair.

'Tell me if I do something wrong.'

'You'll know.'

He hesitated for a moment, looking at her legs, plotting his next move. She was wearing black Chinese slippers. There were dim red splatters on them which he figured must be blood from her head. He touched her bare ankle. It was warm. He took that to be a good sign.

'Look, I'm going to try to get your legs out, one at a time. When they're both on the ground, then you can stand up.'

'If you say so.'

They worked slowly. A car passed without stopping, zippering along the wet pavement. They can't see us down here, David thought. He brushed her broken wrist with his shoulder as he placed her left foot to the ground.

'Wow,' she said, recoiling.

'Sorry.'

He kept working, slowly twisting her around in the seat and freeing her legs from the car. The wind kicked up; the tree groaned. David moved a little more quickly. Finally, he had her standing. She was tall, just a few inches shorter than his six feet. Thin, with long legs and a long neck. In the fading afternoon light he could see that her eyes were a strange color, lighter than brown, almost amber. Her thick, dark red hair fell crazily over her thin shoulders. She wore black pants and a simple white blouse. No jewelry, not even a watch. Another sphere of blood welled on her forehead.

'All right?' he asked.

She nodded weakly, her injured arms crossed loosely in front of her stomach.

'Why don't you sit down?'

'No, I have to . . .'

'Have to what? Look, what is it you have to do?'

She began to sway. The pain was really coming now, he could see it on her face. He put steadying hands on her shoulders.

'Maybe you're right,' she conceded.

He took off his sports jacket and spread it on the ground. She grimaced as he helped her sit. She was light, easy to maneuver.

'I'm going to call now, all right? But don't worry. I'll be back with the cavalry in two shakes.'

'I'll be here.'

Getting up the hill was difficult. The rutted earth was too slick, so he scrambled up the unbroken ground beside the tire tracks, clutching at the long grass. When he reached the top he looked down. She sat perfectly still, staring at the ground, her arms crossed in her lap. The car's blinker still flashed. He hesitated, wondering if he was doing the right thing, if perhaps he shouldn't stay with her, wait for someone else to come along. But that might be a long time. He didn't know if she was bleeding inside or had a concussion or what. No, best to get some help. So he jumped in his car, driving off with the sweet abandon of someone who has a reason to break the speed limit.

He had to go nearly five miles before he found a phone booth outside an abandoned gas station. It worked, even though the glass was shattered and the receiver swung from the hook like a hanged man. He called the operator, who said she'd put him through to the state police. As he waited to be connected it began to rain. He thought of her back there and suddenly regretted taking her out of the car. What had he been thinking? That tree wasn't going to fall. And why hadn't he given her his raincoat before leaving? Now she was going to catch pneumonia because of his stupidity.

The cops came on. He told them his story and when they asked for his location he realized he didn't know. The dispatcher said she'd trace the call and send a cruiser to the booth. Not wanting to leave the woman in the rain, David told her to have them proceed east and keep their eyes peeled for a vintage green Mustang. Then he headed back. It began to rain harder, not quite pouring but coming down steadily enough to soak anyone who hadn't taken cover. As he arrived at the site he had the feeling that, despite the blunder of pulling her from the car's shelter, he was on top of this now, that he really was going to get this woman some help.

17

He'd surfed halfway down the slope before noticing she was gone. The car door was still open, his jacket lay there in a tangle, the blinker flashed. But no woman. Raincoat in hand, he walked up to the sedan and looked in. Nothing. He searched its far side, even stared beneath it. Nothing.

'Hello?' he called.

There was no answer. He stood in the rain, utterly confused. Someone else has come along, he thought. Someone who knew what the hell to do. Applied first aid, carried her up the hill, got her out of the rain. But that was impossible. No one could have got her away that fast. Not alone, not in this weather. And the cops couldn't have already come.

He looked at the foliage beyond the splintered oak. It took him several seconds to make out the small building, hidden by twenty feet of thicket. Not knowing what else to do, he headed toward it. The going was tough, a tangle of unbreakable ivy and camouflaged stickers. Root-shot earth collapsed beneath him with every step; stinging rain ripped through the canopy above. The further he went, the more he doubted she'd come this way. Not with her wrist busted so badly, maybe some ribs as well. When he broke through the thicket he could see that it was a disused, swaybacked chicken coop. He stepped through a hole where a section of wall had caved in. Beams of wan light crossed the room, illuminating motes of dust and hovering feathers. Rain hammered the corrugated roof.

'Hello?' he shouted, his voice quickly swallowed in the storm's din.

There was no response. He stood still, slowly becoming accustomed to the dark. The rain came harder. And then he saw her, slumped just inside the entrance.

'Christ, there you are . . .'

He stopped when he saw that her eyes were closed, her head lolled slightly to the left. He squatted in front of her, placing an ear a few inches from her face. She was breathing slowly, he could feel it on his raindamp cheek. He touched her shoulder and shook her gently, as he'd done back at the car. But this time she didn't move. Someone passed quickly on the road and he wondered if it was the cops. Despite the rain, he didn't want to stay in here and risk being missed. But he couldn't abandon her again. So he covered her with his raincoat and carefully picked her up, making sure her crossed arms didn't tumble from her stomach. Her ribs felt thin and brittle – he wondered if they were broken too. Her body was warm, not feverish, but warm like a lover's. To his surprise she didn't wake, didn't even moan or sigh as he stumbled through the hole in the wall, as the rain began to strike them.

He carried her back to the car, laying her carefully across the front seat and wiping away the drops of water that had fallen on her face. She wasn't very hard to move now that she was unconscious. He didn't have to be so careful. After she was settled he stood in the rain, staring down at her. The wound on her head seemed to have turned benign, washed of blood by the rain, glistening with histamines. Every few moments David would lean into the car and place his damp hand near her lips to make sure she was still breathing. Doing so, he brushed them once or twice. They were soft and warm.

The rain stopped abruptly a few minutes later and then, as if that were some sort of signal, a cruiser arrived. It was the police from the river. The joker and his partner. David nodded familiarly to them but they were all business. The joker took David aside while his partner examined the woman.

'So what's the deal?' he asked after taking David's name and address.

Before he could answer, David had a brief vision of what the truth would bring. He'd be out here for at least another hour, getting everything on paper, going over it with the cops, measuring skid marks, drawing diagrams. They'd want to know why he took her out of the car, how she got to the coop. And when it came to light he'd swayed from his lane there would be insurance forms, lawyers, maybe even litigation. He looked at the woman lying serenely in the car.

'I don't know, really,' he said. 'She must have lost control.'

'Road this slick . . . ' the cop offered.

David nodded.

'When I came down here she was pretty much out of it. Woozy, you know. So I went for help.' He shrugged. 'When I came back she was passed out. So I kept an eye on her until you guys got here.'

The cop nodded, flipping closed his pad.

'Well, it's just lucky you were here. She coulda been down here a long time before anybody saw her.'

An ambulance and a fire engine arrived. David watched as they ran a line to the car, strapped her into a stretcher's cocoon and winched it up the hill. All the while she remained unconscious, her face perfectly still, perfectly composed. As the rubber-gloved paramedics worked the clouds cleared, though there was no sun. It had already dipped below the horizon. David began to shiver, the day's warmth washed away by the storm.

'Where they taking her?' he asked the joker after the ambulance sped off.

'Burleigh County, most like.'

'You need me for anything else?'

'Nah, you can go.'

'Thing is, I'm not sure of the way.'

The cop explained the route. It was so easy. How could I ever have strayed, David wondered as he made his way back up the hill.

Memories from the site zoomed through his mind as he drove home. The bad break of her wrist. The warmth of her body as he carried it through the thicket. Her eyes, so light and serene. What he couldn't figure out was how she'd made it all the way to that shack. It seemed like such a tremendous effort just to get out of the rain. It wasn't surprising, though. That was a pretty bad bump on her head. She'd seemed confused as hell when he first found her – she couldn't have been thinking straight.

As he neared Burleigh he began to feel bad about denying his part in the accident. It was a lousy thing to do, especially given the shape she was in. But he knew how these things could turn out, how a simple admission of a small guilt could reverberate through a person's life. Better to keep quiet for now; see how she was, what she remembered and what she said. Take it from there. He tried to reassure himself that few people would even have stopped to help, though he wished that thought were more consoling.

His doubts increased as Burleigh's meager downtown appeared on the horizon. He began to wonder if he'd done the right thing lifting her from the car. If it had been smart to leave her alone and then carry her through that tangle. He wondered if by helping her he'd done more harm than good. Passing County, he decided to check on her. Just to be safe.

As he hoped, Rowdy was working Emergency, having just come on duty. David sent in a message and then went to the waiting room, pacing nervously among the rows of chairs, drinking half a coke, trying not to think about the last time he'd been here. A few minutes later Rowdy burst through the swing doors like a halfback going off tackle. Muscle rippled beneath his white coat; his razored hair shimmered in the track lighting.

'What brings you here?' he asked, surprised to see David. 'Nothing's wrong with . . . '

David shook his head quickly.

'I was wondering about that girl they just brought in.'

'Which, the car wreck?'

'That's her.'

'Why?'

'I was the one that found her.'

'No shit. Lucky you. You get some?'

David ignored the remark.

'What's her condition?'

Rowdy whistled.

'She's a Betty, that's her condition.'

'Nice, Rowdy. Very professional.'

'You want professional?' he asked, massaging the thick cords in his neck. 'Check this out. Fractured left ulna. Bruising to the ribs but none broken. Contusion to the forehead. That's a bruise to you, the layman. No immediate evidence of any closed head injury but we're going to run a few tests anyway, just to be sure we make a profit offa her.'

'So she's going to be all right?'

'I reckon. Though she's pretty much out of it.' Rowdy's small eyes squinted suspiciously. 'Why, what's all this to you?'

'I don't know. I guess I feel . . . I mean, I moved her some to make her comfortable and I was just worried if I'd done the right thing.'

Rowdy punched him lightly on the shoulder.

'Hey, don't sweat it. She's in good hands now that I'm through messing with her. You done good.'

He snapped his fingers and pointed at David.

'By the way, she wouldn't have happened to tell you her name?'

'Her name?'

'Nobody could find any i.d. on her.'

David shook his head.

'I only talked to her for a second. Cops check the car?'

'They said they did.'

David shrugged. Rowdy whistled softly.

'Ho, boy. Admissions are going to love this.'

David thought about what she'd said back at the crash. Something about wanting to get back to Will's. Whoever he was. He decided not to mention it, still wary of getting too involved.

'Something'll turn up,' he said.

'What are you, an optimist?'

They laughed for a moment.

'Hey, you wanna hear a good one?' David asked, remembering the joke he'd heard back at the flood.

'Go for it.'

There was a commotion behind them, the sigh of automatic doors, the squelch of a radio. Two paramedics wheeled in a stretcher that held a teenage boy with a wad of bloody cotton taped to his neck.

'Let me guess,' Rowdy said.

'Gunshot wound,' the paramedic answered laconically.

'Hey, now there's something new.'

Rowdy pointed at David.

'Gonna have to take a rain check on that joke,' he said before following the stretcher into the Emergency Room.

David watched him disappear through the swing doors, thinking about what he said, about the woman having no i.d. He stood there for a moment, wondering if there was something more he could do, some other way he could help her. But he quickly realized there was nothing. This wasn't his business any more. Cops and doctors were involved now. The pros. He took one last look through to the Emergency Room, then he turned and headed home.

Mary Beth came through the front door just as David stepped wearily from the Mustang. She waved when she saw him and bounded down the porch steps.

'And here I was thinking . . . '

Her smile disappeared when she noticed his filthy clothes.

'Hey, what happened to you?'

'There was an accident.'

'An accident?' She reached out, her hand stopping a few inches from his arm. 'David . . . '

'No, I'm all right.' He brushed idly at his stained pants. 'You should see the other guy.'

'Bad?'

'This woman. She hit a tree. Messed up her hands pretty good.'

'Where'd all this happen?'

'I was driving down from Elk Run and got diverted on to a backroad on account of the floods. And I . . . well this car went off the road, right in front of me.'

'Gah.'

'She was awake for a moment but then she passed out. They took her to the hospital.'

Mary Beth hugged him loosely, careful not to dirty her clothes.

'You be careful out there, David. I don't want to lose you.'

They looked at each other for a moment, mortality flickering between them.

'Hey, come on, I'm all right,' he said, breaking away. 'Not even a scratched bumper.'

'So who was this woman?'

David shrugged.

'Nobody knows. I stopped by the hospital to check. She's in a coma or something.'

He decided not to tell her about drifting into the other lane. He'd keep that quiet for now. Mary Beth had enough to worry about for the next few weeks.

'So where you off to?' he asked, noticing her briefcase and work clothes.

'The station. It's a madhouse down there.'

'Really?' David asked, trying to mask his disappointment. 'I didn't think the fun started until tomorrow.'

'The joys of management. You know how it is.'

'How late will you be?'

'Closing, prolly. Why, what is it, honey?'

'No, it's just, I'd reserved *Blade Runner* at Blockbuster.'

She rolled her eyes.

'We've only seen that like half a trillion times.'

'It's the new version,' he protested feebly. 'They took out the happy ending.'

'Come on, David. You know what this drive's going to be like.'

He held up his hands in capitulation.

'All right, sorry.'

'So you'll be OK then?'

'Sure.'

She kissed him again and began to walk to her car.

'Hey, you want to hear a joke?' he called after her.

'Is it long?' she asked, glancing at her watch.

'Sorta.'

'Can it wait? I'm late as it is.'

She was gone before he could answer.

David passed the evening restless and alone. He drank two beers on the porch, watching night fall, thinking about the accident, wondering in vain what he might have done differently. He fixed dinner in the microwave, then sat fruitlessly in front of the Apple for two hours trying to write his copy. Nothing came and so he finished off the six pack in front of the TV, watching the Braves lose to Chicago. He was in bed by eleven, figuring that maybe a good night's sleep might break his block.

But he was awake just a few hours later, his heart pounding, his skin clammy. He looked at the clock. Not yet four. Outside, it was raining steadily. Mary Beth slept soundly beside him. He lay still for a long time, the nightmare that had woken him running through his mind. It was a killer, the worst he'd had in a long time. He'd been driving fast down the mountain in a car that wasn't his own, a windowless jalopy as cramped as a space capsule. The speedometer reached nearly a hundred before he noticed it had no brakes. There wasn't even a pedal for them. The emergency brake snapped off like kindling when he pulled it. Mary Beth was on the radio, reading out some sort of warning, though there was too much static for him to be sure what she was saying. He gained momentum, the car performed a few miraculous spins, a short flight. He passed several crash scenes, twisted metal and bodies everywhere. Finally, just as he was about to lose control completely, he came to a truck escape lane. He turned up it. The car slowed but not enough – he realized that he was going to hit the sand wall, hit it hard. He braced himself. And then, just seconds before impact, he saw the woman from the crash, buried up to her neck in the sand, her face trapped at bumper level. She stared at him with those amber eyes, trusting, amused, as if this were a joke and he was going to stop at the last moment. He woke just as the car plowed into the dune.

Shit, that was a good one, David thought. He looked over at Mary Beth – she slept, obliviously. That was good. He looked back at the ceiling and began to think about the woman. The feel of her long legs as he gently levered them from the car. How light she had been when he lifted her in the coop. Her deep calm as she lay unconscious across the seat. The fact that no one seemed to know her name. He wondered if she were awake yet, if she was telling anyone her story.

He got out of bed, showering and dressing quietly, not wanting to wake his wife. She'd returned sometime after he fell asleep. The more she slept now the better. The next ten days were going to be hard for her. He went downstairs and brewed some coffee, drinking it while watching Headline News. Nothing much had happened overnight. Europeans bickering, Third Worlders dropping like flies. The floods up on Mud River got a late mention. When it was over he flipped to the shopping channel, where a woman promised 'an adventure into the lesser gemstones'. Everything else was the Evangelicals. They looked particularly smug today, as if the rising waters confirmed what they'd been saying all along. Don't these people ever sleep, David wondered. He turned off the television and as its picture disappeared he decided to go back to the hospital. Just to check. Just to be sure.

Rowdy was still there, nearing the end of one of his epic shifts.
'What a star,' David said, surprising him as he surveyed a chart.
'Damn, you're up early,' he said, checking his watch.
'Quiet night?'
'Quiet enough.'
'So how's she doing?'

'The Jane Doe?' He rubbed at his scalp line with an eraser. 'She's a toughie. I can't get her to come around. She's still in ICU.'

'Isn't there a technical term for not coming around?'

Rowdy nodded distractedly.

'Yeah, you'd think she's in a coma, but she shows no pathological signs of it. All the tests were negative. Spinal X-ray, cat scan. Her brain's fine, far as we can tell. I thought with those bruised ribs she might have a liver or a spleen but she doesn't. I was thinking about hitting her with some smelling salts but, I don't know. Something about her makes me want to go easy for the time being.'

'And you still don't know who she is?'

'Nope.' Rowdy checked his watch. 'Come on.'

They took the elevator up to the Intensive Care Unit, a dozen rooms emanating from a central desk. It had the spectral glow and spooky hum of serious hurt. The first room they passed contained a man lying perfectly still, his bare chest crossed with wires and tubes.

'DNR,' Rowdy said, nodding toward him.

'What does that mean?'

'It means check, please. Do Not Resuscitate.'

She was in the next room. David looked down at her in the artificial light while Rowdy scoured charts and took readings. She looked even more fragile and pained than she had at the crash. There was a fresh cast on the lower half of her left arm. The other was wrapped in an Ace bandage. The welt above her eye had solidified into whorls of dark purple and dull black.

'Yo, Sleeping Beauty,' Rowdy said loudly.

He touched her cheek with the back of his hand. She didn't respond.

'See what I mean?'

'So what do you think?'

'Beats me. The head's a funny thing. You fuck with it and you just don't know what's going to come out in the wash.'

'What are you going to do with her?'

'Well, the neurologist wants to punt, send her to the head-shrinkers on the assumption this might be some kind of hysterical deal. But my superiors have this problem treating uninsured Jane Does with negative tests.'

'So what happens?'

'State hospital.'

'That doesn't sound so good.'

'Not unless she's writing a book on Dickens.'

David looked down at her.

'This is so strange,' was all he could think to say.

They stood in silence a moment longer.

'Anyway. Wanna grab some chow?' Rowdy asked. 'Your treat.'

'Nah, I better get going. I got lots of work to do.'

'Work? Vous? At the Redwine Group?'

'Give me a break,' David said.

Rowdy's beeper sounded.

'Saved by the bell. The halt and the lame need my attention.'

They walked away from the bed.

'You coming to the party tonight?' David asked when they reached the door.

'Wouldn't miss it for the world,' Rowdy answered over his shoulder.

David watched him until he was swallowed by the elevator. He looked around. A nurse sat scrawling something on a pad, the other patient lay perfectly still. And then, without really being sure what he was doing, David walked back into the room. He gripped the cool metal of the safety rail and stared down at her. Jane Doe, he thought. Her eyes flickered and he wondered for a moment what people dream about when they're in comas. If they dream at all.

'Hey,' he heard himself saying out loud. 'Are you waking up?'

He gently touched her shoulder.

'Can you hear me or . . . ?'

And then her eyes fell open and she looked at him with the same lucid calm she had when she first woke at the crash. They stared at each other for a moment. Something about her eyes told David she hadn't been unconscious at all, that she'd been awake the whole time they'd been speaking.

'What are you?—'

'Excuse me,' a voice said from the doorway before David could finish his question.

He turned. The nurse.

'I was just . . . look, she's awake.'

'Awake?'

The nurse frowned and pushed by him. He looked back at the injured woman. It took him a moment to realize that her eyes were shut tight. The nurse examined her, then looked at David, a scowl constricting her features.

'Her eyes opened,' he said. 'I swear they did.'

'What are you doing here, sir?' she asked sharply. 'Are you an immediate relative?'

'No, but—'

'Who are you then?'

'Nobody. I'm just . . . checking on her.'

The nurse's demeanor hardened.

'Sir, you'll have to go now. You shouldn't be doing this. You shouldn't be here.'

'But she woke—'

'I press a button and security's here like nobody's business.'

David looked once more at the sleeping woman, at her closed lids. They seemed like they'd never been open.

'That won't be necessary,' he said.

2

David moved slowly through the sparse crowd, an Anchor Steam in one hand, a Sam Adams in the other. He pretended to be looking for someone, though the truth was that both beers were for him. It was a trick he'd recently started using for getting through business parties. Not only did it cut down on trips to the bar, but it also provided an excuse to break off unwanted conversations. All he had to do when trapped was raise the supplementary beer and nod to a vague point in the distance. As if there was someone waiting for him. It worked every time.

As he wandered through the loose human gel he was aware that this was the first time he'd used the two beer trick at a party that wasn't related to his job. He wondered what was wrong with him – he'd been looking forward to the WBRR bash for weeks. It was usually one of his favorite nights of the year, but now that he was here he couldn't wait for it to end. It must be the accident, the bad night's sleep. He'd been strangely distracted all day, that woman's amber eyes burned into his mind. He couldn't stop thinking about how she'd looked like she wanted to speak to him at the hospital. He'd called over there in the late morning but all they'd said was that there was no change in her condition. After that he'd been stuck in meetings, and then there was the party.

The party. He looked around the guests, feeling an unexpected wave of dislike for them. The last of Burleigh's cultured elite, he thought sardonically. Ex-hippies who had made a killing by incorporating their kilns or leather presses, newspaper people and enlightened lawyers, hustling real estate agents hoping to transform the region's warehouses and derelict farms into subdivisions or business parks. There was even a clutch of Burleigh Tobacco executives who'd been parachuted into early retirement and now spent their days pretending to be consultants, their nights attending functions like this. And there were a few newcomers as well, earnestly affable young biochemists and computer programmers who worked in the ground-hugging, anonymous buildings that had begun sprouting on the outskirts of town. All dutifully rolling out for listener supported radio.

David caught sight of the 'Ten Days of Giving' banner, no more than a painted sheet draped along the front of the bunker-like station building. Things were definitely low-rent this year, he thought. Cheap Chinese lanterns ringed the small lawn, spluttering brown light. Dinner was homemade salads instead of the usual catered spread. The bar was do-it-yourself and a solitary hammered dulcimer rang weakly where a seven-piece bluegrass band had once jammed through the night. The plywood thermometer perched totemically on the edge of the lawn registered nothing yet, of course, and for a moment David harbored a grim thought – that was just the sort of reading you'd expect from a corpse. In fact, there was something of a wake about this year's party, the festive giddiness of previous years replaced by a muted tension, a sense of weariness and even doom.

The crowd shifted and Mary Beth came into view, looking nervous and hopeful amid a group of would-be sponsors. This was her first fundraising drive as station manager. It was also potentially the last in WBRR's history. It had been in trouble since the Burleigh Tobacco break-up five years earlier had deprived the station of its major corporate funder. While the station used to meet its target easily, nowadays its employees had to hustle just to make enough to pay off the interest on their debt. If they didn't make their mark this year then that would be it. They would lose their public radio franchise.

Usually the drive lasted one week, but due to the crisis they'd added three extra days. Just a few years ago there would have been seven or eight hundred people attending the launch party, which would have been held at a museum or country club instead of a souped-up parking lot. Tonight, however, David reckoned there couldn't have been more than one fifty, and that included station employees and volunteers who'd be working the phones. Still, Mary Beth was trying, giving it everything she had. A special benefit concert had been set up for the weekend. Noah Adams and Susan Stamberg had recorded earnest little fillips that would be broadcast continually during the drive, sermonettes about the importance of public broadcasting. There had been talk about Keillor himself coming down to help out but there was a last minute scheduling problem.

Watching his wife now, David couldn't help but think back to the first of these parties he'd attended, eleven years earlier, not long after they'd started living together. Mary Beth was a junior announcer and he had just begun working for the Social Fund. Which meant it had now been twelve years since he first heard her voice. A dozen years, David thought. One sixth of my allotted span. Christ, how could such a big chunk of time slip away like that? He moved close enough to hear her and was struck by the sudden realization that her voice sounded exactly the same as when he first heard it. The only thing about her that hadn't changed. About them.

It was during his senior year in college that he'd first heard her. He was living off campus with Rowdy and some other guys at the time. That night, he'd been at a reception for some visiting poet, returning home slightly drunk. Armed with a six pack, he'd sprawled on his bed and tuned his boom box to WBRR. There was a new show on the eleven until closing slot that night, the time when student trainee deejays were turned loose to play New Wave or New Age. This one was called *The Rose and Thistle*, featuring traditional music from the British Isles. David had never paid much attention to that sort of music but all those jigs and reels suddenly resonated with his slightly addled brain, coming through the receiver like a revelation. Better still was the announcer's voice. He could tell she was a rookie and he was immediately drawn to the willed boldness that just about succeeded in masking her natural timidity. He loved the way her soft accent made its way through the perilous Celtic consonants, the way she'd give a grim, self-deprecating laugh when she messed up. By the end of the show, when the voice said it belonged to Mary Elizabeth Covington, he was hooked.

He listened faithfully for the next few months. Always alone in his room, a little bit drunk, books spread lamely on his desk. It wasn't until the eighth or ninth show that he started to dance. It was no big deal, just a brief, disjointed shuffle as he went for another beer. When he came back she had put on a particularly frantic tune and, more than a little drunk now and hidden from sight, he found himself dancing. If that's what you could call the jumps and twirls he performed until his heart was pounding and his T-shirt was drenched with sweat. When the song ended he collapsed on his bed, listening carefully as she explained what it was he'd been dancing to.

It would have been easy to meet Mary Elizabeth during this time, though for some reason he didn't make the effort. Maybe he was afraid he would be disappointed, afraid meeting her might spoil the voice, ground it, rob it of its allure. Sometimes, walking across the busy quad, he'd try to guess if one of the faces he saw was hers. But that was the extent of his search. He was involved with someone else, anyway, a sullen art major and radical vegetarian named Andrea who spent her days assembling great mounds of recovered garbage into shapes vaguely resembling barnyard animals and her nights drinking cheap beer with David, listening to his spiel with a bemused and slightly distasteful expression, until it was time for them to go to bed and make furious love. No, Mary Elizabeth's voice and his dancing were enough for him that fall and winter.

By spring he wasn't seeing Andrea any more. One night, at a Mexican restaurant, they'd fought over his fondness for animal flesh, a drunken verbal brawl which climaxed with her announcement that their relationship had 'passed its pull date'. She walked out just as the waitress brought her plate of vegetarian enchiladas. David was devastated for about three days. He took some comfort in the fact that Mary Elizabeth Covington was now doing several shows a week, not just her Wednesday night gig but daytime classical segments and early evening jazz. He'd listen to her faithfully, secretly, dancing whenever the urge came upon him.

He finally met her at the Welcome Spring festival on the quad, on one of those days where the sweet and sickly smell of curing tobacco wafted over Burleigh like spilled perfume. It was the usual college party – carbonated beer and trebly loudspeakers and frisbees being tossed to dogs that wore paisley kerchiefs around their necks. There was a half-hearted attempt at erecting a tent city to protest the college's tenuous links with South Africa. Some communications majors had set up a sound system to provide the tunes. Elvis Costello, The Specials, Blondie. The moment David arrived he heard her voice on the loudspeakers, connecting it with the girl behind the mike.

32

He wandered over. He wasn't surprised by how she looked because he'd never really got around to conjuring a mental picture of her. Long, almost black hair and deep brown eyes. About five six, maybe a bit shorter. Full breasts and hips that gently puffed out the flanks of her peasant skirt when she moved to get another record. He waited until she took a break and then introduced himself, saying he was her biggest fan. She gave him that come-off-it look he would later grow to know so well, but stayed there with him, accepting his dinner invitation. They went to the same Mexican restaurant where Andrea had dumped him. David's mind was ripe for comparisons and Mary Beth, as she was called, won hands down, ordering spicy beef tostadas and matching him Margarita for Margarita.

She told him about her family. Her father was a progressive lawyer who had clerked for Sam Ervin and now had a successful practice in Raleigh, where ten per cent of his billable hours were *pro bono*, the rest two-fifty per hour. He'd run for Congress a few years back and been duly swamped by a Republican with a corny nickname and unprovable links with the Klan. Mary Beth had four older brothers, three of them lawyers in practice with her dad, the fourth a Peace Corps trainee. Her mother did things with the museum, drank lots of decaf. Despite her parents' liberal credentials, Mary Beth had gone to a country day school, owned a pony, taken ballet lessons. At sixteen she rebelled, dating a black guy and smoking pot behind locked doors. Her mother simply sprayed her room with Glade, her father offered James a summer job filing tomes in his firm's library. By seventeen Mary Beth was through rebelling.

David listened, enraptured, keeping quiet about his own bland surburban past. For some reason he didn't kiss her when he dropped her off at her dorm, confusing and infuriating her. A few days later he came by the WBRR studio and watched her through the double glass wall of the broadcasting booth. She beckoned him in when she finally saw him. He clumsily knocked a mug off her table as he sat.

'That's David,' she explained to her listeners when it finished clattering. 'He's in love but has a funny way of showing it.'

The next night they went to see *The Deer Hunter* at the campus film club. She cried during the final scene with an energy that surprised and frightened him. Later, they made love for the first time. It was better than he could have hoped, tender and a bit confused. Especially after the mechanical rigors of Andrea, who had used her strong hands to manipulate his head and hands and cock, as if she were sculpting her orgasms. But with Mary Beth he could soon feel the walls of self-consciousness tumbling down. When they were finally still he noticed that it was past midnight. Outside he could hear the revving cicada, the rumble of interstate trucks. *The Rose and Thistle* was on, turned so low it was barely audible. He realized they had been listening to the jigs and reels all along. But the voice on the radio was unfamiliar. Male, Yankee, cocksure.

'Hey's, who's that?'

'Oh, some new kid,' she explained. 'I got him to stand in for me.'

'Why?'

She jostled David.

'So I could do the dirty with you, genius.'

He turned off the radio, feeling a vague and utterly inexplicable disappointment. It passed a few minutes later when they were making love again, though now, twelve years later, watching her at the party, for some reason it was that unexpected disappointment he most remembered.

He drained a beer and was now holding two empty bottles. He tossed them into a dumpster, noticing that its puckered metal wall was plastered with a WBRR poster. 'Broadcasting Into the Future.' Typical Burleigh sleight-of-hand, David thought. Cover the rot with paper promising better times. He wove his way to the bar, where Rowdy was downing a beer.

'Hey, don't you ever sleep?'

'Sleep, let's see. Yeah, I used to sleep. Gave it up, though.' Rowdy looked around, his thick brow furrowing. 'Hey, you ain't seen my future ex, have you? Somebody said she'd be here.'

'No, I think she's working.'

'Good. She's been trying to hit me with these fucking papers.'

David accepted a beer, waved away the glass. He didn't say anything. Normally, he'd have provided Rowdy a shoulder to cry on, but he just didn't feel like it tonight.

'So,' Rowdy said. 'M-B's big night. You think they'll reach the target?'

34

'It's going to be tough. The donor base just keeps shrinking and shrinking.'

'That's funny,' Rowdy said, shaking his head. ''Cause mine keeps getting bigger and bigger.'

David sipped his new beer.

'Tell you what, though. They better.'

'Why's that?' Rowdy asked.

'If they don't then the board says . . . ' He drew a finger across his neck. 'Check, please. DNR.'

'That bad?'

'They've been hurting ever since the Burleigh money went away.'

'Who ain't, bro. Who ain't.'

They both looked at Mary Beth, then took simultaneous pulls from their beers.

'Hey, guess what,' Rowdy said, flicking David's tie. 'Your Jane Doe's gone.'

David pulled the beer quickly from his lips. An unexpected pulse of energy ran through him, something he didn't recognize, didn't understand.

'She died?'

'No, no. My patients don't die without written permission. She's absconded.'

'Absconded? What the hell is that supposed to mean?'

'It means she left our care without being formally discharged or settling her bill. She bolted.'

'So you're telling me that she just woke up, got dressed and split?'

'Hopefully in that order.'

'Jesus. How'd she get by everyone?'

'Very skilfully, it seems.'

David gestured with his beer.

'You know, it's funny, because after you left I could have sworn she opened her eyes and was looking right at me. Like she wanted to say something. But when the nurse came in she was out of it again. It was weird. I tried to explain but she just wanted to sic security on me.'

'Well, just because somebody's got their eyes open don't mean they're awake.' Rowdy shrugged. 'On the other hand, she could have been faking it.'

'Faking it?'

'Happens. I usually let them have their little charade until they get tired of it. Though she seemed a bit more motivated than most.'

'Don't you have an address or something?'

'An address? Hell, boy, we never even got a name.'

David thought for a moment.

'What about the car?'

'Yeah, I asked about that. It's a rental is the best anybody could come up with. Admissions called the cops who said they'll keep their eyes open but, you know, they see it as a civil matter. They don't care, they got better things to do.'

'So what happens now?' David persisted.

Rowdy shrugged.

'Nothing, I guess.'

'But is it safe for her just to go like that?'

'No. I mean, that was a pretty nasty bump she took and you have to admit her behavior has proved a tad, uh, erratic.' He took a long drink. 'I'll tell you what, though. Wherever she is, she must be one hurting puppy. I never could give her a painkiller, not till she joined the living.'

David contemplated this in silence.

'Don't look so worried, hombre,' Rowdy said. 'You did your duty.'

'Yeah, I know.'

They drank in silence for a while.

'Hey, by the way, there's this thing I want you to try,' Rowdy said, smiling conspiratorially. 'Paintball.'

'What's that?'

'Come on, you heard a this. It's a pursuit game. Mostly singles but we have a few of the living dead, too. We do it up in Nowheresville. Sneak in there. Everybody gets these guns with paint bullets in them. And you divide into two armies. We shoot them, they shoot us. When you're hit, you're shit. They got a whole league. We're in second but we need some more guys.'

'What makes you think I'd want to do that?'

'Come on, David, you're the sneakiest motherfucker I know. We could use a Yankee on our team. Give us a little of that cold-hearted

Sherman action. There's too much gallantry afoot as it is.'

'How'd you get in there, anyway?'

'Oh, there are ways in.'

'What's it like?'

'Very creepy. Lots of those buildings are still standing. Rumor is there are still some people living there.'

'No way.'

Rowdy shrugged.

'So what do you think?' he asked.

'After the drive, sure, I'll give it a whirl. I wouldn't mind blowing someone away.'

'That's the spirit.' Rowdy looked around. 'Well, if I'm going to get laid I'd better get busy.'

'Hey,' David said, snapping his fingers. 'You wanna hear that joke now?'

'Always.'

'Well there's this old guy who lives alone. And one day there's this flood—'

'David?'

It was Mary Beth. David held up a finger. He really wanted to tell someone this joke. She smiled and mouthed 'now'.

'Go on,' Rowdy said. 'Your jokes suck, anyway.'

David joined his wife.

'Hey, where've you been?' she asked. 'I've been looking all over for you.'

'Mixing.'

'Well, mix with humans, OK? I'm like to die here.'

'Come on, you'll do great.'

David gave her back a reassuring rub. He could feel her bra strap scroll and unscroll beneath his palm.

'You think?' she asked.

Someone started talking to her before David could answer. He hung around for an obligatory stretch of nodding, then drifted off, thinking about what Rowdy had said about the woman from the crash. Although he knew he should feel relieved that he now wouldn't have to answer for the accident, what he really felt was strangely unsettled. He thought of the look in her eyes when she'd stared at him back in the ICU. He wished that nurse hadn't shown

37

up, that they'd been able to speak for a moment.

'David Webster.'

He turned to be confronted by the pure white hair and jet black beard of Donnie Redwine. And he only had one beer.

'Hello, Donnie.'

'Nice party.'

'So how was your trip?'

Redwine sighed.

'Tell you what, we sailed right across the Bermuda Triangle and not a cot-damned thing happened. Except I caught a shark. Little sucker, only about three foot.' He measured it with his hands. 'What's the use of being a shark if you're only yay big?'

David obliged him with a laugh. The wind seemed to be picking up.

'So how'd you do with my ad?' Redwine asked.

'Pretty good.'

' "Pretty good," he says. Thing of it is, I thought I'd have some copy on my desk this afternoon.'

David smiled feebly.

'I'm getting there.'

Redwine stroked his close-cropped beard.

'Because we're getting real close to the wire here, David.'

'I know. That's the way I like to work.'

Redwine grimaced dubiously.

'Tell you what, let's you me get together first thing tomorrow and shoot the shit.'

'Fine.'

'About nine?'

'Can we make it ten?' David tried.

'What the hell,' the older man said, smiling convivially. 'Let's make it nine.'

With that, Redwine wandered off toward a group of retirees. A few moments later the crowd grew quiet as Mary Beth stepped up to the microphone. There was muted applause. She mock-scowled, turned up her palms and bounced her hands a few times. The applause increased, there was some laughter.

'I'd like to thank everybody for coming out,' she began. 'I know we've had a few tough years but I think this is going to be the start of our comeback, the city's comeback. Maybe, I don't know, it's been a blessing in disguise, a way to break free from our traditional dependency on corporations, to empower the average listener. Maybe we needed a few lean years to get our priorities down right. And I guess I don't have to tell you how important a one public radio is these days. I mean, there's no reason for me to stand up here and preach to the converted . . . '

David felt a drop of rain on the back of his neck. The wind gusted, knocking over a few chairs.

'But what would be nice would be if every one of you would tell a friend . . . '

The microphone groaned with the wind. More drops fell. A few of the cheap paper lanterns went up in flames, scattering rogue embers among the partygoers. Some people broke for cover.

'Urge a friend to . . . and, well . . . '

She was smiling nervously, losing her way, confused by the wind. Thunder rumbled and sourceless pulses of blue light began to flash. David took a step forward, wondering what he could do to help her. Short of making the storm stop, not much.

'So . . . the thing is . . . '

And then the rain came, great sheets of it that obliterated the remaining lanterns, bent trees and knocked over chairs and tables. Everyone broke for the station's lobby. For the second time in as many days David could feel rain soaking through to his skin. Once inside he elbowed his way through the crowded lobby, finding his wife by the coke machine.

'Saved by the storm,' she said wryly.

Ironically, the party now began to pick up, laughter and occasional whoops resounding through the lobby's confines. The door flew open as Rowdy led a salvage expedition back to the toppled bar. The wind was really blowing now, the water whipping down like a shaken blanket. There were cheers when the doctor and his men reappeared, soaked but laden with booze. Everyone seemed giddy, like children allowed to stay up late. The storm outside increased, pumping water into the glass doors, causing the big antenna on the roof to moan with metal fatigue that shivered through the building's structure. Lightning flashed continually, so muddled with thunder that it was impossible to tell which flash went with which peal. Someone started to sing and people joined in but they stopped before the song was over. And then the power went out. There were more whoops, scattered applause. Emergency spots came on and flashlights were found and soon the room was full of laughing bottom-lit faces.

David watched Mary Beth sip wine from a bottle. Her damp hair, cut short now, hung across her temples; her dress clung to her breasts and thighs. She smiled forlornly when she met his gaze and shook her head. He took the bottle she offered and drank from it, still watching her over the horizon of tinted glass. She seemed relaxed now that the onus of speaking had passed, almost girlish as she watched the people jostle and laugh. Suddenly, in the building's near darkness, he was reminded of when they first became lovers, the nights he would join her while she worked the graveyard shift. The studio was usually empty of everyone except a bored technician dozing in front of Letterman in another room. They would turn off the lights so there was only the red of the mike's indicator bulb and the subaqueous glow from the instrument panel. And then they would make love in the swivel chair, Mary Beth's peasant skirt covering them like a tent. Slow and emphatic and daring, the chair's hydraulic stem panting beneath them. David loved doing it so close to the mike, just that on-off switch standing between them and discovery by the enlightened listeners of northeastern Carolina. Or if there were too many people around they would sneak into the record storage vault, lying between the stacks of discs, Joe Strummer or Yo-Yo Ma staring down at them. She would often have to rush back, taking her seat just in time to avoid dead air. David would stay where he was, listening to her voice over the speakers.

She met his gaze.

'You know what I'm thinking about?' he asked.

'What?'

'Those times.'

She knew right away what he meant.

'Pervert,' she said.

'Come on.'

'I don't think so, stud.'

'Come on, Mary Beth.'

She looked at him for a moment, noted his intent, then took a

40

long pull of wine.

'All right,' she said, her voice infused with dare. 'Keep in mind I don't have my thingamajig in.'

'I'll improvise.'

'Yeah, I bet you will.'

David confiscated a flashlight and they moved quickly through the crowd. Mary Beth punched the code into the key lock and they were into the studio, walking down the short flight of stairs to the basement broadcasting area. There were three people in the big booth, staring forlornly at the dead equipment. David checked the heavy door to the record vault. It was unlocked.

'Come on.'

She hesitated.

'I don't know, David. Maybe we should go back up.'

'Please?'

She shrugged tentative assent and he led her in, locking the door behind them. She set the flashlight face down on the chair – it glowed oblique and red. They dropped awkwardly to the carpet and began to kiss. From where he was David could see the last record in the stack. Some prodigy whose smile had become a smirk in the dim light.

He could feel Mary Beth's reluctance but pressed ahead, peeling off her wet clothes, layer after layer, like some archaeologist of desire, his mind alive with how she was those nights years ago. The room smelled of old vinyl and rug shampoo but soon all he could sense was her wet flesh.

'Wait, David.'

'What?'

'I don't think this is . . . '

'Please.'

'I think I hear something.'

'It's just the storm.'

'No, there's someone out there.'

'I locked the door.'

'Get off,' she said, not kidding. 'Please. Something's wrong. There shouldn't be people down here.'

She gently pushed him off her. He listened. There were voices, footsteps, some just a few feet away. They quickly fastened their

41

clothes, bumping into each other several times in the near dark. When they opened the door there were a few dozen people milling around, whispering somberly. No one noticed them step from the vault.

'What's going on?'

'Tornado,' someone said.

'It was a watch,' another explained. 'Now it's a warning.'

'Warning, hell. My ears just popped.'

Mary Beth and David looked at each other. A few more people filtered in.

'You should see it out there,' one of the newcomers said, laughing nervously. 'It's really blowing.'

Thunder sounded as the last of the guests crowded in, filling the booths, the vaults. No one was talking, no one was laughing. There was nothing to do but wait now, crushed together in the rapidly heating room. And so they waited, listening to the wind blow just a few walls away.

It was a half-hour before the all-clear was given. The party was over. People left quickly, exhausted by their spell sheltering in the small studio. David and Mary Beth went home as soon as they could. Soaked leaves and branches lined the streets, but there was no sign of a tornado. When David pulled up to the house he could see that everything was all right. Two arm-sized limbs had fallen on the roof and a shutter had come loose, but that was all. The alarm system's spotlights strobed the lawn, its motion sensors having mistaken the wind for a host of intruders.

'I'll go check for damage,' he said.

Mary Beth nodded distantly. They hadn't spoken much since their abortive grapple, since the party's collapse.

'I'll be upstairs.'

After turning off the alarm he began a slow circuit of the property, checking for broken windows or damaged tiles. Wet, the house looked even more dense and solid than usual, its gutters like a tank's armor, its wood slats as durable as cut granite. Nothing can hurt this place, David thought without pride or pleasure. It'll stand until long after I'm gone.

They'd coveted the house on Ivy Street from the moment they

saw it was for sale, just after Mary Beth became pregnant. The varnished wood floors, the period fixtures, the high ceilings. All those rooms. It sat a good twenty-five feet above street level, its pachysandra-shrouded front yard so steep that it looked like a wall. Three storeys, the top one a big attic. There was a wraparound porch and, out back, a broad lawn shaded by an implacable elm. Its previous owner was a senile old woman who was in the process of being packed off to a nursing home by her shamefaced sons, fat Baptists who refused to budge from the asking price they would use to bankroll her supervised dotage. It was beyond their reach at first but they saved and borrowed and were eventually able to make it happen. They couldn't believe their luck – it was twice the house they'd planned on buying.

The idyll had almost been ruined, however, when they began to find the turds. Small human offerings, stored in ziplock bags and hidden away in the house's nooks and crannies. Some were calcified with age, others still soft as putty. Mary Beth had retreated to her parents for two days while David searched them out, collecting nearly three hundred small pouches of the woman's fecal legacy in all. She moved back when he declared the house shit free, though for several months David led the way whenever they entered a new area.

Their progress through the house was vertical. At first, before they had enough furniture, they lived in a back room on the ground floor. Next it was the room on the second floor that was to be the kid's. Then the attic became the master bedroom. It was where they now lived, a room as long as the house, with a sloping ceiling and irregular windows that admitted ever-changing patterns of morning light. The house was too big for them, especially now. They sometimes flirted with the notion of taking in boarders, grad students maybe. But there was really no reason. They were all right. The simple fact was that, at the age of thirty-three, David found himself living in a house he would never have to leave, a house he could neither outlive nor outgrow. Sometimes it scared the hell out of him.

He finished his circuit, having found nothing that a good raking couldn't handle. The last of the storm front was passing as he stepped up on the porch, the wind chimes of Ivy Street sounding its retreat. He listened to the gentle cacophony with mild distaste. The chimes had become the rage a few years back, handmade by some ex-banker who'd decided he didn't need the rat race any more but still wanted to pull down six figures. They came with a customized pitch. David had heard of streets where everyone was in tune, though at least the good folk of his block kept it chaotic. Still, the chimes used to drive him crazy, especially in the early summer, when the nights were cool enough to turn off the air conditioner and open the windows. He eventually got used to them, however, giving in to Mary Beth and buying a set for their own porch. He'd messed up the assembly, so that they were silent in anything but gale-force winds, and then produced a jarring dissonance. She'd stripped them down and started over from scratch.

David stepped up on to the porch, untwisting the Greenpeace banner that hung in the American flag holder. Seal pups, grinning uneasily. Then he surveyed the city, the interstate and then the small downtown, little more than the empty art deco Burleigh Tobacco building surrounded by a few tinted-glass hotels and bank towers. The storm's dying winds carried the sound of multiple sirens from somewhere to the north. For a moment they blended with the chimes, sounding a bizarre city symphony that David found strangely pleasing.

And then, from nowhere, he was struck by the unsettling thought that she was out there somewhere, dazed and injured and confused, caught in the storm. An almost photographic image of her standing in the wind and the rain flashed through his mind, as quick and brilliant as the retreating lightning. And then it was gone.

He stood there for a while longer before walking back into the house. He crept up to their room, hoping to pick up where they'd been interrupted back at the studio.

'Mary Beth?'

But his wife was asleep, the covers pulled up to her neck like a layer of fresh snow. He stared at her for a long time, until rain began to rattle the windows. Another storm, fresh on the trail of the last one.

3

There was a hole in the bottom of Donnie Redwine's snakeskin boot. It looked like a wound in his sole. The ruined rubber could have been broken flesh, the shredded inner lining torn muscle, the white sock exposed bone. David briefly wondered if he should tell his boss about it but decided not to, reasoning that Redwine's pride was more important than his comfort. Besides, with all the rain they'd been having, he'd find out soon enough.

'So,' Redwine said, crossing a second, unholed boot over the first, so that both feet now rested on David's desk. 'What you got for me, son?'

David hesitated. The short answer, of course, was nothing, though he knew that wasn't what the man wanted to hear. Redwine had expected a thousand words of seductive prose on his desk when he returned yesterday and instead all David had given him were lame excuses. For over four years he had been able to coast through this job, avoiding the bursts of temper that had withered nearly everyone else in the office. Now he knew it was time to put up or shut up.

'Well? Let's hear it, son.'

Donnie Redwine was a former NASCAR driver who hadn't won a race in ten years on the circuit, his best result third place at Daytona when he was a rookie. But despite his poor record he had become famous for his spectacular wrecks, bringing out more yellow flags than any other driver in the sport's history. In fact, after causing an epic pile-up at the Firecracker 500 he'd earned the nickname 'Crash', though it was something no one was supposed to call him. After retiring broke and battered he decided it was time to get rich. He'd started out in billboards, soon controlling over half the space in the city, then branched out into real estate, making a killing in the dark days after the Burleigh Tobacco takeover. With an irony he didn't allow to be lost on anyone, he'd finally become a success during the recent property market crash, thereby justifying the moniker he'd always hated.

He now lived in a sprawling house with his third wife, twenty-five-year-old Kimberly May. David had been there only once, for Redwine's fiftieth birthday party. It was a maze of pastel colors, Lladró figurines and plush pile carpeting. The light fixtures in the den were naked men with on-off switches situated between their legs. There was a regulation batting cage out back for Redwine's sons from a previous marriage, who visited one weekend a month. The day's crowning moment came when Kimberly May ushered everyone into the master bathroom to show off Donnie's gift – his own personal urinal. For a moment David thought Redwine was going to christen it right there, in front of everyone. But then an almost-famous country band started playing in the back yard and the guests trooped out for a fireworks display that eventually drew the attention of the local volunteer fire department.

David never fully understood how Redwine had profited from Burleigh's transition into a ghost town, though he believed it was a combination of brilliant business instincts, opportunistic betrayal and downright crime. There were rumors that in the bad days just after the crash he would buy the houses of laid-off Burleigh Tobacco employees dirt cheap, insure them for their surveyed worth, then collect when they mysteriously burned to the ground before State Farm or the city could reassess them. Recently, however, he'd begun to leave such shady practices behind as his projects grew larger, culminating with the massive Elk Run resort.

David had started working for the Redwine Group several months after losing his job at the Social Fund. He was communications director, a title Redwine had dreamed up after sitting next to Pat Buchanan at a banquet. It simply meant that David was in charge of all the company's public utterances. Print ads, billboards, flyers, letters to buyers. Overseeing the occasional television commercial or radio spot. Promotions such as lip synch contests or the ill-fated raft race down the Mud River that had ended up with a dozen snakebit and dehydrated fraternity boys being Medevaced to hospital. It was an easy job most of the time, though sometimes, like this morning, David was expected to earn his pay.

'Well, I know you don't want to call it a retirement community,' he started, 'so I kicked around pre-retirement for a while . . . '

Redwine scowled.

'Exactly,' David agreed. 'It sounds like something you'd need ointment for. Then I thought about semi-retirement . . . '

'That's what they call people who just been laid off. *You* should know that, son.'

David ignored the comment.

'So what I thought was, well – how does New Beginnings sound to you?'

Redwine's bushy eyebrows began to flutter in thought.

'It's sort of Christian without being too heavy about it,' David added.

'So how would that go?'

'Elk Run – a place of old-fashioned values where new beginnings can be made. I mean, that's rough, but something like that.'

Redwine began to stroke his impenetrably black beard, an obsidian canopy that covered the lower half of his face like a moonless night, made to seem darker still by his head of white hair.

'Run that by me again?'

David repeated the phrase. As Redwine pondered it, David's eyes drifted out the window to Main Street. The first thing he saw was a meter maid ticketing a Trans Am. The second thing was a just-squashed pigeon, its feathers flapping in a parody of flight as a car passed over it. The third thing he saw was the woman from the crash, standing perfectly still on the far side of the street, staring right at his building. Her cast-covered left hand was held flush to her abdomen, awkwardly supported by her bandaged right one.

'Donnie?'

Redwine stopped stroking his beard.

'Listen, I just remembered something,' David said quickly. 'I gotta go.'

'Go? The hell? We're meeting here, son.'

'Family business.'

Redwine nodded solemnly, once, wanting further explanation.

'I'll call you . . . ' David said.

He stood quickly enough to send his chair spinning behind him, again looking out the window. She was staring down the street now, alarmed, as if she'd seen something she didn't like. Then she turned and began to walk away. David grabbed his jacket from its hook and strode quickly from the office, barely noting that Redwine was still staring at the empty, whirling chair.

When he burst through the front door she was turning down one of the small, depopulated streets that laced downtown like blocked veins. The badlands where he'd been mugged. He started to run, stepping in the flattened pigeon as he crossed the street, sliding and almost falling in the goo. People watched him race down the street – Burleigh wasn't the sort of city you ran through. He stopped abruptly when he turned the corner. There was no one there. Just two long rows of boarded-up shops. He walked quickly along the street, his shoes ringing on the pavement. There was no way she could have made it to the street's end, even if she'd been running. And the way she'd stood outside his office made him doubt she was capable of that.

About halfway along he saw something in a doorway. A stew of clothes and flesh and hair, with two brilliant eyes floating on a sooted face. One of Burleigh's burgeoning population of sidewalk people. David stood above him.

'I'm looking for a woman.'

'And I'm waiting on the Dispensation,' the man snapped back.

'I'm sorry?'

'The Lord's Dispensation, fool. I'm settin' here waiting for it.'

David nodded, hoping for further explanation.

'She had a cast on her arm,' he said when he realized there wasn't going to be any. 'Red hair.'

The man stared, unblinking.

'Give me a dollar,' he said.

The smallest David had was a five. He handed it over. The tramp tucked it away without noting its denomination.

'She went in there,' he said, pointing to a shop across the street.

It was called Mary's Originals, formerly a wig boutique, now a ruin like everything else on the street. Two coiffed silhouettes faced each other on the marquee, as if they were about to kiss. One window was soaped, the other smashed. David pushed through the plywood-covered door. There was rustling in the corner.

'Hello?'

There was no answer. He took a few more steps in and saw a pale

48

face a few feet away.

'I saw you on the street,' he said to it. 'I followed you here.'

The face didn't respond. David's eyes grew used to the light and he saw he was talking to styrofoam. He looked around. Dozens more model heads stared at him, like some dumb jury. There's no one here, he thought.

'What do you want?'

He recognized her voice right away. It was hushed with pain. He turned in its direction.

'Do you remember me?' he asked. 'From the accident?'

He heard more rustling and then she stepped out of the shadows.

'Sure, I remember you. What do you want?'

She looked bad. Her face was pale, dewy with cool-looking sweat, crossed by strands of hair and straw. The pants and shoes she wore were the same as when he'd found her, though the hospital green gown and rust-colored Naugahyde jacket were recent additions. The cast was scored with mud, the Ace bandage on her other wrist was slightly ruffled. The welt above her eye had darkened into a black hole that seemed to suck the color from her face.

'I saw you on the street,' he said. 'Outside the building where I work.'

She was giving him the same searching look she had at the hospital.

'I was worried about you,' he continued.

'Why?' she asked quickly.

He gave a short, incredulous laugh.

'Why do you think? I run you off the road and then I go to see you in hospital where you're in a coma and the next thing I hear they say you'd absconded.'

'And that's all?'

'Well, yeah.'

'There's nothing else? Nothing you know or . . .'

She didn't finish the sentence.

'I don't understand what you mean.'

'Look, I need your help,' she said after a moment.

'My help?'

She nodded, sucking air through her teeth.

'You gotta tell me where it happened,' she said.

49

'What, the accident?'

'No, the moon landing,' she said, wincing with pain.

'Well, yes, sure. Why?'

'I think my stuff is up there. My money and my license. Everything.'

'I don't remember seeing anything like that.'

'But you remember where it was? The crash?'

'I think so.'

'If you could tell me where it was then I could grab a cab up there and . . .'

'A cab? Up there? It'll cost you a fortune. *If* you can find one. This town isn't that big on cabs.'

'I could pay if I found my stuff.'

'What if you don't?'

She looked down at the rubble-strewn floor and he could see a small dead leaf in her hair.

'Then it really doesn't matter a whole hell of a lot, does it?'

'Look, I'd forget about a cab if I were you. They wouldn't take you up there, anyway. Not the shape you're in. Not without something up front.'

'I'll rent a car.'

'Do you have any plastic?'

She looked around the ruined shop.

'Fuck,' she said quietly.

Her face was drawn with pain and exhaustion – it looked to David like it hurt her just to breathe.

'Look,' he said. 'Maybe I should take you back to the hospital or—'

'No,' she said sharply. 'If that's why you've followed me then just leave me alone.'

'That isn't why I followed you,' he said quietly.

She stared at him and for a moment he wondered if this woman was crazy, if he should just walk away, make a call and let the pros sort her out. But he'd been around plenty of crazy people in his last job and he was suddenly sure she wasn't one of them. There was a lucidity to her desperation, a purpose. And he still couldn't shake the feeling that he was somehow responsible for this.

'All right, listen – why don't I give you a lift up there?'

She seemed as surprised at the suggestion as David.

'Really?'

'It wouldn't be a problem.'

She gave him a long, searching look.

'When could we go?'

David thought of Redwine, wondering if he was still sitting there, staring at the empty, spinning chair. He found the idea deeply gratifying.

'Whenever you want.'

'Now? Could we go now?'

'Yes, of course,' he said. 'There's one condition, though.'

Her eyes narrowed as she waited for it.

'You have to tell me your name.'

'My name?' She exhaled slowly, laboriously. 'My name is Sara.'

For some reason he felt elated to learn this simple thing, like it was some sort of revelation.

'All right, then, Sara. I'm David. Let's go for a ride.'

He got the Mustang without telling anyone what he was doing. She waited for him at the shop, claiming that to walk any further would hurt too much. As he helped her into the car he could sense how painful it was for her simply to sit.

'Is that all right?'

She nodded without saying anything.

'I'd better do up the seat belt.'

'OK.'

He pulled it gently across her, the back of his hand brushing her breasts as he did. They were loose beneath her hospital gown. She remained perfectly still as he locked her in. The symphony on the radio progressed to the next movement.

'Tell me if you need something,' he said. 'You know. Food or pit stop or whatever.'

'Just to get my stuff and get the hell out of here,' she said grimly.

He put the car in gear and headed off.

'Can I ask you something, Sara?' he asked a few blocks later.

She looked over at him, her amber eyes neutral, expectant.

'Were you awake yesterday morning? When I was in your room?'

She looked back at the window, nodding almost imperceptibly.

'But you didn't want the nurse to know it.'

She shook her head even more gently.

'And you left the hospital . . . '

'To find you. I heard you guys say something about this Redwine place. I thought it was a brewery or something but then I saw that building.'

'You must really be anxious to get your stuff.'

She didn't respond. David drove.

'So you just walked out, I mean, without telling anyone?'

'I don't have any money, remember? The last time I checked you needed money to be well in this country.'

'I'm sure they could have come to some sort of accommodation.'

'Accommodation,' she said ruefully. 'I've had enough of those.'

'Look,' David continued. 'Your doctor's a friend of mine. He was concerned about you. I'm sure if I had a word with him—'

'I'm all right.'

'But surely your hands must—'

'I'm all right,' she said impatiently. 'They're set. I can handle it.'

'I'm sorry. I'm just trying to help.'

She sighed.

'I know. I should be the one saying sorry. Making you drive all this way.'

'It's not a problem.'

'Not for you,' she muttered.

They drove in silence for a while. The music on the radio stopped.

'I thought I'd just bring you our first grand total of the drive . . . ' Mary Beth said.

David switched it off. He looked over at her, a tentative smile appearing on his face.

'What?' she asked warily.

'I was just admiring your jacket.'

She looked down at it.

'Yeah, it's been in my family for years. We're dumpster divers from way back.'

'So where are you from, then?' he asked.

'From?'

'I mean you don't sound like you're from these parts.'

'No, I'm not,' she said, struggling to find a comfortable position.

52

He waited for more but none was coming.

'Where were you going?' he asked finally.

'Away.'

She closed her eyes before he could ask anything else. David kept quiet for a few miles, thinking she might be falling asleep. He took the opportunity to study her face. She had a high, strong forehead; eyes that seemed big even while closed; a mouth pouted into natural disdain. Her nose was small, fragile looking. Dark red hair sprouted thickly along her temple, flowing into a long tangle at the back.

And then she opened her eyes and he realized she'd been combating a period of pain.

'Hurts,' he said, nodding.

'I can handle it.'

'So where did you spend the night?'

'Around. I found an open car and slept in that for a while. The windows got all fogged, it was like being in a dream or the womb or something. It was good.'

He took his eyes off the road again.

'Wait a minute. You mean you were out there during the storm?'

She nodded.

'Jesus, it must have been an awful night.'

'Yeah, I never thought there could be so much rain.'

'There was a tornado, you know.'

'No shit.'

He nodded.

'Then it's official,' she said, shaking her head. 'I've lived through everything.'

'It really is crazy your worrying about hospital bills and such.'

'It's not so crazy.'

They were in the countryside now. Gone-to-seed fields lined the road, alive with insects and wild flowers. Those tilled were studded with nascent soy.

'Those are pretty flowers,' she said.

'They used to grow tobacco but now most are fallow.'

'Like in *The Wizard of Oz*,' she continued, as if she hadn't heard him.

It took David a while to find the roads he'd been on two days earlier. Last night's storms had been heavy up here – pools of

53

standing water lined the road, big branches crackled beneath his radials. Some fields were almost completely flooded. He took a curve too fast and she placed her sprained hand on the dashboard for balance. Dirty pink fingertips wriggled from the bandage like a brood of something just born.

'Not much further,' he said.

Two miles later he saw the Adopt-a-Highway sign and pulled on to the shoulder. They both stared down the slope, neither of them speaking for nearly a minute.

'Are you sure this is the place?' she asked finally, her voice thin.

'Look at the skidmarks,' he said, pointing at the chewed earth.

'I don't fucking believe this. I don't fucking . . . '

She placed her wrapped hand over her eyes.

'The river must have burst its banks,' he said. 'Maybe a dam broke. Something. All that rain.'

Muddy water covered the crash site. The splintered tree seemed to be floating above the ground; the only part of the coop still visible was its swaybacked roof. She removed her hand and stared at the floor, her eyes pained and distant.

'How deep do you think it is?' she asked.

'Six, eight feet. Maybe more. Why?'

'Perhaps we could, you know, wade out or something.'

'I don't think that's such a good idea, Sara. The water's too murky to see anything. Including the exact number of snakes swimming around beneath the surface.'

He looked over at her.

'I mean, credit cards and stuff like that, you can replace them, right?'

She looked at him like she didn't know what he meant.

'Was there a lot of money?' he asked.

'Enough.'

'Well, someone might have picked it up.'

She didn't answer.

'Maybe we could talk to the people who were here,' he said. 'The cops or whoever.'

'No. I'd know if they found it. They would have brought it to the hospital, I mean,' she added quickly.

'Well, I can check anyway.'

'Unless someone ripped them off,' she said, ignoring him.

'I don't think anyone stole them,' he said. 'There were just cops and paramedics up here.'

She laughed mirthlessly.

'And you don't think they could have stolen something? What planet did you say you were from?'

They looked at the site for a while.

'Why did you go into that coop?' he asked.

'What?'

'The shack there. That's where I found you when I came back from calling the cops.'

Her eyes narrowed.

'I don't remember that. The last thing was you driving away for help. Then I woke up in the hospital.'

David watched the water for a while.

'Who's Will?' he asked finally.

She looked at him, her eyes unrevealing.

'What?'

'When I first found you you said maybe I should take you back to Will's place.'

She didn't answer.

'I was just thinking, I could take you there now, if that's still where you want to be.'

'I don't know any Will,' she said, looking back at the flood. 'You must have heard me wrong.'

David knew he'd heard her perfectly well but decided not to press the point. She was upset enough as it was. They watched the muddy water roll by for a while.

'Do you remember it?' he asked. 'The crash?'

She nodded.

'I came too fast around a bend and was in the middle of the road and all of a sudden there you were . . . '

Her eyes narrowed, remembering.

'It's funny, they say in a crash it seems like everything's going in slow motion but actually it went really fast. Way too fast. And then the next thing I remember you were standing there.' She looked over at him and smiled weakly. 'I'm glad you stopped. Most people wouldn't have. If you hadn't, then . . . shit, who knows.'

They looked at the flood. A car passed, dovetailing leftover water.

'So what do you want to do?' he asked.

She gave a brief, bitter laugh.

'You know, I honestly don't know.'

'How about your car? We can go check that.'

'It's not my car.'

David remembered what Rowdy had said about it being a rental.

'So isn't there anywhere I could take you?'

'Not really.'

'Back to town?'

She shrugged.

'All right, then,' David said. 'Town it is.'

He pulled a U and they drove in silence for a while. She sat slumped against the door, staring at the fields, the billboards, the houses.

'God, look at all those satellite dishes,' she said.

'It's the state flower.'

She didn't smile.

'If there's someone you want to call you could use my phone back at the office. It's a WATS line so . . . '

She looked at David as if the idea had never crossed her mind.

'Not really.'

They drove on, heading back to Burleigh. David soon began to worry. There's obviously something going on here, he thought. Something he shouldn't get involved in. It was inconceivable that a woman like this would have no one to call. There was clearly some purpose behind her evasiveness, some drama in which he didn't need anything more than a walk-on part. He'd helped her, given her a ride – he owed her that much. But he couldn't get involved in this any more. They were quits. He had work to do, a busy wife to help. Enough was enough.

'Look,' he said. 'Since you don't have anywhere specific in mind, I think I will just take you back to the hospital. We'll find Rowdy, the doctor. He'll make some sort of arrangement about—'

'No,' she interrupted.

'I know you think you don't want to go back there but since you won't give me any alternative—'

'There's an alternative.'

56

'Such as?'

'Stop the car.'

'What?'

'Stop this fucking car right now.'

Her sudden ferocity made him do as he was told, rolling to a halt on the shoulder.

'Unhook this for me,' she said, nodding at the seat belt.

He did it.

'And the door.'

'Listen . . . '

She tried to open it with her bandaged hand but couldn't get enough leverage. Her arm began to quiver with the pain and effort. So he reached across and opened it for her. She looked at him.

'Thanks for the lift,' she said coldly.

And then she simply got out of the car and started to walk. It was a particularly deserted stretch of road – just scraped billboards and rusted pylons and trees heavy with the recent rain. David watched her in disbelief, expecting her to turn around and come back. But she just kept on walking. After she'd gone about fifty yards a pickup appeared on the road's horizon. Sara stepped in its path and waved it down with her bandaged hand. The truck flashed its lights and started to slow.

'Holy shit,' David said aloud.

He put the Mustang in gear and drove quickly down the road. By the time he reached her she was talking to the driver, a fat man with a greasy beard and impossibly small eyes. There was a passenger as well, his smiling teeth covered with a gray caulk. David rolled down his window.

'Ass, gas or grass,' the driver said. 'That's what a ride costs out here.'

The other man cackled agreement.

'Sara,' David said.

She didn't turn.

'Sara, come on. Get back in the car.'

The driver looked at David, who realized this could go one of two ways. Either the men would press their advantage or they'd decide this wasn't worth the grief. The driver's eyes went from David's face to Sara's damaged hands, her bruised head. Then he smiled and gave

David a complicitous nod.

'She's all yours, good buddy.'

As the truck peeled off David knew he'd won the showdown for one simple reason – the man thought he was the one who'd done all that to her.

Sara was still standing in the middle of the road.

'I'm sorry,' he said to her back. 'I was wrong to press you like that. We'll do it your way. Please get in.'

She stood where she was for a moment, then, without looking at him, walked slowly around the car and got into the passenger seat. David didn't bother fastening the seat belt this time. They sat in silence for a moment.

'What'd you say your name was again?' she asked finally.

'David.'

'Look, David, you're clearly a decent guy and everything, but I'm not kidding around when I say I do *not* want to get involved with hospitals and shit like that. If you have a problem with that, well, that's cool, I don't blame you. Just drop me off at the next gas station or whatever.'

She looked over at him, her eyes sparkling with determination.

'No,' he said. 'I don't have any problem with that.'

They entered Burleigh ten minutes later. Flagging down the pickup seemed to have sapped her remaining energy. By the time they reached the city limits she was leaning back in the seat, her eyes hooded, her mouth slack as she took long, slow breaths.

'I still don't know where to take you,' he said.

'Is there a bus station?'

'Bus station?'

'I thought maybe I could . . . '

She closed her eyes in weary acknowledgment of the improbability of whatever she was planning. For a moment David entertained the notion of taking her to his house. There was all that room, after all. Mary Beth would understand. In fact, she would have insisted if she knew what was going on. But he quickly realized there was no way he could have this woman in his home, not after she'd run away from the hospital, not without knowing what she was fleeing. Christ, she could be anything. And yet he couldn't just dump her at the bus station.

'Look,' he said finally. 'Since you don't want to go to the hospital, I mean, why don't I lend you the money so you could stay in a hotel? Just for tonight. You look bushed and it's crazy for you to have to decide anything now. You could get some sleep and then in the morning you'd probably have a better take on what you want to do. If there's someone you want to call, I don't know. But after last night and now this, the main thing is I think you should get some rest.'

She looked across at him.

'A hotel?'

'Sure.'

She mulled it over. They were approaching a Motel 6.

'How about that one there?' he asked.

She didn't take her eyes off David as he pulled up to the office.

'Yes or no?' he said as he put the car in park. 'We're in a no standing zone here.'

She looked through the lobby's glass doors.

'And I could just chill out for a while? No questions or answers or . . . '

'Of course.'

'I guess since I really don't have a choice, the answer's yes.'

'Good,' he said, pushing open his door. 'Wait here.'

He used his company credit card to pay. The bill wouldn't clear for a month and he'd have time to think of a way to bury it by then. They drove around back. The room was like any other. Twin beds, Pay Per View. That smell. Prayer card on the pillow. The light through the curtains was pale green.

'Will this be all right?' he asked.

'I've stayed in worse.'

She was supporting her cast with her bandaged hand.

'That looks painful.'

'Fucker's really getting heavy.'

'Here, let me . . . '

He looked around for something to make a sling with, settling eventually on his tie. He carefully looped it beneath her cast, then double knotted it behind her neck.

'Thanks,' she said, testing it. 'Yeah, that's a lot better.'

59

'Can I get you something else? Some food or . . .'

'I just want to sleep.'

He took a ten from his wallet.

'I saw there's a Food Lion across the street. Or you could send out for a pizza.'

She pincered the bill in the stiff fingers of her right hand.

'I'll owe you for this,' she said. 'For all of this.'

'God, don't worry about that. It's the least I could do. Look, you just get some rack. I'll come by this evening, after work. Maybe by then . . .'

'Could you do something else before you go?' she asked.

'What's that?'

'Don't take this the wrong way, but could you undo my pants?'

She gestured with her damaged hands as an explanation. He laughed nervously, then reached out. She thrust her hips forward to help. As he worked the brass button through its slit he could feel the soft, warm flesh of her belly on the back of his hands.

'It hurts like crazy for me to do it.'

When he was through he pulled his hands away, rubbing them together for a moment.

'Now, you get some sleep.'

'All right.'

'And I'll be back around five, five-thirty?'

'I'll be here.'

'Sleep well then.'

He walked to the door. There was a small handwritten sign above the chain slot. *STOP: Have you forgotten anything?* it asked.

Thankfully, Redwine was gone when he arrived back at the office, up at Elk Run for the rest of the day. There were two messages from Mary Beth. He called her at the station.

'Hey, where you been?' she asked.

'Up at Elk Run,' he said without thinking.

'Oh, 'cause Ginger said she didn't know.'

'It was sort of a spur of the moment thing.' He gave an ironic laugh. 'I was looking for inspiration.'

Someone at the station spoke to her and she answered.

'Listen, what do you want to do about dinner tonight?' she asked when she came back on the line.

'I'll cook.'

'I have to be back in at seven so if we could eat at six . . . '

'No problem. So how's it going?'

'We're a bit behind already, I think.' She sighed, bucking herself up. 'But it's early yet.'

'I have faith.'

'You for one.'

After hanging up David felt an urge to call her right back, tell her what was happening. Why had he lied to her? How would it look if she found out he'd just put up a strange woman in a hotel? Innocent as it was, it looked bad. What was wrong with him? But he couldn't bring himself to pick up the phone. It wasn't that big of a thing, he told himself. After some rest Sara would know what she wanted to to do. And then she would be gone. Better not to tell anyone, especially Mary Beth. That could only lead to misunderstanding.

Ginger buzzed with a call and after that he began working in earnest on the insert. Time was running out on that – he'd screwed around enough. So he fired up the Mac and buckled down. And yet, no matter how hard he tried to concentrate, he couldn't shake the feeling there was something he hadn't done. Every time he gave it a moment's thought he came up with his parting image of Sara as she stood by that hotel bed, hurt and confused, looking at him like he knew what it was she should do.

Despite planning to leave at five he wound up trapped at work until five-twenty, haggling with the newspaper's photo editor over color separations. A steady rain was falling as he drove to the Motel 6, further dampening the already-soaked city. He would have to hurry if he was going to get home in time to cook Mary Beth dinner. The smart thing would have been to forget the hotel and check on Sara later that night or in the morning, when everything would be clearer. After all, as she'd said herself, she wasn't going anywhere. But instead of doing the smart thing he found himself standing outside her door, wondering if she were still in there, if she were awake or even alive. He listened for a moment but all he could hear were the trucks hissing by on the slick pavement of the nearby overpass. He knocked.

'What?'

Her voice was weak.

'It's me. David.'

A few seconds later the bolts were working. He winced, thinking how painful it must be for her.

'I was beginning to think you weren't coming,' she said as the door finally came open.

The room was dark and silent and smelled of wet towels. He was shocked by how bad she looked. He thought she'd be better, that his provision of shelter and money would have made her well. If anything, she seemed worse.

'Did you sleep?'

'No. You can't believe how bad this fucking arm—'

'Sara, are you all right?'

'I flooded the place,' she said, ignoring the question. 'The plan was to take a bath.'

'Don't worry about that. How are you feeling?'

She sat gingerly on the bed.

'My wrist feels worse than ever. I keep on expecting it to get better, but it doesn't.'

'Can I get you something?'

'I bought some Tylenol across the street. The kid there opened them. They're useless, though. So I went for some cognac but the prick there wouldn't sell me any without i.d. I said, come on, Jethro, I'm of age. But he seemed to think it was a big deal that I stay sober.'

She looked at David.

'What I need are some real pills.'

'We should take you to a doctor.'

Her faced closed up.

'I thought I explained . . . '

'It doesn't have to be the hospital,' he added quickly. 'I have a family doctor; you can trust him. Or there are these initial care clinics, you know. We could just go in and they would prescribe you something. In and out.'

'No.'

His eyes came to rest on the place where the puddle from the bathroom had dampened the room's carpet.

'All right,' he said eventually. 'I'll get you that cognac. Do you want some food?'

'I couldn't eat.'

He was trying in vain to think of something more he could do to help her, really help her. Nothing came to mind.

'I'll be back in a minute,' he said finally.

The ABC store was across the highway. There was a Woolworth's next door and as he passed it he had an idea. When he came back she was lying on the bed, her eyes slitted open.

'Do you want a glass?'

'They're in the bathroom.'

There were two on a tray. He pierced their seals and splashed in some cognac. When he came back into the room she was propped up on the bed.

'I got you something.'

He showed her what else he'd bought.

'A crazy straw,' she said. 'Jesus. I used to have one of those when I was a girl.'

'So you won't have to keep lifting the cup.'

She managed a smile.

'You're all right, David, you know?'

He was surprised how deeply her words pleased him. He set a pillow on her lap and nestled the cup into it. Then he ripped the straw from its package and placed it in the drink. For some reason he raised his in a toast. She smiled weakly, unable to respond. Cognac was soon making its way through the bends and switchbacks of her straw. He noticed how it matched the color of her eyes.

'Have you thought any more about what you're going to do?'

She raised her chin to swallow.

'I'm really not in the thinking mode, you know?'

'Well, you're all right here for tonight.'

He looked at his wrist before remembering that his watch had been stolen.

'You don't know what time it is, do you?'

She nodded toward her bandaged hands.

'Oh yeah. Right. Sorry.'

He turned on the television. The six o'clock news had just started. They were showing footage of the tornado's wreckage to the north of the city. The usual catalogue of crumpled mobile homes and peeled roofs, flash floods and choked-up women vowing to pick up the pieces. The governor's chopper, a fireman carrying a cat.

Shit, David thought. Six o'clock.

'Look, I have to go,' he said quickly. 'I'll come back first thing in the morning and we'll get you organized.'

'Good luck,' she said sardonically.

He bolted his drink and walked to the door.

'Make sure you get some sleep.'

'Could you . . . '

'What?'

'Forget it. You've done too much already.'

He waited.

'Could you try to get me something for this pain? Something scrip, something real.'

'I don't know how easy that'll be.'

'Well, try, anyway.'

'All right.'

He felt like there was something more he should say, something more he should do. But she'd closed her eyes and placed the crazy straw to her lips, as if he'd already left the room.

The car's digital clock read 6:32 when he pulled into the driveway. Mary Beth was in the kitchen, the phone to her ear.

'Never mind,' she said when she saw him. 'Here he is.'

'Sorry.'

'Where were you?' she asked, a puzzled smile on her face. 'I was starting to get worried.'

'Work, you know. I lost track of the time.'

He shook his left hand, rubbed the wrist.

'I got to get a new watch.'

'But they said you left at five-thirty.'

'Who said that?'

'Your secretary.'

Just tell her, he thought.

'She did?'

'David, I don't want to be a nag but I'm on a pretty tight schedule this week. You know all I got is a bunch of kids down there. We're dealing with feeds from NPR.'

'I'm sorry.'

'No, come on, you don't have to apologize.' She pointed at his chest. 'Hey, where's your tie?'

'Oh, I spilled some coffee on it.'

She moved close to him and sniffed.

'What is that?' she asked, recoiling, the bemused smile on her face shrinking a bit. 'Have you been drinking?'

'Just one. It was somebody's birthday, one of the salesmen. That's where I was. The bar.'

She tilted her head, scrutinizing him but still smiling patiently.

'David—'

'Mary Beth, look, I'm sorry. Just go. You're late enough as it is.'

'But what about dinner? I'm starving.'

Fuck, he thought.

'We could order out.'

'Have you called?'

David stared helplessly at her.

'Never mind,' she said. 'There's no time. They have sandwiches at work.'

'Mary Beth, listen . . . '

She watched him, nodding.

'I'll have something for you when you get home.'

'That won't be till about one. Hey, don't worry about it. I could use to lose a few anyway.'

'I guess this Elk Run thing is getting to me.'

'Well, you got tonight to work on it. Look, I better go.'

'I'm really sorry about this.'

'Will you stop saying that?' she said, shaking her head in amusement. 'It's no big deal.'

They kissed and then she left. After the front door slammed he sat down at the table, his mind reeling. What was he doing? Why the fuck was he lying to his wife? He knew he should feel guilty, though all he really felt was wonder at how easily the lies had come. Like there was someone else speaking them, this other person beating him to the punch before he could tell the truth.

He threw something in the microwave and then sat on the porch, picking over the steaming food as the Ivy Street chimes announced another front of turbulent weather. The word Rowdy had used rattled through his mind. Absconded. Followed by related phrases. Aid and abet. Cease and desist. Search and seizure. Who was this woman? Just what ailed her beside the obvious breaks and bruises? He was struck by a sudden temptation to call the hotel, see if she was all right. But he didn't want to wake her. And if she'd been hitting that bottle she'd be in no shape to talk now. Besides, there was nothing to say to her except ask her how she was doing. And she'd already told him. She was in pain.

He remembered her request for drugs. Maybe if he could get her something to ease the hurt then she could think more clearly, perhaps even explain her situation. And then they could decide what to do. There was probably an easy answer to all this. He went upstairs and rummaged through the medicine chest. Antibiotics, vitamins, water relief tablets. Nothing for pain, not what she must be feeling. He considered calling Rowdy and explaining the situation to him. Rowdy would understand. He was a doctor, after all. Didn't they have some sort of code that would have made him write out a prescription? She would never have to know he'd done it. There was every reason to call him. And yet, looking at the meager relief he and Mary Beth allowed themselves for life's troubles, he suddenly knew that he wouldn't be telling anyone about the woman at the Motel 6.

He racked his brain, finally coming up with the Kellys next door. Of course. Shana was a frail, nervous woman who always joked about her pills. More than once Kyle had turned down an invitation to dinner or a party, saying his wife was 'tranked out'. They must have something in there. All David had to do was ask. They owed him a favor. But if he asked there would be the risk of Mary Beth finding out. And then he'd have to explain why he'd lied about today.

He went downstairs to the bulletin board in the kitchen, where the Kellys' house keys dangled from a Snoopy ring. Woodstock was perched on his shoulder. Countless fingerings had worn the legend beneath them into obscurity. Love means this or that, David couldn't tell. Kyle had let him have them a few months back after locking himself out. Just in case.

David pocketed the keys and slipped out the back door, jumping the fence that separated their yards. Cool blue light glowed from a window at the side of the house. Shit, he thought. They're home. He hesitated at their back door, convincing himself that he could pull this off anyway. Getting through the hallway would be the only hard part. A siren sounded in the distance, the wind gusted. He thought of Sara, the pain she was in. Just knock and ask, he thought. Quit messing around. Just knock and ask.

Instead, he gently eased open the door and stepped in, pausing for a moment before walking quickly through the kitchen to the hallway. He stopped – the family room door was half-open. He could hear the TV playing. A man's voice, a woman's wail, a squishy noise like the last bit of water down a drain. He moved closer and listened.

'In order to prevent premature ejaculation, grip the base of the penis, the fore and middle fingers at the bottom, the thumb on top, and squeeze the seminal vesicle when you feel the impending orgasm. With practice, you or your partner can thereby control the duration of sex, maximizing . . . '

He peeked around the corner. The Kellys knelt on the rug in front of their television, eyes glued to the screen, Shana's hand gripping her husband's semi-erect member as if it were a squash racquet. David relaxed. Feeling suddenly invisible, he moved quickly past the door.

He felt a pulse of relieved excitement when he opened their medicine cabinet. It was three deep with pill bottles. He isolated two likely looking candidates. Prozac and Percodan. One for stress, the other for pain. Sara's situation in a nutshell. Both were nearly full. He shook out ten of each and headed downstairs. A woman's voice was testifying.

'The thought of swallowing sperm used to disgust me, but I soon grew used to it and I now see it as a sort of love snack . . . '

David tiptoed past the door. An image of his neighbors flashed, mouth to crotch, crotch to mouth. A taut, continuous Kelly. Infinite and blindly groaning.

He made sure to lock the door behind him as he left their house.

The phone was ringing when he got home. He picked it up quickly.

'Hi,' he said, trying to sound groggy, just-woken.

'Is your refrigerator running?' a young voice asked.

He looked at it instinctively, bedecked with messages, schedules, reminders.

'What?'

'Better go catch it then!'

There was a shriek of laughter at the other end, followed by the phone's slamming. David replaced the receiver. It rang again.

'Mary Beth?' he asked, convinced that this time it had to be her.

'Do you have Prince Albert in a can?'

'Listen . . . '

'Better let him out, then!'

He hung up and stared at the phone, ready for them this time. But it didn't ring again.

4

David drove quickly through the wet and nearly deserted streets, listening to his wife running down the day's programming on WBRR. She'd been gone when he woke, her side of the bed almost cool. For the rest of the drive she would have to be at work before the six a.m. *Morning Edition* feed from Washington, remaining there with few interruptions until *Jazz After Hours*. The station had been seriously understaffed since the hiring freeze instituted after last year's drive came up nearly thirty thousand dollars short. To make matters worse, her principal sound technician and senior disc jockey had recently joined the exodus from Burleigh. Sometimes, she said, it felt like it was just her down there.

The local morning news came on. It had rained all night in the mountains, further swelling the rivers. There were four flood-related deaths, further evacuations, more reclaimed farmland. Sandbaggers had worked through the night on the upper reaches of the rampaging Mud, though their walls had still been breached in several places. David thought of Sara's possessions, whatever they were, sinking deeper and deeper under the water.

He parked in front of her motel room and stared at the door, wondering what his next step was. He'd been moving on impulse yesterday, letting her pain and confusion dictate matters. Today he'd act differently. Take charge. Let's look at things logically, he thought. She's hurt and disoriented. If she was to be believed, then she has nothing. The responsible thing would be to contact the police. How would it look, David wondered, if it turned out they had been searching for her all along? And now there was a credit card slip proving he'd put her up in a hotel room.

He got out of the car, powered by his resolve to settle this matter right now. He'd tell her she could either give him a name he could contact or he was going to have to call the cops, the hospital. Someone. Lover, brother, friend. Husband. Enough was enough. As he approached he thought he could hear the TV through the door but couldn't be sure – the noise from the overpass drowned out everything else. He knocked. The door's cheap aluminium rattled like an old man's chest. Nothing happened. He knocked again. For an instant the possibility that she had died flashed through his mind. But then the door came open a few inches before being caught by the chain. She recoiled when the light hit her. Her eyes were puffy and unfocused; her hair stuck to her cheeks and forehead as if her skin were charged. She looked at him wearily, her face blank.

'It's me,' David said.

She nodded and closed the door, fumbling with the chain. It swung back open and she moved away from the light, her wrists crossed mummy-like in front of her chest.

'Bad night?' was all he could think to ask.

'Real bad night.'

He followed her into the room, noticing how the hospital gown clung tightly in several places to her thin back. The only clothes she had, he realized. She sat slowly on the crumpled bed. He stood where he was, at a loss how to comfort her. Next door a TV came on too loud, and was immediately turned down. The cognac bottle on the side table was less than a quarter empty. He pointed to it.

'I thought you would have polished that off.'

She glanced over.

'I had a few glasses and then I was just drunk and hurting and awake.'

'Didn't you sleep at all?'

'A bit, I think. It was hard to tell. The trucks kept on waking me. And I get the feeling this is some sort of notell motel. People slamming car doors, laughing. I think there was a fight in the next room.' She squinted at the wall. 'I don't know. Maybe I just dreamed that.'

He sat on the bed beside her. The mattress rocked slightly and this seemed to hurt her. He noticed his tie on the floor. He picked it up and looped in carefully over her neck, then helped her put her arm through it. She looked up at him and said a feeble thanks and he suddenly knew he wasn't going to be forcing her to do anything. Not yet, anyway. Not in the state she was in.

'We could find you another place,' he offered.

'It doesn't matter. I wouldn't have slept much at the Plaza.'

He began patting his pockets.

'I almost forgot. I brought you these.'

She squinted at the baggie he produced.

'Are those what I think they are?'

'Let's see if I can remember right. These ones are—'

'Prozac,' she interrupted. 'And the others are Percs if my eyes don't deceive me. Where did you get them?'

'From a neighbor. She's a bit of a tranquilizer junky. Don't worry. I was discreet.'

Sara smiled with relief.

'Just what the doctor ordered.'

'Yes, what I thought was—'

'I'll have two Percs and one of the tranks.'

'That's a lot, Sara,' he said, remembering the upper-case interdictions on the vials.

'There's a lot of pain, David.'

He hesitated.

'I can handle three pills,' she said. 'Believe me.'

He reluctantly counted them out and placed them on the bedside table, then went to the bathroom and filled a cup with water. When he returned he could see she was having trouble picking them up with her sprained right hand.

'Let me . . . '

He fetched the pill and tried to give it to her. But her fingers were stiff, it tumbled to the floor. He snatched it from among the wiry strands of the cheap carpet. They looked at each other.

'You'd better just feed them to me.'

He placed one pill at a time on her parched tongue, the backs of his fingers brushing her soft, dry lips as he did. She took a long pull of water through the crazy straw after each. When they were gone she closed her eyes and tilted back her head. David stared at the smooth contour of her throat, the lift of her small breasts. He could see the small mounds of her nipples through the stretched cotton.

He realized what he was doing and looked away.

'Sara, I was thinking on the way over here . . . '

'Yes?'

He was flipping the plastic bag over and over, tightening its seal, catching the air inside.

'This room runs out at eleven,' he said eventually. 'I'll pay for another day so you can sleep.'

'That would be great.'

They sat in silence for a moment.

'And after?' he asked. 'Have you thought about that?'

'I haven't been able to think about anything, you know? I'm just trying to keep from . . .'

Something caught in her throat and she closed her eyes. David reached out to touch her and found himself giving a reassuring pat to plaster. He quickly withdrew his hand.

'That's all right,' he said. 'You're OK for now. I was just thinking, you know. If there's something more I can do . . .'

'This is good, what you've done. Real good.' She fell back on the tangled sheets. 'I just want to sleep now. Sleep and sleep and sleep.'

'I'll go, then.'

'Talk to me a minute before you do,' she said, her eyes still closed.

'All right.' His mind was a blank. 'What should I say?'

'Anything.'

'Four people died in that tornado you were in.'

'No, come on, not like that.'

And then it occurred to him.

'You wanna hear a joke?'

She nodded. So he told her about the old man and the flood. To his surprise he remembered every word of it. Usually, he forgot jokes the moment he stopped laughing. But this one had stuck. When he was through she laughed gently.

'That's the story of my life,' she said.

Her eyes were open now, staring at the ceiling.

'How do you mean?' he asked.

'You keep on waiting for something different to happen,' she said slowly. 'Something better to come along. And eventually you realize it won't and by then it's almost too late. So you have to go out and try to find it. And that's when the trouble starts.'

'I'm not really sure what you mean.'

She smiled weakly.

'No, me neither.'

He stared at her, a thousand questions in his mind.

'Try to sleep,' was all he could think to say.

'I don't think it will be too hard.'

'I'll come by tonight. About five? Is that all right?'

'I'll be here.'

'I was thinking, maybe then we can decide what to do.'

'Maybe.'

He started for the door.

'David?'

'Yes?'

'Thanks for the pills. And the joke. And the straw.'

He paid for another day and headed to work, still at a loss what to do with her. Christ, she'd already cost him nearly a hundred bucks and he didn't even know her last name. He couldn't keep on paying for her room – his company credit card was nearly maxed out as it was. He could use his own money, of course, but then he would have to tell Mary Beth what was happening. And that would be tricky. The best thing would be to get her out of that dive, put her somewhere she could rest up and recover for a few days. David thought of all the friends he had with spare rooms, all the people he knew who owed him favors, who'd be glad to help him out. There were plenty of them. Dozens. Good friends. People he could rely on. But even as he drew up a mental list he knew that he wouldn't be using any of them. Not now. Not with her. Not until he knew something more.

When he arrived back at the Redwine Group he sat for a while in his parking space, staring at his sign. *Reserved For D. Webster*. It was a simple white cross that he'd always jokingly referred to as his grave marker. He'd kept on meaning to get it changed but never had. His mind shifted back to Sara. Maybe now that she's taken the pills she can decide what she wants to do. Maybe that's all she needs, for the pain to go away.

He got out and walked into the rambling wood frame house that was the Redwine Group. It had been owned by a senior Burleigh Tobacco executive before the company was broken up. Inside, David made his way past offices filled with splenetic young salesmen and women, all of them perched on the edge of chairs, shouting the same things into phones. Ginger was whiting something out.

'Donnie's looking for you,' she said without looking up. 'Energetically.'

There was a piece of paper taped to his chair. A note from Redwine. It was to the point.

'Today.'

He balled the note and tossed it into his trash can. All this with Sara and he still had to write the fucking article. It was going to be a long day. He sat at his desk, booted up his computer and looked at the blank screen, the wavering lines washing gently over his eyes.

And then it came to him. What he was going to do to take care of her.

He worked hard for the rest of the morning to finish the ad, digging deep for the first time in a long while, tapping that reserve of energy and concentration that had rested undisturbed since he'd left his last job. By noon he was done. He reached Redwine on his cellular, telling him he had something for him. They agreed to meet for lunch at a place called the Hot Chili Bordello, a cavernous restaurant done up to look like someone's idea of an Old West whorehouse. The waitresses wore Belle Starr costumes, the effect diminished somewhat by their powder blue Reeboks and fluorescent Swatches. The walls were decorated with daguerreotypes, antique guns, wanted posters. They met in the parking lot. Redwine led David straight past the long line, acting like he owned the place. Which he did. The hostess broke off a phone conversation to show them to a table inside an ersatz Wells Fargo wagon.

'You want a drink?' Redwine asked as a waitress hovered.

'Iced tea,' David said.

'Two Long Island Iced Teas,' Redwine said. 'And two bowls of your best.'

She was gone before David could object, her sneakers squeaking on the polished floor like just-hatched birds.

'So, you get your problems sorted out?'

'Sorry about that,' David said.

'Just don't make a habit of it.'

The waitress brought their drinks.

'Cheers.'

The alcohol shot straight into his system. His second unexpected drink in as many days. He handed the copy to Redwine, who read slowly, stroking his beard. When he was done he looked off to the side for a few seconds worth of theatrical deliberation, then met David's eyes.

'That's good, David. I especially like the title. A New Life in a Familiar Place. I mean, that's *real* good.'

'Thanks.'

'I want to tell you, son, this is the sort of thing I always knew you were capable of.'

'Yeah, well,' David said, smiling slightly. 'I was inspired.'

Redwine nodded his approval and took a long drink, his rugged body-jewelry clanking. When he put his glass down he noticed David was still staring at him.

'Anything else you wanted to see me about?'

'Donnie, listen, I wonder if I could ask you something.'

'Here we go. I give him an attaboy and now he's gonna hit me for a raise.'

David smiled.

'Thing is, I need a favor. A personal favor.'

'Yeah?'

David took another sip. This one went down more easily.

'I have this problem that I was hoping you could help me out with. I have this friend. And, well, she's sort of in trouble and needs a place to stay for a few days. Maybe a week. And she doesn't really have enough money for a hotel.'

'Who does?'

'And I was wondering if perhaps you knew of somewhere she could crash. Stay. I mean, some empty house or something. Nothing special.'

Redwine's face was impassive. The waitress arrived with two big bowls of chili and a plate of parchment-like soda crackers. David took one, broke it in half, put it back.

'Well, sure,' Redwine said. 'I know places. We got tons of rentals, you know that. Some are pretty cheap, if you don't mind little critters for company.'

'You see, Donnie, that's the thing. She's broke. I mean, stony. She's had some tough luck. And she's hurt her hands pretty good. I

75

spotted her some money but now that's gone and . . . what I was thinking is if there was some place that was just sitting there and she could have it, you know, until she gets on her feet.'

'You mean for free?'

David nodded. Redwine looked around the place.

'God, I hate that word.'

David waited. There wasn't anything more for him to say.

'Well, there are lots of places, sure. I mean, your best bet would be an eviction.'

'An eviction?'

'Yeah.' He snapped his fingers. 'In fact, I do believe we picked up a place at auction the other day. A little home over in North Burleigh, a real nice place. It's right up near Nowheresville. That the sort of thing you had in mind?'

'I don't want to put anybody out.'

Redwine laughed.

'You're not putting them out. The bank already done that. It would be pretty down and dirty, though. I mean, there's water but no juice.'

'That would be great, Donnie.'

'Sure, I can let you have it for a week or so. But I don't think I can give you much more than that. We're going to have to move on it 'fore long to make our margin.'

'No, it'll just be a few days. Just till she's back on her feet.'

A smile ruffled Redwine's beard.

'Back on her feet, huh?'

David looked at his steaming chili.

'It's not like that.'

'Oh yeah? Then what *is* it like?'

'I honestly don't know.'

'Well, what's her problem?'

'She was in an accident.'

'They got hospitals for that, last I heard.'

'She doesn't want to go to a hospital.'

'You ever get to thinking there might be a reason behind that?'

David shrugged noncommittally.

'I'm just doing her this favor.'

'Shee,' Redwine said.

'Could she move in today?'

'Man, you are chompin' at the bit.' He rubbed at his beard with a napkin, then looked into its folds, as if seeking the answer there. 'Well, sure. All right. The keys are at the office. Somebody'll drop 'em by.'

'And, Donnie, you know, I think this should just be between thee and me.'

'You got my word, hoss,' Redwine said, raising a bejeweled right hand.

David took another sip of his drink, suddenly feeling giddy, like he'd just done the deal of the century. He couldn't wait to get back and tell Sara.

'Now, eat your chili and tell me what you think,' Redwine said.

David tasted it for the first time. He sat perfectly still for three seconds, then dropped the spoon and reached for his iced water, which he downed in one gulp. Redwine sat back in his chair, spreading his arms expansively.

'God, I love burnin' those virgin buds.'

David was tempted to go right over to the Motel 6 to tell Sara what he'd arranged, but decided against it, not wanting to disturb her much-needed sleep. Better to wait until after work, check the place out first. So he went back to the office. Mary Beth called just as he got there, full of news and worry about the drive, reminding him about their dinner plans for the evening. She asked if he would help with the phones the following morning. They were short of volunteers. David, feeling guilty about his petty lies to her, readily agreed.

After hanging up he started to think about Sara. If only he knew something more about her, maybe then he might be able to understand how to purge this growing feeling that she was his responsibility, that it was up to him to look after her. And then it came to him. The car. Of course. It took him a while to find the pound where it had been towed. The man there said it had been recovered by the rental company. David called them, explaining that he'd helped the driver after her accident.

'I'm just concerned about her, I guess.'

'Yes, we recovered that vehicle on Wednesday,' the man

77

explained.

'Could you tell me the name of the person who'd rented it? I just wanted to see if she's all right.'

'That's not our policy.'

'But you've reported this to the police?'

'Reported what? They had the car.'

'I just thought since she'd abandoned it.'

'There's no reason, really. We're not pursuing her. The damage is covered by the insurance she took out.'

'But what about the additional charges? Mileage and stuff like that?'

'We just ran it through on her Amex.'

'And it cleared?'

'Sure. It was gold.'

'It must have been a lot of money.'

The man didn't answer.

'Does this happen often? People just abandoning cars?'

'Enough so we don't make a federal case of it.'

'So you're not, like, looking for her?'

'Not as long as she had enough credit to cover the costs.' He paused. 'I mean, technically, she should come in and fill out an accident report but that's really for her own protection.'

'So the fact that she's disappeared doesn't matter to you?'

'Not as long as we get what's owed us. I mean, everybody disappears, if you look at it a certain way.'

Great, David thought. A philosopher.

'Have the police talked to you about this? I mean, are they interested in her?'

'No. Why would they be?'

'She absconded from a hospital.'

'Well, I imagine they got better things to do, what with all these storms.'

'I guess you're right.'

David hung up in disappointment. The car was a dead end. He thought about calling the hospital but doubted that would get him anywhere. Running out on a bill was a civil matter. Like the man said, it'd be a long time before the county sheriffs got off their asses to come looking for her, if ever. The hospital would probably just eat the charges, anyway. They were doing big enough business these days. But at least he'd learned one thing. She had enough credit to absorb the kind of serious change the rental company must have extracted. A gold card. Despite everything she tried to make him think, she didn't come from nowhere, after all.

There was nothing much to do after that. He touched up the Elk Run copy and sent it over to the newspaper to be typeset. Then he made some phone calls to radio stations, sent off a few letters. There was a short meeting with a freelance photographer who snapped houses that had just come on the market. He was done by midafternoon. After that it was just a matter of passing time until five. Yet another day at the office, David thought. Like all the other days.

He'd been unemployed for six months when he finally took the job with Redwine. Six months of wandering the house, flipping channels and composing phonily cheery letters. He stripped and shellacked the downstairs floors even though they didn't need it; he joined the Y and was able to bench press his body weight after only a dozen sessions. He spent an hour a day in the reference room at the local library, a once barren crypt suddenly crowded with men in suits and ties who wouldn't meet each other's eyes as they passed around the Help Wanted sections of newspapers from Phoenix or Seattle or San Diego. Every once in a while one of them would disappear, having experienced a spell of one kind of luck or the other, only to be replaced by a new guy.

Before that, for over six years, David had worked as a case officer at Burleigh Tobacco's Social Fund, a heavily endowed and supposedly independent foundation that dispensed grants to various charitable organizations throughout the South. Teen pregnancy programs, hostels for battered women, drug rehabilitation centers, job schemes for high school drop-outs. Guilt money from death peddlers, Rowdy called it. David knew it but he didn't let that worry him. He understood the good they did. His job was simple – he would sift through the mountain of applications and choose those most worthy of a visit. He'd fly in, check the books, talk to the directors, meet those who would be helped. If he liked what he saw, he would then submit a report to the Fund's board for their consideration, presenting the case like a lawyer addressing a jury. A friendly air of competition existed among David and the two other officers to see who could get the most projects funded. David won, year in and year out. It was becoming clear that he would be made director when the slot opened in a few years.

He loved the job. He'd taken it shortly after graduating from college, having aimlessly kicked around for a while, temping, waiting tables, harboring vague plans about doing some sort of writing. But the rejection letters he got to the few poems he sent to magazines and the utter silence that greeted a film treatment he sent to an LA agent put paid to that plan. Any disappointment he'd felt was quickly assuaged when, with the help of Mary Beth's father, he landed the job. He loved being able to fly in to Chattanooga or Savannah, meet with people he admired, help them if he could. That was the best part, that moment of stunned and gratified silence when he called Hattie Mae or Reverend Scales to tell them their application had been approved. He even got used to writing rejection letters.

It was after he'd been in the job for about five years that they bought the house on Ivy Street. Mary Beth was newly pregnant and they decided to buy big so they wouldn't have to mess around moving later. The house was beyond their modest salaries but Mary Beth had recently been given access to a trust fund set up by some antique aunt. They used that for the downpayment and then finessed a big mortgage from a banker who was a devoted WBRR listener. Soon after they moved in Mary Beth was promoted to program director. Everything was fine. They were doing well and they were doing good. They were on their way.

And then, less than a month after closing on the house, utterly out of the blue, the Burleigh Tobacco takeover happened. It began when the company's chairman, N. Wilton June, had made a friendly bid for the company in an effort, he claimed, to raise share values. At first, no one was worried. Common wisdom held that diversification and streamlining were in order, especially in the increasingly turbulent tobacco market. Any debt incurred could easily be paid off from the more efficient company's profits. Employees at the Social Fund were assured that they wouldn't be adversely affected by the deal. In fact, it was hinted that once the company was running more smoothly there would be even more money made available for charitable purposes.

But then the local newspaper had uncovered a memo which proved that June personally stood to make forty million dollars from the deal. The whole thing was a con, a shell game. A bemused board invited rival bids, and what had started as a friendly management buyout became a frenzied takeover battle, with several rival investment firms entering the fray. The modest increase in share values became wildly inflated, so that when the bidding was finally won by a rapacious gang of dead-eyed arbitrageurs, Burleigh Tobacco was saddled with so much debt that there was nothing left to do but break it up, sell off everything that wasn't nailed down. Farmland was dealt to a Saudi/Japanese soy consortium, the company's headquarters was moved to Atlanta, its profitable distribution network and textile subsidiaries peddled to other corporations. The city of Burleigh was gutted. The small clique of shareholders who'd profited from the deal fled for Florida or the West Coast or anywhere else that wasn't Burleigh. And then, as a grimly ironic *coup de grâce*, a Wall Street lawyer discovered a clause in the Social Fund's charter that allowed the new owners to raid that as well, using its two hundred million dollar endowment to help retire their junk bond debt. The city of Burleigh wasn't even going to be left with its own charity, its own source of grace.

And, all of a sudden, like so many others in town, David was out of a job. After a few weeks of shock he began to look for new work, hoping to find something at least marginally related to what he'd been doing at the Fund. But there was nothing in Burleigh and leaving town was out of the question. It would have been both crazy and unfair for Mary Beth to give up work, especially since she was set to be promoted to station manager eventually. Besides, as he scoured the papers and journals David began to suspect he'd lost his taste for foundation work.

And then, just when he thought nothing else bad could happen, Mary Beth lost the baby. The fact that she'd had such an untroubled pregnancy made it all the more of a shock. No morning sickness, no back aches, just the occasional bout of weariness. She'd worked straight through to month nine, boasting she wanted to be at the mike when the contractions started. David knew it was a cliché but she really did seem to get more beautiful, her skin flushed, her eyes crystalline with extra life. Even her voice seemed to be affected, lowering fractionally, filling out the airwaves. They did all the right things – taking the classes, performing the exercises, cutting back on the booze. After losing his job David even began to harbor a secret fantasy of using the child's birth as a pretext to stay home, to postpone the humiliating search for work so he could look after the kid while his wife ran the station.

The baby was a week late when it happened. David was at the Y, swimming laps. He did fewer than usual that day, swimming faster, diving deeper, not wanting to be away from home for very long. Especially since Mary Beth had been worried that morning. The baby had been kicking crazily the night before, rippling the stretched and veiny flesh of her stomach like a sheet drying in the spring breeze. But at breakfast there was nothing but doldrums. He hadn't wanted to go for his swim but she insisted, claiming that his hovering was driving her nuts. David told her not to worry as he left, assured her that the baby was probably just sleeping.

When he got back to Ivy Street, his ears clogged with chlorinated water from an ill-judged dive, there was no one home. No note. He figured she was at the station. Then the phone rang, just as he was about to call her up. It was Rowdy, saying there was a problem. David couldn't understand what was wrong – the water still blocked his ear cavities. Something about a C-section, about a cord and a neck. Mary Beth was unconscious, there didn't seem to be any complications. She'd be fine. That much he could understand.

David drove quickly to the hospital, pounding the sides of his head furiously all the way, unable to clear the trapped water. He went in and sat by his wife but she was way, way under. He stared at her for what seemed to be hours, until the sound of his own breathing rattling inside his sealed ears began to get to him. Why wouldn't this fucking water drain? He went out into the hall and began to slap his head so hard that his skull began to ring with pain. People cast furtive glances at him as they passed, a few said things he couldn't comprehend. Still, he kept slapping his ears, thumping his temples, trying to get that fucking water out. Finally, Rowdy appeared, grabbing David's hands, asking what it was. After he'd explained Rowdy grasped the sides of his neck and gently levered his head forward, turning it first one way, then the other. The water cleared immediately. It was that easy. David would always remember how good it felt running over his neck and chest – body temperature, waxy, cleansing.

Mary Beth came home a few days later. David took care of her; she got better. He rented the whole *Thin Man* series and they watched them curled up against the brass headboard. He cooked her favorite dinners. Friends came by. Her mother. David snuck out with the baby stuff they'd purchased, donating it all to a shelter. Sometimes he wondered if he should have stored it for when they tried again but it wasn't a time for logical thought or long-term strategies. He'd had enough of that for a while. The woman at the shelter wouldn't meet his eye. She knew this drill – young dad lugging in the bitter paraphernalia of his once undentable future.

Things changed after that. Silence entered their lives. Suddenly there were things they couldn't talk about, couldn't even name. Unexpected emotions, like David's bouts of anger with Mary Beth for not taking it easy at the end, for the stubborn show of strength that had caused her to stay home that last night. And he knew she felt the same way about his brief absence. But there were no words for any of this. Their few attempted conversations were quickly strangled by everything they couldn't say, by all the pain a simple phrase could conjure. They'd lost the habit of truthfulness, learning instead how to keep what they felt to themselves. And even after the feelings of recrimination faded, David found it easier to lock away the bitterness and frustration he was beginning to feel with his life. Once that first silence was embraced, others came easily. That explained yesterday's ready lies, he now realized. Five years ago it would have been inconceivable to hide what he was doing with Sara. Now, keeping her a secret seemed almost second nature.

A few weeks after the stillbirth, David began to consider selling the house, whose size and emptiness had become a constant reminder of what had happened. They could get somewhere smaller, he thought, or maybe leave town altogether. Buy a brownstone in some big city. He met secretly with a real estate agent who gave him the bad news. The collapse in Burleigh house prices meant that they were now saddled with a mortgage worth sixty thousand dollars more than their house. The man kept on using the phrase negative equity. Even in the unlikely event they were able to find a buyer they would still owe the bank more cash than either of them could beg, borrow or steal. To put it bluntly, they were stuck on Ivy Street.

As the debt began to pile up, David readjusted his sights. He'd take anything now short of slinging burgers. But his re-entry into Burleigh's forlorn job market was unspectacular. There were only a handful of jobs, none of them good. Finally he saw the ad for a communications director. He could communicate. No sweat. The next day he met Redwine. To his surprise he liked the man. And Redwine reciprocated, impressed by David's previous job. At the end of the interview the developer was lovingly stroking his black beard.

'Well, son, we'd love to have you. About time we had some class around the place.'

At four-thirty a salesman came by David's office with two sets of keys. The address was written on each. Eighteen Locust Lane. David went by the house before going to the hotel, just to make sure everything would be all right. It was in a quiet, sparsely populated neighborhood. Small homes built of the ubiquitous Carolina brick. Lawn art and carports surrounded them; downed branches and flattened leaves from the storm still littered the grass and sidewalks. The repossession was a small, single-storey deal with unshuttered windows and a gone-to-seed lawn. Unlike most of the other houses on the street, this one was made of wood, painted flaking gray. None of the immediate neighbors seemed to be occupied.

The auction sign was still in the front yard. David yanked it up and placed it in the front hall. Inside was clean and anonymous – scuffed wood floors, eggshell walls, a brick fireplace. A small screened porch at the back, an overturned trash can. He was surprised to find a massive sofa in the front room. A half-dozen people could have fit on it. Too big to move, he thought. He ran his hand over its dark green upholstery – it was smooth, like the fur of some big slumbering mammal. He tested the cushions. They were comfortably collapsed. She could sleep on this. No problem.

There were two empty bedrooms as well. Blistered wallpaper, mounds of dead bugs filling the corners. He closed them off, figuring he could set up camp for her in the more welcoming front room. There was even a framed picture on the wall there, a bad watercolor of a fawn drinking in a glade. He went into the kitchen. There were squares of grease where appliances had once stood; strips of undulating formica on the counter. He worked the faucet. After a few gasps, cool water streamed out. This will do, David thought. This will do.

Sara looked better when she answered the motel room door. Her eyes were clear and her face seemed less pale, less puffy. She'd managed to pull her hair back, fully revealing the fine, wishbone curve of her cheeks. The welt above her eye no longer had that vivid, painful sheen. Nor did she stand in that slightly stooped way.

'Did I wake you?'

'No, I got up a half hour ago,' she said. 'The maid came in. I forgot to put out a sign.'

'You look good.'

'I feel like I've slept for months. When I woke up I didn't know where I was.'

'That must have been a shock.'

She managed a weak smile.

'I sorta liked it.'

They stared at each other for a moment.

'Pack your bags,' David said.

Her face collapsed in disappointment.

'Oh. Yeah, well I guess it wasn't going to . . . '

'I've found you somewhere to stay.'

'Really?' Her surprised was tempered by suspicion.

'It's a house,' he explained. 'You'll be much more comfortable there.'

'A house?'

'It's furnished. Well, kinda. There's water but no electricity. But we can get candles and stuff. It'll be fine.'

'I couldn't—'

'Look, I can't let you stay here,' David laughed softly. 'I can't afford it, for openers.'

She averted her eyes in embarrassment.

'Whose house is it?'

'I'm borrowing it.'

'And the owner . . . I mean, is there anybody else there?'

'Don't worry about that, Sara. No one will bother you.'

She stared at the floor, deliberating, running through options.

'All right,' she said eventually. 'But are you sure you want to do this?'

David nodded.

'And you're not going to end up paying for this?'

'Positive.'

On the ride over she grew more animated. David wondered if it was the result of the sleep or the drugs or the fact she was able to leave the hotel room. Probably a combination of all three. Whatever it was, he felt responsible for it, and that made him feel good.

'This is such a strange town,' she said, looking around. 'It's like there's no one here.'

'When I first came down here it was different,' he explained. 'Real different. It was your basic prosperous small city. Recession proof, we liked to say. People driving gunmetal blue Volvo station wagons filled with strapped-in kids. Lots of good restaurants. Symphony orchestra, a dance company, a Shakespeare Festival. We were even maybe going to get an NBA team.'

'So what happened?'

'A few years ago there was a takeover of the company that employed about half the people here. Burleigh Tobacco. The chairman sold out to these Wall Street sharks. At first it seemed like it was a good thing – dividends went up, everybody had more change in their pockets. But then the new directors announced they were breaking up the company. They sold off some of it, moved the rest away. The few people who had made a killing got the hell out of Dodge.'

He gestured at the city around them.

'It was real bad the first few years. People losing their jobs, moving out. Crime, things closing. We became like an occupied people, always talking about life before the takeover, life after it. The only thing they've built around here since then is a bypass for the interstate. And then there were the fires.'

'What fires?'

'Arson. Lots of landlords suddenly realized they were saddled with several tons of useless timber that only had value if it didn't exist any more. Some nights, man, some nights that first summer I'd sit on the porch and it would be like looking over a battle zone. They burned a big warehouse once. It took two days for that to go. It was like Gone With the fucking Wind.'

'But this doesn't happen any more?'

'Not so much. Most of the things that were going to get burned have been. The people who were going to leave have gone. Most of what had to be sold has been sold.' He laughed. 'There's not much pickings left on the carcass. Actually, it's starting to get better now. New companies are moving in, new people.'

'Why did you hang around?'

'Me?'

'When all this bad shit was happening.'

'Negative equity,' he said, smiling privately.

She gave him a puzzled look but he didn't explain. They stopped at a Winn Dixie near the house. She waited in the car as he bought some bread and peanut butter and cheese and cokes. Basic things to help her get her strength back. Grapes and bottled water. He also found some candles, small and cloudy white. For Lent. He told her that later he'd try to find her a lantern, some source of portable light. Maybe a heater. For now there was a blanket in the back seat which he shook out for her to use.

He helped her out of the car when they got to Locust Lane. She didn't say anything as he showed her around the house.

'So what do you think?' he asked finally.

'When do I have to go?'

'Go?'

'How long do I have here?'

'Don't worry about that. You can stay here until you know what you want to do.'

'Who lived here?' she asked, looking at the painting of the fawn.

'Somebody they threw out.'

He nervously worked a light switch. Nothing happened. She turned at the noise.

'Like I said,' he explained. 'There's no electricity and no phone.'

'I don't need a phone. Or electricity, for that matter. Just walls you can't see through.'

He rattled the keys in his pocket and looked at the door. He was supposed to meet Mary Beth and some WBRR people for dinner. He didn't want to be late again.

'You're not going?' she asked.

'I'd better.'

'You're always running off on me.'

For the first time since he'd met her there was a hint of playfulness in her voice, a carefree note. He looked around the place.

'Yeah, well, you know, work. Look. I'll stop by tomorrow. Bring some more stuff.'

'All right.'

'Maybe we could get you some threads.'

She looked at her soiled gown.

'That would be great.'

'You're sure you'll be all right here?'

She shrugged.

'As sure as I am about anything.'

'Keep the door locked.'

She smiled.

'I can take care of myself, David. Contrary to appearances.'

'Is there anything else?'

She looked around.

'Could you light one of those candles?'

'Sure.'

He had a book of matches he'd picked up from Redwine's restaurant. The candle burned dull and steady, a holy, unostentatious flame. She slumped on the big sofa and stared at it.

'I'll bring a radio or something,' he said. 'Just rest. Tomorrow we'll get you set up properly.'

She didn't answer. For an instant David was struck by the strange feeling that she was listening to someone else, a voice he couldn't hear.

'Sara?' he asked.

'Yeah, fine,' she said finally. 'Fine.'

He left her there, staring at the flame, as he went to meet his wife for dinner.

5

David sipped scorched coffee and stared at the phone, willing it to ring. He hadn't taken a pledge since *Car Talk* had ended a half-hour ago. The calls just weren't coming in. And when they did the sums were paltry. Ten dollars, twenty-five. After a while he began trying to coax money out of people, talk them up a few bucks. It seldom worked. In fact, several callers got mad and hung up without pledging anything. There were cranks, as well. People offering a million bucks, wanting to donate organs. Jokers.

Six years ago the drive had been very different. The phones never stopped ringing. David left his sessions in the pledge room with a hoarse voice and a cauliflower ear. Not that the money he took really mattered – the basic grant from Burleigh Tobacco covered the station's operating expenses and then some. Everything else was gravy. There had been a festive atmosphere back then. During the breaks you could hear volunteers laughing and chatting in the background. In the first two years after Burleigh was gutted it was still all right – there was all that dividend money floating around, all those golden parachutes to be sliced up. But gradually those people had filtered away, leaving behind citizens who had more on their minds than whether or not they were plugged into the American Public Radio grid.

This year, everyone knew that if the thermometer outside didn't top out then the station would either have to close or change radically. The atmosphere in the pledge room was fraught, there was little laughter. As David waited over his slumbering phone he watched Mary Beth in her glass booth, trying to hold things together. There was a speaker above him – he could see her as she spoke, as she introduced and informed and beseeched. It felt strange to him, like it wasn't really her talking, like her voice and body weren't related. A stupid thought. The sort of thing that pops into the mind when you're stuck in front of a quiet phone all morning, when you'd rather be some place else. Once she looked at him and he smiled, gave an ironic little wave. When she didn't respond he realized that she couldn't see him through the opaque reflections on her side.

At noon he was replaced, receiving a free T-shirt for his efforts. *WBRR: Broadcasting into the Future*. He told Mary Beth that he might be out with Redwine in the afternoon, just in case she called. It was unusual for him to work weekends but she didn't say anything. She had other things to worry about.

He stopped by his house before going to Locust Lane. It took him a while to find everything he needed. They hadn't been camping since before Mary Beth lost the baby – the equipment was packed deep. As he searched the big basement he was besieged by inescapable thoughts of the long weekends they had spent hiking the Appalachian Trail or meandering over Grandfather Mountain, where hang gliders would sometimes swoop like birds of prey, arcs of color against an impossibly blue sky. They went nearly every weekend back then, leaving after class or work, unable to keep their hands off each other once they were up there. They'd just search out the first spot off the beaten path and get down to it. Once or twice they had been discovered by strangers and, after the initial embarrassment, this had only served to heighten their intensity.

The memories came thick and fast with every musty breath of the unused gear he tugged from storage. The time they were caught in a storm whose thunder was so close they could feel the percussed air; the morning they woke to a single beam of light falling between them, a bullet hole caused by a gunshot they'd never heard puncture the tent's moist skin. And then there was the afternoon they sat stoned on a bluff and watched a hang glider plummet several hundred feet, disappearing into a canopy of fir as if it were the ocean. The pilot emerged into a clearing three minutes later, while they were still doubting the data of their red eyes, still trying to decide what to do. He saw them and waved. They simply waved back.

The last time they went Mary Beth was six months pregnant. She insisted they go, refusing to become inactive until she had to. It turned out to be a rainy weekend which they spent huddled in the tent. Every time they ventured out for a hike the rain would ambush them and they'd have to rush back. That night they got uncharacteristically drunk, made the wrong kind of love. David remembered rearing back as he drove into her, his head brushing the tent's top, providing a conduit for rank, freezing water that left them soaked and miserable and shivering for the rest of the night. They returned home at dawn, the pealing bells of the churches they passed piercing the car's grim silence.

When they got back Mary Beth took a long bath as David packed the gear straight into a remote corner of the basement, before it was thoroughly dried. Which, he supposed, was why it smelled so strongly now, why it was lobbing these memory grenades at him. After that trip everything had changed. The takeover, David's job, the baby. They never went camping again, never even talked about it, having, he reckoned, reached another unspoken agreement about what the future no longer held for them.

It didn't take David long to find everything he imagined Sara would need for her short stay on Locust Lane. A lantern and a two-burner propane stove. A big flashlight and a sleeping bag; a survival blanket and a Swiss Army Knife. In the front hall closet he found his old boom box. As he loaded everything into his car, Shana Kelly walked by.

'Going camping?' she asked.

'Sort of.'

'How can you sort of go camping?' she asked, her left eyelid twitching through a complex neurotic code.

David smiled and nodded goodbye, leaving her to wait in vain for an explanation. He stopped at a hardware store on the way over, buying batteries for the radio, fuel for the stove and lantern. Then he went to Rexall for shampoo and toothpaste, soft drinks and ice. It was two-thirty by the time he reached Locust Lane. He knocked on the front door.

'David?'

'Yes.'

'It's open.'

She was sitting on the sofa, drinking warm coke through the crazy straw, surrounded by small glaciers of wax. The room smelled of candlesmoke.

'I was beginning to wonder if you were ever going to come.'

'I had to stop for some stuff.' He looked over his shoulder. 'You know, I really think you should lock the door.'

'All right, Dad.'

He smiled and dropped the gear, then joined her on the sofa. He looked into her eyes for a moment. They seemed calm now, sparkling and intelligent, that hunted look washed away.

'What have you been doing?' he asked.

'Thinking.'

'What about?'

'What I'm going to do.'

'And?'

'I think I'm going to hang here for a couple days, if I can. It's sort of nice. Quiet. Besides, I'm in no condition to go anywhere. That crash really took it out of me. I walk across the room and it's like I've run a marathon.'

He nodded, surprised how pleased he was that she would be staying. She began to pick at a frayed section at the top of her cast.

'It's been a long time since I've been away from, you know, everything. All those expectations.'

Something in her demeanor stopped David from asking what she meant.

'How did you sleep?'

'Artificially.'

'Is that good?'

'Good enough,' she said.

'OK, check this out.'

He showed her what he'd brought, moving around the room like a salesman. She watched in silence as he fueled the lantern and the stove. When he was done he met her gaze. It was intense, curious. Like she couldn't figure out who he was, what he was doing here.

'And, for our first caller, there's this fabulous prize,' he said, showing her the WBRR T-shirt.

'Ah, great.'

She took it from him with her stiff right hand.

'Do you need help?'

'No, I think I can handle it.'

She smiled shyly and motioned for him to turn away. He walked over to the storm window, looking out at the quiet street.

'Can I ask you something, David?' she said, her voice suddenly serious.

'Sure.'

'I've been wondering – why are you doing all this for me?'

He listened to the rustle as she changed.

'I guess I feel like I put you in the deep end,' he said. 'I mean, running you off the road . . . '

'You didn't run me off the road. I was an accident waiting to happen.'

'Well, I still feel like I did.'

'Are you sure that's all?'

He didn't answer.

'I'm such a wreck,' she continued. 'I mean I know it can't be because—'

'I'm not even sure there is a reason,' he interrupted.

'I'm just, I'm having a hard time figuring you out, you know?'

'Well, it seems like that should be pretty low on your list.'

'You got that right,' she said. 'OK. You may behold me now.'

He turned around. The T-shirt hung loose on her thin shoulders. She was gently levering her hair from inside it, her chin describing a languorous circle as she did.

'You ready to go shopping?' he asked.

'Shopping?'

'For clothes.'

Her eyes lit up.

'God yes.'

He stayed in the unfamiliar neighborhoods of North Burleigh to lessen his chances of running into someone he knew. They drove slowly down streets lined with For Sale signs and weedy lawns.

'Nice wheels, by the way,' she said. 'I meant to tell you the other day. What is it?'

'A Mustang.'

'No duh, David. I meant the vintage. What, Sixty-nine?'

'Sixty-eight. I got it two years ago.'

She nodded appreciatively.

'You know about cars?'

'I know about people who like nice things,' she said distantly, the jut of her chin making it clear she wasn't going to elaborate.

'It's my consolation prize,' he said after a while.

'For what?'

He smiled, pleased that it was his chance not to answer. They turned down a road that dead-ended against a big, barbed fence.

'What's with that fence?' she asked. 'It reminds me of the Berlin Wall with those no trespassing signs all over it.'

'That's Nowheresville,' David said as he turned the car around. 'It used to be a neighborhood called something or other, I can't even remember. Lots of the people who worked in the tobacco factories lived there. Neat, boring little houses. Mini-malls. Churches everywhere, lube places. The sort of place you never really go, never really notice. After Burleigh Tobacco split most of the residents began moving out, voting with their feet. Arizona, Oregon. Before long there was hardly anyone left. This is where most of the fires I was telling you about were. Vagrants started moving in, squatters. People from the hills. Crack houses and child snatchings and triple homicides. All the amenities of modern life. When we had our first drive-by, well, gosh, we were all so proud. So then the city council came up with this great plan. They decided to downsize the city.'

'Downsize? What the hell does that mean?'

'It means they simply moved out any old timer still left, ran off the riff-raff, built a big fence around the whole deal and said, that's it. This is no longer part of Burleigh. This is no longer part of the civilized world. No water, no electricity, no sewers, no cops. Mothballed. It cut the city budget by nearly ten per cent. The idea being if there's a recovery they'll open it back up, redevelop it.'

She looked at the fence.

'Downsize. Yeah, I like that. So no one lives in there?'

'Who knows? It's illegal to go in, it's still city property, though on the other hand it's not like there's anyone checking too close. You hear rumors about hillbillies, sidewalk people. Citizens go in there sometimes, you know, dirtbiking or hiking. To play.'

She stared at it for a long while.

'This is such a very weird town,' she said quietly.

'I used to think so. Now I think it sort of looks like the future.' He looked across at her. 'So what are you telling me here, you've been to Berlin?'

'Sure.' She shrugged. 'I've been just about everywhere.'

'What, London, Paris . . . ?'

She nodded.

'Borneo?'

'No, but I've been to Tahiti.'

'What were you doing there?'

They were passing a decrepit mini-mall.

'Pull in here,' Sara said.

'Here? I don't think . . . '

'I saw something.'

There were only a few open shops. A drug store, a hair salon, a martial arts video rental. The place Sara had seen was cattycornered in the shadows. The sign above the door read 'Twins Used & Antique Clothes'. There were no shoppers inside, just the proprietors, two elderly black women, identical twins who greeted David and Sara with big, weary smiles.

'So what's the program?' Sara asked them.

'You get a bag now, honey, and then you can fill it up.'

'Not with the jewelry, though,' the other one said, indicating an open display case in front of them.

'Now how's she gonna wear jewelry with her hands all like that?'

'It's five dollar a bag.'

'I think one will do,' Sara said.

David took a bag. They walked slowly down the first aisle, Sara's eyes wandering over the piles of old clothes. At the end she pointed to a sweater. David fetched it for her.

'Hold it up for me.'

He shook it, then held it aloft.

'What do you think?' she asked.

'It's you.'

'No, it isn't,' she said as she walked away. 'Which is precisely why we're going to buy it.'

It took ten minutes to find everything she wanted.

'You found some nice things here, honey,' one of the women told her as David paid.

'Thanks,' Sara said distractedly as she looked over the jewelry display.

'Anything there you want?' the other twin asked.

'Too rich for my blood,' Sara said, looking up.

'Oh, we got some fine bargains in there.'

'Go on,' David said. 'It's all right.'

'No,' she answered, joining them. 'The clothes'll do.'

'Do you have a pen or something?' she asked as they drove back to the house.

He found one in the glove compartment. She gripped it awkwardly in her sprained hand and began to probe beneath her cast with it.

'Itchy?'

'Not really.'

She gently removed the pen just as they reached the house. She held up her left arm.

'Reach in there,' she said. 'Carefully.'

It was a tight fit. Her flesh was warm and moist beneath the cast. An inch in he touched something that he thought for an instant was bone, though he quickly realized it was metal. He pulled it out. A watch's clasp, followed by a watch.

'Where did you . . . ?'

She smiled cagily. He looked at it. Cartier, with a Roman numeral display and a fatigued leather band. The small tag hanging from the buckle said twenty dollars.

'You just took this?'

'Pretty slick, eh ? Those biddies don't even know what they had there. I bet that thing's worth two thousand bucks, minimum. It's yours, David.'

David looked at her.

'You said someone ripped off yours,' she explained.

'Yes, but Sara, that doesn't . . . '

'Hey, don't worry about it being real. It is. If I'm lyin',' she said, 'I'm dyin'.'

He looked up at the house.

'No, what I mean is, you shouldn't have just taken it.'

Her smile vanished.

'Why not? They won't miss it, not what they were selling it for. They think it's a fake. It would have been wrong to pay them what they were asking.'

He looked at the watch.

'Come on, David, I owe you. Since I don't have anything this is the only way I could think of paying you back.'

He fingered the worn leather in silence.

'Fine,' she said, holding her bandaged hand across the seat. 'If you don't want it, give it back to me and I'll hock it. I can definitely use the bread, and you know what?'

He looked at her.

'I can get a lot more than twenty bucks for it.'

'No,' he said, pulling out the dial and setting it by the digital display on the dashboard. 'I want it.'

They spread the clothes throughout the front room, covering the floor and the sofa, draping them from the naked curtain rods. There were a few Oxford shirts, two thin sweaters, a knee-length skirt, two pairs of white painter's pants. Deck shoes and sandals. A black cocktail dress she'd laughingly chosen. David refused to put it back when she told him she was kidding, saying he wanted to see her in it one day, a statement which drove them into an uneasy silence for a few minutes. The last thing she'd chosen was a book from the table of paperbacks. *A Good Man is Hard to Find*. Figuring Sara out, David was beginning to suspect, was going to take some time.

'So what do you think?' he asked, gesturing to their bounty. 'What're you going to wear first?'

'Before I put on anything I'm washing this hair.'

She stared at him.

'You want me to help,' he said after a moment.

'You *are* quick.'

He set to work. First, he found a big pot beneath the sink and half-filled it with water, which he heated on the kerosene stove. The odor of gas quickly filled the small house. When it boiled he carried it to the bathroom, mixing it with tapwater until it was lukewarm. Sara came to the door a few moments later. She'd taken off the T-shirt, holding it flat against her torso. It swayed with her movement and for an instant David could see a deep bruise on her lower ribs, rings of lightening color, deep purple in the center, amber like her eyes on its outer edges. He helped her sit cross-legged, her back to the tub. The flesh of her shoulders warm in his palms.

'Tell me if it's too hot,' he said.

'You'll hear the screams.'

He balled the towel they'd taken from the hotel and put it on the edge of the tub as a cushion for her neck. She leaned back and closed her eyes. Her ribs and collarbone rose gently beneath her skin. Kneeling beside her, he gently arranged her long hair so it dangled into the tub, then began to scoop up water with his hands. Her shoulders immediately pocked with raised flesh. At first the water didn't penetrate, sliding off her hair like it was waterproof fabric. Gradually, however, it began to soak in. David poured out a coin-sized dollop of the shampoo and worked it in. Reluctant suds came up and then dirty runoff swirled down the drain. Her scalp shifted slightly beneath his fingers and a rivulet of foamy water ran down her neck. He collected it just before it reached the T-shirt, still draped over her chest.

'Your hair's so thick,' he said.

'It was shaved once.'

'Why?'

She shrugged.

'That's just how it worked out.'

He didn't ask any further. He knew that tone by now.

'All right,' he said after a minute. 'We rinse.'

He scooped up more water. Soon what ran down the drain was as clear as glass. She sat forward and he placed the towel over her head.

'Thanks,' she said. 'I got it.'

He arranged the towel so it draped behind her shoulders and walked to the front room, where he stared out the window at the quiet street, taking several long, calming breaths, the feel of her skin still on his hands. He took the watch from his pocket where he'd put it and fastened it on his wrist. Its old leather felt good, almost living. She came out, her crossed arms still holding the T-shirt to her naked chest. For a moment he glimpsed the pale side of a crushed breast.

'Now,' she said, looking at the clothes. 'I think, let's see . . . this and this.'

She nodded to a plain gray skirt and thin white pullover. He handed her the sweater first, standing behind her as she worked her damaged hands through the big sleeves. The thin muscles of her

98

back shimmered as she lifted her arms. He straightened it for her, letting his hand linger on her shoulder for an instant. He felt her freeze, like something caught in highbeams.

'There,' he said, pulling his hand away. 'The new you.'

She was still facing away from him, standing perfectly still.

'I'll do the skirt,' she said flatly.

He wondered if he'd made a big mistake, touching her like that.

'Do you want a coke?' he asked to break the tension. 'I have some cold ones in the car. I almost forgot.'

'All right,' she said, her voice still distant.

When he returned she was wearing the skirt, its side clasp open like a breathing mouth. He wondered if it had hurt her to put it on but she wasn't showing any signs of pain. She sat on the sofa, her legs gathered up beneath her. The towel was off her head and her wet hair hung limply, bringing up small patches of damp on the sweater's shoulders. She didn't meet his eyes as he approached. He twisted open a bottle and gave it to her. She used her cast as a support, cradling it gently with the slightly crooked fingers of her right hand.

'That feels better,' she said, shaking her head.

'I bet.'

'I'm almost human now.'

She took a drink. He looked at the floor, at the things she'd been wearing, the hospital gown and the black pants. And the shoes. Once again he noticed the pattern of dim red stains on them. He looked back at her. She was watching him warily.

'How are your hands?' he asked.

'Better,' she said. 'Those drugs really hit the spot. Like drugs so often do.'

'You know,' he said, looking into his bottle. 'Rowdy, the doctor who treated you, said that he couldn't be sure he set your hand right. Because you were so gonzo when he did it. I think he wanted to see it again.'

She tossed some wet hair over her shoulder.

'Well, he can't.'

'But it would be a shame if it didn't heal right.'

'Yeah?'

'Well, sure.'

'I'da thought it was a blessing in disguise,' she muttered.

He looked up at her.

'What do you mean?'

'Nothing.'

He took a deep, resolving breath.

'Sara, look, I know you don't want to talk about this, but since we're here and you're going to be hanging around for a couple of days, I have to ask. I mean, what's going on with you?'

'Going on?'

'I mean, you show up out of nowhere and—'

'I didn't show up out of nowhere, David.'

'You know what I mean.'

'It just seems like that to you.'

'Fine. Whatever. My question remains.'

She sighed.

'I told you. I lost my stuff in the crash. Someone ripped it off or it's gone in that flood. So I'm stranded. It's not that much of a mystery.'

'But I don't understand how there can't be anyone for you to call.'

She looked down at her bottle.

'Why can't you understand that?'

'So you mean to tell me there's no one on the face of the earth you could call?'

'There are people I can call. Just not any I want to.'

'So what are you saying?' He circled his bottle to indicate the room. 'That you plan to keep on living like this indefinitely?'

'David, you can stop helping me any time. I'll survive. I always have.'

'I don't want to stop helping you, Sara. I want to figure out how to do it better.'

She met his eyes, her defiance giving way.

'Look, all right. I'm sorry. You deserve some sort of explanation. I know that. It's just . . . ' She was gently tapping her cast with the bottom of the bottle. 'There was, I was in, well, it was a really bad situation. I was getting lots of static from this person I was with and so I ran away. I just bolted. It was the only way I could get out of there. A clean break.' She looked at her cast, smiling briefly at the inadvertent pun. 'I didn't even know where I was going, who I was going to stay with. I mean, it was pretty intense for a while there and I sort of lost track of my life, of people. It was just . . . us. So after I got the nerve to split I was just moving. On instinct. What does the song go like? "No particular place to go." That's what I was doing when you found me. Running.'

David wasn't saying anything.

'And so that's why I don't want to be in the hospital or call people I know or start trying to replace credit cards and stuff. Because everything was in this person's name. And, well, this is going to sound paranoid.'

'Go on.'

'Well, he'll try to find me.'

'Is it . . . ?'

'No, it's not the cops, if that's what you were going to ask. It's private.'

That wasn't what he was going to ask, but he let it go.

'How private?'

'Real private. More private than you can imagine.'

'Will?'

'Will what?'

'Was that the guy's name? Will? Was that what you meant about going back to Will's place?'

The pale flesh of her neck and upper chest reddened.

'You know,' she said after a moment. 'Names and . . . it's probably better if we don't go into all that.'

'And you didn't know where you were going?'

'I just wanted to disappear.'

She looked at him.

'You can do that, right?' she asked softly.

'I don't know.' He nodded to her new clothes. 'At least you're dressed for it.'

She laughed gently, though her face quickly grew somber again.

'But now this accident has fucked things up. Without any i.d. or money, well, it just seems like the only thing to do is go back, which is the one thing I am *not* going to do.'

'It must have been pretty grim. For you to leave like that, I mean.'

'Grim. Yeah. That's one way of putting it.'

She looked up at him before he could ask her anything else.

'You know, you've been just as big a mystery about your life as I have.'

'Have I?'

'I mean, what is it you do that allows you to spend so much time looking after strangers?'

'Me?' He was peeling back the bottle's label. 'Nothing, really. I work for a property developer. I guess I'm not too motivated.'

'You sell real estate?' she asked, scowling dubiously.

'No, no. I write ads and stuff. My boss refers to me as his LAT specialist.'

'What's what?'

'Little a this, little a that.'

'I see. You like it?'

'It's a job. There's not much of anything else around.'

She stared at him for a while.

'So what is it you really do?' she asked finally.

'Why do you ask that?'

'You seem like somebody who isn't doing what he's supposed to.'

'Well, I used to work for a foundation, if that's what you mean.'

'A charity?'

'We weren't supposed to call it that, but yeah.'

'What, for artists and stuff?'

'No, we supported, you know, drug rehab centers, hostels, head start programs.'

'Yeah, I thought you were too good to be true,' she chided.

He smiled.

'Well, I don't know. Sometimes it seemed like I got more from the people I helped than they got from me.'

'So what happened?'

He shrugged.

'We were bankrolled by Burleigh Tobacco. When they sold out the company all our dough went south. Or north, I guess I should say.'

'So can't you get another job like that?'

'I suppose. I have to confess the whole thing left me a bit, what, jaded.'

'How so?'

'I thought we were making a difference but now I think it was just a big fucking shell game. And I was this shriveled little pea being swirled around.'

'You and me both.'

She smiled sardonically and raised her glass.

'Here's to jade,' she said. 'A beautiful and enduring gem.'

They touched bottles, the styrofoam wrappers muffling the sound.

'It's not like this is your home, though,' she said. 'You're not a southerner.'

'Is it that obvious?'

She smiled and nodded.

'You're right,' he said. 'I'm from Jersey.'

'Oh yeah. Which exit?'

'You got it. I came down here for college, you know, for a change. Stayed on. I like it here.'

'What do you like about it?'

'Let's see. Diners where they serve breakfast anytime. The mountains this time of year. The way the women talk. The men when they get old. Stuff like that . . . '

He stopped, realizing that if he told her much more he would either have to tell her he was married or lie to her. She flipped her hair back off her shoulders and took another long drink. Once again he found himself staring at the long curve of her neck, the lift of her small breasts. He suddenly knew if he stayed here much longer, this close, out of everyone's sight, he would soon try to kiss her, to make love to her. He looked at his new watch. It was after six. He didn't have to be anywhere for two hours.

'I gotta go.'

She dropped her head and looked at him in disappointment.

'Really?' she said.

He stood quickly.

'I don't think I'll be able to come by here tomorrow. Work.'

'You're joking,' she said. 'You mean I'm going to—'

'You should be all right with these things now,' he said, bulldozing over her astonishment.

'David . . . '

'I mean you got a radio and a book and food and . . . '

'David,' she said.

He stopped.

'I'll be all right. I'm used to being on my own. Believe me.'

He nodded glumly, not meeting her eye.

'Where are you going?' she asked.

'I just have, there's this thing I have to go to. This concert.'

'Oh well,' she said, looking away, seemingly indifferent. 'Enjoy it.'

'I'll come by on Monday morning and then maybe we can start thinking about, you know.'

She looked up at him, as if she didn't know at all.

He drove around for two hours after that, stopping only to buy quarts of beer he drank still wrapped in their paper bags. He couldn't stop thinking about the feel of her warm shoulders and thick hair; couldn't stop seeing that gently crushed breast. He hadn't expected this, the speed and intensity of his desire for her. Everything was going too fast. Before doing anything else he had to try to sort out what was happening, figure out what he was feeling. Two days ago he'd just wanted to help her out and now he found himself unable to stop imagining them making love in that small, anonymous house.

He switched on the radio. Mary Beth was on, interviewing one of the musicians who would be playing at the benefit concert that night. She sounded smart and sexy – David tried to focus on her voice, let it calm his jangled nerves, let it work the old magic. But his mind kept drifting back to Sara.

'Man, what the fuck are you going to do?' he asked himself out loud.

'We're going to play a tune from the new album,' his wife answered from the dashboard.

By the time he got to the concert he was drunk. Not falling down, just unfocused and slightly disoriented. The place was packed with the usual Burleigh crowd, supplemented by people from Charlotte or Chapel Hill who'd made the drive to see Widening Gyre, a veteran Irish folk group heading the WBRR benefit concert. David moved quickly through the restaurant, past the fading murals by local artists, the ferns hanging from crocheted ropes, the pizza oven

104

that glowed an infernal orange behind the bar. There were two rooms, one crowded with booths, the other a performance space. He ordered a draft and stepped into the back room. Mary Beth was sitting at a long table stacked with transmitters and amplifiers for the remote broadcast. People from the station surrounded her.

'Sibilance,' she said. 'Sibilance.'

David nodded to someone he knew and downed his beer, the carbonization fizzing through his guts like static electricity. Then he saw his wife looking at him. She cocked her head quizzically.

'David?' she said, her voice echoing over the intercom.

The place grew silent. Everyone looking at him. He walked over.

'Lurking in the shadows, huh,' she said playfully as she removed her headphones.

He nodded terse helloes to the people at the table.

'So what have you been doing with yourself all afternoon?' she continued. 'I called a few times.'

'Working.'

'But I called the office.'

'We were in the wilderness,' he said, helping himself to a refill from the sweating pitcher at the end of the table.

She gave him a long look.

'Have you been drinking again?'

'I'm under the limit,' he said without really thinking.

'The limit? What limit? What are you talking about, David?'

'Nothing.'

'Hey, you sure you're all right?'

'Sure I'm sure.'

She stared at him dubiously for a moment longer, then donned the headphones and returned to her work. He took a seat at a nearby table, spilling some of his beer on the floor as he dropped into the molded chair. A while later the band took the stage. Five middle-aged Irishmen with ragged tweed clothes and graying mutton-chop sideburns. They looked out over the crowd with suspicious smiles as they were introduced. After a spell of welcoming applause they began to play. The audience sat quietly through the first tune, a few people trying unsuccessfully to get some rhythmic clapping going. David's beer-soaked mind was swept back to those nights in college listening to Mary Beth. The song ended and there was enthusiastic applause. The seemingly bemused musicians looked into the crowd. Two whispered together, shaking their heads.

'We should dance,' David heard himself saying out loud, to no one in particular.

People at nearby tables flashed him guarded smiles. Mary Beth was staring at the stage, the flesh on her cheeks bunched by her headphones. She hadn't heard him.

'We should dance,' he repeated generally. 'Come on.'

Another song started, a jig, wilder than the first. The audience remained seated, staring up at the band, hazarding brief slaps on the sticky surface of their tables. David drained his beer. The tunes seemed to be whirling faster, just like they had those nights a dozen years ago, when he sat alone in his room, falling in love with Mary Beth before he even knew anything about her.

'We should . . . ' he said, his voice inaudible in the raucous music.

And then he was on his feet and he was dancing, jerking around the small floor, chasing the music. The fact that he didn't know how to dance was irrelevant. He was just moving. The faces in the audience were a blur; the sound seemed to be coming from everywhere. He stumbled and almost fell, but this only got him whirling faster. Soon he could feel sweat on his skin and pain in his cramping legs. But he kept moving, even after the music stopped, his momentum carrying him through several seconds of silence.

Then there was applause and he found himself facing the audience. Not many people were looking at him. Some students smiled conspiratorially, that was all. He took an unsteady step back toward the broadcasting table. Mary Beth was biting her lips, fiddling idly with dials.

'Steady on, lad,' one of the musicians said, and there was laughter from the stage.

He sat and reached for the pitcher, but only managed to knock it over. It was empty.

'What are you doing?' Mary Beth asked when the music started up again, her earphones pulled down to her neck, a hand covering the microphone in front of her.

'I was just dancing,' he said. 'I mean, that's sort of the point, isn't it?'

'Making a fool out of yourself is the point? Of what?'

He shrugged.

'This is so unlike you.'

'Come on, Mary Elizabeth,' he said. 'I was only dancing . . . '

'I think you should go home, David. *Walk* home.'

'I got my car.'

'We'll come for it in the morning. David, do what I'm saying. Please.'

Her voice sailed through the floodplain of beer to some small island of sobriety within him.

'Yeah, I could use some shuteye,' he conceded.

'That's a good idea.'

'Sorry.'

'Don't apologize. You're only drunk. Just . . . go home.'

'All right.' He looked at her. Tell her, he suddenly thought. Just tell her everything. Stop this now. Make it right with the truth. 'Mary Beth?'

But she'd put her headphones back on.

'This is WBRR,' she was saying, 'bringing you live music as part of our . . . '

He moved unsteadily toward the door.

'Drive friendly,' someone said.

'Fuck off,' he answered.

He walked by the glowing pizza ovens to the bathroom, pissing copiously on a disintegrating chlorine disk. Beneath it there was a plastic filter inscribed with the words 'Just Say No'. David tried to imagine what sort of puritanical zealot would think of that. Let's catch them when they're pissing, Nancy. Just get 'em by the bladder and the hearts and minds will follow. He looked up at the moonscape of boogers on the wall, the misspelled obscenities. Don't look here, someone had advised, the joke's in your hand. You don't say, he thought. When his bladder had drained he walked unsteadily out to his car and drove back to Locust Lane.

He parked on the empty street and looked up at the house. His head was no longer spinning – the dancing seemed to have knocked the drunkenness out of him. Suddenly, he just felt empty. Wan light flickered in the window. He stared at it for a long time before he got out of the car and walked up the steps. The door was locked. That's good, he thought. She's taken my advice. Nobody could bother her this way, nobody could harm her. He used the spare set of keys to enter.

She was asleep on the sofa, the irregular light playing over her thin body. Music played softly on the radio. The Irish band, still live and in concert. The room smelled of candlewax and kerosene. He stood above her and it occurred to him that he could do anything to her now. He could make love to her. Abandon her. Smother her. No one would know. Here she was, this woman. No one around here knew her name, no one knew where she was. His secret.

'Hey.'

He touched her shoulder like he had back at the crash site but this time she didn't move. He looked at her damaged hands, at her long neck and placid face. Then he perched on the edge of the sofa and began to touch her lightly, running his hand over her hair, over her shoulder, over the exposed flesh of her neck. This roused her a bit. She changed position slightly and the sweater he'd bought her rode up until he could see her thin belly. He touched her there, careful to avoid the bruise on her ribs. Her flesh was so warm, warmer than it had been when he'd carried her from that ruined shack.

Her eyes fell open just as he was pulling his hand away. She stared at him for a moment, as unsurprised as she'd been back at the crash. Her face was creased with sleep.

'Hello,' she said sleepily.

'I thought I'd . . .'

'What?'

'How are you?' he asked.

'Feeling no pain,' she said languidly.

She stretched her damaged arms above her head. The sweater rode up even higher – he could see the beginnings of her breasts. He looked away, focusing on the boom box's dancing graphic equalizer. The music continued to whirl.

'What time is it?' she asked.

'Late. Past midnight.'

'I had a bath after you left, then passed out. How was the concert?'

'It's still going on,' he said, nodding toward the radio.

She smiled.

'I'm glad you came back.'

'I was worried, you know. I was thinking about you.'

'David?'

He could see the drugs in her eyes. The fiery, desperate resolve of the past few days had been smothered by the chemical blanket he'd provided.

'Yes?'

'Everything's all right, isn't it? I mean, when you left I was worried that . . . you're going to keep helping me out here until I'm myself again, right?'

'Yes, I will.'

'I mean, because I'm in some very deep shit here.'

'I figured as much.'

She closed her eyes and nodded a few times.

'That's good,' she said. 'Because I'm really . . . '

She didn't finish the sentence. After a while she opened her eyes and they said yes and so he kissed her. She pulled away after a moment, staring at him, as if she wanted to be sure of something. It made him uneasy, so he kissed her again and this time he could feel her kiss him back. Her mouth was soft and dry. He began to run his hands gently over her body. She was so thin. She shuddered when he tried to put his weight on her.

'My ribs.'

So he knelt on the floor, amid the clothes still scattered there. She closed her eyes and lifted her arms above her head, letting him undress her. When her sweater was off he could see all of the large bruise over her ribs, starting just below her left breast and running almost to her hipbone. The skirt slipped off easily – it was unclasped, a size too big.

'What should I do?' he asked when she was naked.

'Just keep kissing me.'

He kissed her mouth for a long time and then he began to kiss her body. It was so different from his wife's, so brittle. He tried to be as gentle as he could, afraid of hurting her, afraid of putting pressure on her ribs or her hands. A few times his lips didn't even touch her. He slowly worked his way down her long neck to her breasts, circling her nipples with his tongue until they hardened. Bits of soap and patches of talc still clung to her flesh from her clumsy bath. Then he gently kissed her bruise, touching her as softly as he could.

Suddenly he realized what he was doing and he pulled back.

'No, that's all right.'

He pressed until he could feel her tense, then he pressed a bit harder and she recoiled. So he moved his tongue over her hipbone and around the horizon of her thigh and kissed her there until she came in a great, silent exhalation. He stood and quickly removed his clothes. He was hard, she didn't have to touch him. Not that she could. He tried to lie on top of her but she said no and maneuvered him gently on to his back on the floor with her useless hands. She straddled him and then they were making love. She pressed down hard, dwelling there for a few seconds each time before rising. The music on the radio was swirling faster and faster. Soon she was rising more quickly, he was following her. And all the while she didn't touch him with her useless hands, one perched weightlessly on the sofa, the other dug lifeless into the floor by his head.

When they were finished she placed her head on his chest, stretched her body along the length of his. Beneath the sofa, he could see the silhouettes of things people had lost and hadn't cared about enough to find.

'I thought this was going to happen,' she said after a while.

He didn't know what she meant by that; if it was an accusation or a simple statement of fact.

'It's not why,' he tried to explain. 'I mean, it wasn't what I had in mind when I brought you here.'

'That doesn't matter.'

'No?'

'There's nothing wrong with being desired.'

They lay still for a while.

'David?'

'Yes?'

'Come see me tomorrow, all right? I don't think I could spend a whole day on my own.'

'I'll try.'

'Don't try. Just come.'

'All right,' he agreed.

They lay still for a long time and then he knew that she was asleep. The concert ended and there was applause, meager but impassioned. Then Mary Beth came on. Her voice sounded giddy, drunk with the music. David gently extricated himself from Sara. It wasn't hard, with her thin frame, her ungrasping hands. He carefully lifted her to the sofa, placing two blankets over her naked body.

As he dressed, Mary Beth signed off. He wasn't worried – she had to pack up her equipment, count the proceeds. He'd beat her home by a good fifteen minutes. He turned off the radio, not wanting to run down the batteries. Then he looked at Sara one more time before he left the house, making sure to lock the door behind him.

6

David woke on the floor. His elbow and hip stung; his thumping heart rattled his ribs. He looked around in confusion at the expanse of burnished wood surrounding him, the dropped clothes and toppled shoes. It took him several seconds to remember that he was in his own room. Then he figured out what had happened. He'd fallen out of bed.

He smiled and shook his head. Like some fucking kid. After rubbing the pain out of his elbow he sat up and looked across the mattress. Mary Beth slept calmly, her back to him. She hadn't noticed his fall. The clock beyond her said it was nearly nine. Church bells were ringing somewhere, summoning the faithful.

And then David remembered what had happened the night before. He jumped to his feet and began to walk quickly from the room. He made it as far as the top of the stairs before he was caught up by the knowledge that this was where he was supposed to be. He walked slowly back to bed, the wood cold on his bare feet. After a moment's hesitation he slipped gently under the covers, careful not to wake his wife.

He stared at her sleeping form for a long time. You've cheated on her. The word echoed through his mind. Cheated. Cheated. It was such a strange term to use. As if he'd been trying to win something. It was scary – no matter how often he went over last night he couldn't figure out how it had happened. Yes, the act itself was there, there was no doubting that. Every move, every sensation. The taste of her flesh, the way their eyes had held as she rose and fell above him, the sway of her long hair. But the hours and days leading up to it were a blur. Everything he had done for her had seemed so logical at the time, so benign. What anybody would have done. And yet, eight hours ago, he had betrayed his wife with a woman he knew nothing about. A woman who might have been from anywhere, who might have done anything. Lying there in the big bedroom, the morning light spilling in, David slowly realized how crazy it all was.

Mary Beth's breathing was deep and regular. He reached out and touched her black hair. It was finer than Sara's, less tangled and confused. It was once as long, though she'd cut it when she was pregnant to keep cool and had never grown it back. He touched her shoulder, ran his hand down to her hip. It was so familiar, her flesh. So sound, so comforting. Soft and strong. Nothing like Sara's damaged and mysterious body.

When he pulled his hand away she reached blindly behind her.

'No, keep doing that,' she said sleepily. 'I like it.'

Later that morning they went to the Burleigh Newsstand. Mary Beth wanted to linger in bed but David insisted. He had to get out of the house, move around, be among people. She didn't have to be at work until noon – in Burleigh, only churches solicited on Sunday mornings. As they drove David volunteered to spend the afternoon working the phones. At night they would meet friends for dinner. Fresh pesto and CD reissues and California Merlot. Despite his promise to Sara the night before, there would be no trips to Locust Lane today. Not until he figured out what was going on and what he was going to do about it.

The Newsstand was a combination coffee house and book store, run by five shy sisters who had inherited a small fortune from their parents. Like the Redwine Group, it was built in an abandoned frame house just on the outskirts of downtown. The tables were situated among the stacks of books. Mary Beth and David grabbed their usual place in the travel section, beneath a fading poster of Tibet that had been there for as long as anyone could remember. He went off to order breakfast and pick up their reserved copy of the Sunday *New York Times*, walking numbly through the throng, nodding vague helloes, stopping for brief, disjointed chats. Most of the people he saw had been at the concert the previous night, at the party on Wednesday. A few joked about David's dancing, others asked how the drive was going. As David spoke to them he gradually began to feel that he was returning to some semblance of his normal life. When he reached the counter the waitress wrote down his order before he could speak. Espresso, cappuccino, onion bagel, *pain au chocolat*. What they ordered every week. Their thick paper was at the register, the name Webster penciled in the upper right corner. This was good, David thought. He was where he belonged. Everything was going as it should.

Mary Beth smiled up at him when he got back to the table. And suddenly it occurred to him what he had to do. Tell her. Tell her everything, right now. It was so obvious. That was the only way. You cannot live with someone and have this sort of secret from her. A secret which was, with every passing second, becoming as much a betrayal as anything he'd done with his tongue or his hands or his dick. That's it, then, he decided. Tell her everything, the whole story, ending with last night. That was how he could bring this mess under control. It would be hard, as close to impossible as anything he'd ever done. But once Mary Beth knew then there would be nothing more he could do with Sara, no more compulsive visits to her. He would lock the doors to those distant rooms he seemed to be intent on entering, strobe those dark corners free of mystery. His wife would be furious at first, there was no doubting that. Maybe he'd have to spend a few weeks in the minors, on Rowdy's hide-a-bed or at an Elk Run model home. But she'd forgive him, because she'd believe him when he told her it wasn't going to happen again. After all, this wasn't the nineteenth century. He'd fucked up, sure, but he wasn't going to repeat the mistake. That was the thing to keep in mind here. And once she knew that, it would be easy not to go back to Locust Lane. He'd have no choice.

He sat down.

Tell her.

'I got you the last *pain au chocolat*,' he said.

'My hero.'

They dismembered and divided the paper along the usual lines. Tell her.

'Mary Beth, listen . . . '

'What?'

'Look, I'm sorry I got so tanked last night . . . '

'I just wish you hadna driven home.'

Tell her.

'Yeah, me too. Listen . . . '

'Well, if it isn't Hope and Michael.'

It was Rowdy, scraping up a third chair. He wore camouflage

114

pants and a Hornets T-shirt. Stubble glistened on his cheeks. He smelled of sleeplessness and sweat.

'Wow, you look like you been rode hard and put away wet,' Mary Beth said.

'Just pulled an all nighter.'

'How's it going?' David asked.

Rowdy rubbed at his muscular neck, then ran a hand through his blond crew cut. His bulging bicep kicked and shimmered like a bent hose.

'Ah, the usual parade of human misery and malfeasance. I patch 'em up and tell them to sin no more but do they listen?'

'My guess would be not hardly,' Mary Beth said.

Rowdy looked around.

'You guys seen Cath?'

They both shook their heads.

'Why?' David asked.

'She's still after me with those fucking papers.'

'What papers?' Mary Beth asked.

He made a gun with his fingers and put it to his head.

'Final settlement,' he said, dropping his thumb.

David and Mary Beth glanced at each other, then looked back at their news. No one said anything for a moment.

'So how was the concert?' Rowdy asked finally.

'Great,' Mary Beth said, turning a page. 'David here was the main attraction.'

'How so?'

'Oh, he got shitfaced and then danced all by his lonesome.'

Rowdy looked at David, amused.

'Yeah?'

'Hey, I can't help it if everyone else in this town has a sharp stick up their ass.'

'Insurance covers that now, by the way,' Rowdy said.

'Uh, the stress is on the second syllable,' David joked.

'The hell it is,' Mary Beth responded.

Rowdy picked up the magazine, flipping to the lingerie ads.

'Hear anything more about your girlfriend?' he asked.

David's smile wavered.

'What's this?' Mary Beth asked, wanting to get in on the joke.

'Didn't David tell you about his nocturnal visit to the ICU?'

'His what?'

'He came by in the middle of the night to see that babe he found out there in the boonies. I think David likes them in comas.'

'I went by to check on that woman from the accident,' David explained with mock forbearance. 'What was her name?'

Rowdy shrugged.

'Never did find out. We call her the Mystery Date.'

Mary Beth was looking at David now.

'I just wanted to make sure we weren't going to get some personal injury asshole showing up on our doorstep,' he explained.

'He's so responsible, our David,' Rowdy said.

'What ever happened to the days when you could just help people out without worrying about lawyers?' Mary Beth asked.

Rowdy made a sign of the cross.

'Don't talk to me about lawyers. Cath has got this guy on my ass like ugly on an ape.' He looked at David. 'But seriously – you will let us know if you hear something about her, will you?'

'You after your money?' David asked.

'Fuck that. I don't work on commission like you property boys. I just want to make sure she's all right. She was still my patient last time anybody checked.'

David nodded sullenly, not too happy about the property boys remark.

'But I guess if you ain't heard anything from her people by now you ain't gonna. Looks like you gone dodged a bullet, Mr Webster.' He tossed the magazine back on the table. 'By the way, what ever happened to that joke you've been dying to tell me?'

David shrugged, still smarting from the remark.

'Forgotten it.'

'Well, listen to this one. Where can you find a turtle with no legs?'

'Where?' Mary Beth asked gamely.

'Right where you left it.'

Everyone laughed, though Rowdy stopped abruptly when a small, fiercely pretty woman with near-white hair and deep blue eyes pulled up a fourth chair.

'Oops,' Mary Beth said beneath her breath.

'I just heard a song on the way over called "All My Exes Live in

Texas",' the woman announced. 'I guess some people are just lucky.'

'Hey, Cath,' Mary Beth said.

'Hey yourself.' She pointed a small, tapered finger at Rowdy. 'You been avoiding me, shit heel. I checked everywhere you might be. Even the cheerleader tryouts at the junior high. They said you'd just left.'

Mary Beth couldn't help a stifled guffaw.

'I'm not avoiding you, Cath,' Rowdy explained sheepishly.

'Bullshit you ain't.'

'I wouldn't shit you,' he tried. 'You're my favorite turd.'

No one laughed. Cathy placed a small finger against Rowdy's bulging pectoral. It gave like kneaded dough.

'You better sign those fucking papers, zipper head, or there's going to be a hostage situation at your place of employ.'

Rowdy looked around for support, quickly realizing he wasn't going to get any. He held his hands aloft in mock surrender as he stood.

'Well, David, M-B, it's been real,' he said, turning to go. 'Cath, always a pleasure.'

'I'm not kidding, Ronald. Sign or I'm going to haul your ass before the judge.'

He stopped and turned back to face her.

'Don't call me that,' he said quietly.

'Oh gosh, I'm sorry, Ronald. Did I hurt your feelings, Ronald?'

He stalked away before she could say any more. She looked at David.

'What are you smirking at?'

'I'm not smirking.' He pointed to his mouth. 'Mary Beth, is this a smirk?'

'More of an incipient shit-eating grin,' she said.

Cathy shook her head.

'Why won't he sign the damned papers?' she whined. 'I know he's a muscle head but how hard can that be? They've trained chimps to do it, sign their names.'

'Maybe he doesn't want to,' Mary Beth offered. 'You know, deep down inside?'

'Ronald doesn't have a deep down inside. It's solid in there. Hit him with a bar – there's no echo. I've tried it on many occasions.' She snorted. 'Ah, fuck it. So, Mary Elizabeth, how's the drive going?'

'Fair to shitty.'

'Hey, you'll be all right. The gods smile down upon you. Both you two.'

'You want a coffee or something?' David asked.

'Yeah, I'll get it in a minute.' She squinted at him. 'So how's life with Crash Redwine?'

'Not so bad,' David said, his eyes making their way back to the newspaper.

'I hear he's going to put in a bid for Nowheresville.'

'News to me.'

'Yeah, I bet it is. I still can't believe you're working for that land raper.'

'He's all right,' David said, shrugging.

'All right? Jesus, five years ago you wouldn't have given him the time of day.'

'Well this isn't five years ago,' David said sharply. 'You know, I don't see why I have to—'

'Hey, Cath, come on,' Mary Beth interrupted. 'Give David a break. You know it's just a temporary thing.'

She relented, shaking her head.

'Yeah, sorry. I don't know what's got into me these days. The Mouth from the South. This divorce thing's got me goin' nuts.' She placed a hand on his arm. 'Hey, David? You still love me?'

'Passionately.'

He returned to his paper as Cathy and his wife began to speak, trying not to show how deeply he'd been stung by the criticism. This confession thing wasn't going right. He began to wonder if he was going to be able to do it at all. Cathy's beeper went off a few minutes later.

'Sounds like I'm needed. See you kids later.'

She left as quickly as she'd arrived.

'Christ, what's she running on?' David asked.

'High octane spite,' Mary Beth said. 'You done with the front page?'

David handed it to her, trying to think of a way to steer the conversation back to where he could tell her.

'Where did you get that?' Mary Beth was pointing to his outstretched arm.

'This?' he said, turning his wrist, as if he'd just noticed the watch for the first time.

She didn't answer. David wound and unwound it a few times.

'Hello? Earth to David.'

'I bought it.'

'You bought it? When?'

'Yesterday. When I was out.'

'Where?'

'At this antique shop.'

She screwed up her face, trying to picture him going into an antique shop.

'Antique shop?'

'Yeah. Just an old junk place, really.'

He smiled weakly.

'It seemed like a good deal.'

'David, you never buy yourself anything.'

'Well, I thought it was a good time to start.'

'And what the hell were you doing at an antique shop, of all places?'

'Hey, Mary Beth, come on. It's just a watch.'

'That's not really the point.'

'What is the point?' he asked. 'Why are you getting so bent out of shape about a watch?'

Somebody they knew passed. Greetings were exchanged and there was a short, strangulated conversation.

'What is it with you?' she asked when they were alone, her voice low now.

'What do you mean?'

'Late for things and all this drinking and then last night you're jumping around in front of everyone. And now you're buying yourself presents. That's what.'

'It's just, I guess I'm just starting to feel . . . '

'What, David?'

'I don't know, this job and stuff, it's starting to get me down. Cath's right. I mean, it's like there's a part of it that's not a joke any more. Like I'm working for the other side or something.'

Everything about Mary Beth softened into sympathy.

'David—'

'Nah, forget it. I'm just feeling sorry for myself.'

'No, it's all right. Look, I understand, hon. Nobody wants you to work that job forever. I just thought we decided, you know, for a while . . .'

She double-patted his hand, resolving something.

'Listen, after the drive, let's both just take a few weeks off,' she said. 'We can go camping.'

He was staring up at the poster of Tibet.

'David?'

'No, yeah. That'd be good.'

'If your boss has left us any wilderness.'

'There's still some.'

She let go of his hand and he stood and kissed her over the table. Her mouth tasted good to him, so deep and warm. And he knew he wasn't going to tell her. Not now. It would be all wrong, after lying to her about the watch, after her sympathy. As he sat his arm hit something, the coffee the waitress was placing on the table. Some of it sloshed out.

'Oh,' she said.

'No, my fault.'

She didn't argue the point. David tried to mop it up with the napkin they gave him with his bagel. It was too small, though, too glossily waterproof.

'Use this,' Mary Beth said, handing him the Book Review section.

It worked well, absorbing the coffee in a matter of seconds. David balled it up and threw the whole dripping mess into the trash can near the kitchen with its scraps of uneaten bagel and coffee grounds. When he got back to the table his wife showed him a wire service photograph of the flooded Mud River.

'Isn't that where you had your crash?'

'Somewhere around there.'

They went straight to WBRR from the café. The big cardboard thermometer had barely risen since yesterday morning. Even though only three people worked the phones there were still long stretches between calls. Sitting there, waiting for the white lights on

120

his receiver to flash, David brooded over his inability to tell Mary Beth what had happened. Sure, it had been a madhouse at the café, but that was no excuse. Maybe he really didn't want to send Sara away. Maybe his attraction was deeper than he'd reckoned. But that couldn't be right. She was a complete stranger, he knew nothing about her. The only thing they had in common was an accident. And when she got over its effects they wouldn't even have that any more.

His phone rang. An anonymous pledge of five hundred dollars. It was the biggest non-corporate donation so far. They had a little celebration and when David got back to his chair the word anonymous began to sound through his mind. And then he knew what he was going to do. Anonymous. That was the clue he'd been waiting for all day. He'd been looking at this wrong. The question wasn't whether or not to tell Mary Beth. Jesus, do that and they'd probably end up like Rowdy and Cath, bickering and ruined, hopelessly compromised. The whole thing could be resolved more simply than that. All he had to do was keep what had happened secret. Just be more careful about it – sporting the wristwatch had been inexcusable. Tomorrow, first thing, he'd tell Sara this had gone too far, tell her he couldn't help her any longer. Last night had been strange and wonderful and utterly unexpected. He'd have to settle for that. He knew it would be folly to try to repeat it. And then it would be over and he could go back to his life, back to Mary Beth, to his house and his friends. Find another job, maybe. And that secret now growing out of control would gradually starve, would soon shrivel up and die, some husk of it preserved in the clay and peat of his memory. So that was the way he was going to play it, then. Get Sara on her way before he got any more involved with her.

It seemed like the phones began to ring more regularly after that. At eight they closed for the day – nobody would give anything on a Sunday night. In honor of the big pledge he'd taken, they let David fill in the thermometer, four solid inches of deep blue ink. Then he and Mary Beth drove off to dinner with their friends. The place they were going was nowhere near Locust Lane.

121

PART TWO

7

David had to rush to make it to work on time. He'd stayed up late the night before, drinking too much wine, toking a few times on an atavistic joint someone had produced. He'd been thoroughly drunk by the end of the evening. But there was no dancing this time. And, as planned, no trips to Locust Lane. At home he and Mary Beth had grappled for a moment in bed before exhaustion and inebriation separated them inconclusively. When he woke the next morning she was gone and he was late. There was no time to make coffee or fetch the newspaper from the porch. Just shower, shave, and out the door. It only took a few minutes to get to the office – it had been a long time since there'd been a rush hour in Burleigh. Before going in he decided to pick up a big cappuccino from his local deli, the Bottomless Cup. Something to clear his head, get his blood flowing.

Despite his mild hangover, there was purpose in David's stride as he crossed the street. Today would be the end of his involvement with Sara. He had the whole thing planned. First, he'd finish the work he'd neglected last week. Proofs of the Elk Run insert were due back from the printer's that morning and there would be the usual corrections, additions and rewrites. A few hours of effort, tops. After that he would be free for the day. He'd call Mary Beth to let her know he'd be out, make excuses to Redwine, and then head over to Locust Lane to tell Sara that he couldn't help her any more. Carefully, tactfully, he'd explain that the other night had been a mistake, an impulse he could no longer follow. It would be tough, but she'd have to understand. He'd gently force her to come up with a plan that would get her out of the house and out of his life. If she needed money, a lift, that was fine. But this couldn't go on any longer. Something had to change.

As he passed the newspaper box outside the deli he noticed that the headline was larger than normal, a snare of ink and language that made him deviate from his plan by feeding a couple quarters into the machine's pursed mouth. It took him a moment to realize what he was reading.

N. WILTON JUNE FOUND DEAD AT MOUNTAIN ESTATE

Former BT Head Was Under Indictment for Tax Fraud

by Cathy L. Hunt

Former Burleigh Tobacco chairman N. Wilton June was found dead at his remote mountain home above Ivanhoe yesterday after it was raided by officers of the Internal Revenue Service's Criminal Investigations Unit, seeking June's arrest on tax evasion and conspiracy charges. There is as yet no determination of the cause of death.

'We won't be saying nothing until our coroner has a look-see,' claimed Ivanhoe County Sheriff William 'Bob' Swisher.

June, 57, chairman and CEO of Burleigh Tobacco Corporation from 1981 to 1988, had virtually disappeared after he controversially offered the company for sale to a group of Wall Street investors. It was a move that left the tobacco giant saddled with debt, resulting in the sale of many of its profitable manufacturing subsidiaries, widespread lay-offs in Burleigh, and the relocation of BT headquarters to Atlanta. Although the figure was disputed, June was believed to have made upwards of $40 million from the transaction.

'Will June killed Burleigh, and now he's dead,' a former BT executive said last night. 'Maybe there is some justice in the world.'

David stopped reading. Will June. Will. *Maybe I should go back to Will's place first.* He read the quote again. It said the same thing. Someone bumped into him. He was blocking the way. He folded the paper and walked quickly back to the office, ignoring Ginger as she waved pink message slips at him like a race starter. He went straight to the conference room, to the survey map hanging on the wall. It took a few moments to find Ivanhoe, forty miles north of Burleigh. The spot where she'd crashed was just a few miles due south of it.

'Jesus Christ,' David said aloud.

'You rang?' a wisecracking salesman said as he passed in the hall.

David walked slowly back to his office. He looked down at his desk – the proofs were there, ready for his attention.

'Donnie wants to know when you'll have the copy ready,' Ginger said from the doorway.

'All right.'

There was a pause.

'All right?' she asked. 'That's an answer?'

But David was already past her and on his way back to the Mustang.

Locust Lane was as quiet as ever. He sat outside the house for a moment, thinking about N. Wilton June, scouring his memory for something that would help him here. But the images that came were uselessly generic. The tall handsome man with impeccable suits, flawless manners and that icy calm. The long face with its grey eyes that peered unblinking through rimless spectacles. The lovely and poised wife who'd died suddenly of an unspecified cancer. The city's gentle patriarch, the aloof benefactor of most every cultural institution in town. David had seen him often at functions for the Social Fund, yearly at the WBRR party. They'd spoken perhaps a dozen times, once at length about the Old Burleigh project David had masterminded. He had always found the man polite and informed; and yet, like others, he occasionally sensed that there was something else beneath the frosty crust, some dark energy that played for a split second through his eyes or injected the odd word into his conversation. When he'd sold out his company David thought that it had been greed, pure and simple. Could it have been him Sara was talking about back at the crash? What the hell could she have been doing with June?

Christ, David thought. N. Wilton June. It was a name he was beginning to think he'd never hear again. No one knew what had become of him after the takeover. He'd disappeared altogether, fleeing with his loot, shrouded in rumor and acrimony as thick as the mists that wafted through the gaps in the Blue Ridge on the mornings after a storm. No society parties or high-profile lovers, no new business ventures or foundation in his dead wife's name. Just silence, a silence which seemed to contradict everything he'd done up to then. His fate had been the subject of a tide of speculation and rumor that had only recently begun to abate. And now he was dead. And Sara might have been with him.

David got out of the Mustang and walked slowly up to the house, wondering how he was going to play this. The best thing would be to simply ask her who Will was. Make her say. No more games, no more evasions. If it was June, if she was in some way involved with his death, that's it, he'd call the cops and walk. If it wasn't him, then David could still go back to his original plan, tell her it was time to find whoever she wanted to think were her people, offer her the help she needed to get her going. Either way, he thought as he stepped up to the small porch, it was definitely time to be done with Sara.

There was no answer when he knocked. He opened the screen door and looked through the fan of small, cloudy windows. He could see the things he'd brought her, the clothes she'd chosen. But not her. He knocked again, harder this time. There was still no answer. He went around back and looked through the kitchen door. The tap dripped steadily, each drop catching the low morning sun, flaring brilliantly for an instant. Otherwise the kitchen was empty.

He walked to the front door and used his spare key, stepping in as far as the auction sign. The radio played softly. He called her name. There was no answer. She's gone, he thought. That's it. Case closed. Despite his resolve to be rid of her and the jolting news of June's death, an unexpectedly intense wave of regret washed over him.

'Sara?'

He searched the front room, looking for some clue as to where she was, finding nothing. He checked the bathroom and the kitchen – nothing there, either. Finally, almost as an afterthought, he opened the door to one of the bedrooms he'd closed off when he first got here. It took him a moment to make her out. She sat in a corner, the darkest corner, her knees pressed to her chest, her hands resting uselessly at her sides, palms up, like a devotee or a beggar. He said her name and there was no answer. He crossed the room and knelt in front of her. Her eyes were open but distant, unfocused.

'Sara? What are you doing in here?'

'I'm cold,' she said after a long time.

'This is a cold room,' he said. 'The heater and lights and everything are out front.'

She didn't say anything. He looked around in vain for something to cover her.

'How long have you been in here?'

'I don't know. Pretty long.'

'Why?'

'I heard someone outside.'

'That was me.'

'No, I mean earlier. When it was still dark.'

'I don't . . . well, there isn't anyone outside now.'

She said nothing.

'What did you hear?' he asked.

'Car doors slamming. People calling out.'

'That was probably just kids.'

'How was I supposed to know that?' she asked, her voice tinged with hysteria.

'You weren't, you weren't. And so . . . you've been in here since then?'

She didn't answer.

'Come on,' he said. 'Let's get out of here.'

'No.'

The angry resolve in her voice stopped him. It was the same tone she'd used when she'd leapt from his car after he tried to force her to go back to the hospital.

'You can't just sit in here, Sara.'

'Watch me.'

'What is it you want, then? What is it you want me to do?'

'Get me something.'

'More painkillers?'

'The others are gone.'

'Is it bad?'

'Worse than ever.'

He shook his head slowly.

'I don't know how easy that will be.'

'Listen to me, David. If you don't get me some right now I'm going to freak. I'll have to try to find something for myself.' She looked up at him. 'Where the fuck have you been, anyway? You said you'd come back. I've been waiting for like . . . how could you just leave me here like this?'

'I thought . . .'

'What?'

'I thought you'd be all right.'

'Well, I'm not. I'm not even in the same zip code as all right.'

He nodded once and walked back to the front room, staring out at the quiet street for a moment. The news came on the radio, leading with the story of June's death. There was still no word as to the cause. David wondered how he could have been so stupid not to have come by yesterday, at least for a minute. What the fuck were you thinking? That she would just vanish? You made love to her. You told her you were going to help her.

And then he thought of something. He walked over to the sofa, looking amid the scattered clothes for the things she had been wearing when he found her, the black pants and especially the stained shoes. They were gone. The hospital gown and the cheap jacket were there, tangled and dirty. But not the other things.

He walked back to the window and looked out at Locust Lane. He suddenly knew he couldn't turn her out now, certainly couldn't let her go wandering the streets in search of drugs. She'd probably get picked up by the cops. Or worse. She wasn't going anywhere in her condition. He had no choice – he had to get her something to calm her down until he figured out what to do. Standing there, the thoughts rattling around in his brain like people rushing for the exit of a burning theater, he grimly recalled the morning's resolve to send her on her way, to neatly end his little adventure. Suddenly that seemed like a long time ago.

He picked up an unused thermal blanket from the things he'd brought her, a shiny survival wrap they handed out to earthquake victims or people who've just finished marathons. He carried it to the bedroom. She hadn't moved. As he placed it over her shoulders his hand brushed her neck. She was corpse cold.

'All right,' he said. 'But you have to promise me you'll stay here until I get back.'

She nodded dully.

'And when I do there are some things you'll have to tell me.

That's the deal.'

'Anything, David. Anything.'

'Will you at least wait in the front room? Where there's light?'

She reluctantly agreed. He helped her to her feet and they went through together. He sat her on the sofa. She looked bad. Worse even than at the crash or the hotel. Her irises seemed to have fractured into a million bits, her color-drained skin was covered with a dew of sweat. His heart ached with pity and anger. He felt like throttling her, like making love to her.

Before he left he made her some herbal tea. She held it like she did, using the cast as a support, letting the steam wash over her face.

'I'll be back soon,' he said.

'Hurry.'

That I will, he thought.

Despite dozens of billboard annunciations fanning out on highways surrounding the city, Old Burleigh was little more than a clutch of brick buildings surrounding a village green, a modest replica of what the city had looked like in the 1740s. It was one of the few cultural institutions in town that still functioned, somehow still roping in bored interstate drivers and elderly day trippers. There were crafts demonstrations, a sound and light show on summer nights, the Burleigh Inn with its 'traditional fayre', watering troughs and a well, and some punitive stocks. Prefab history with plenty of parking.

David walked quickly across the just-scythed green, hoping to hell that Bobby Lee was still around. If he wasn't then he didn't know what he was going to do. The idea of looking for bootleg painkillers on the streets of Burleigh was too much even to consider. Luckily he was there, snug in his apothecary, providing a group of retirees with a demonstration of old-time medicinal practices. He'd just levered a leech from its bottle, holding the viscid insect up to a chorus of yuks. David watched impatiently. He was really making a meal of it, peppering his spiel with thees and thous, letting the gooey bug squirm for an instant on his own thin arm, snatching it away before it could latch on. If anybody noticed the red patches at the crook of his elbow they probably thought it was a work-related rash. Which it was, provided you looked at it in a certain way.

David had got to know Robert F. Lee while setting up the Old

Burleigh project, his crowning achievement at the Social Fund. The idea was simple – to create a historical village that would also serve as a halfway house for paroled prisoners. They could live and work there, the discipline of learning traditional trades such as black-smithing or candle dipping supposedly preparing them for life in the modern world, though David always knew that was the weak link in his argument. Still, the idea was enthusiastically adopted by the board, matching funds easily secured from the city and the Bureau of Prisons. Within two years the project was up and running.

Lee was one of the first prisoners to be accepted into the program. He was smart and likeable, a good candidate for reform. The child of a prostitute who worked out of a mobile home, he had been in and out of institutions on drug and petty larceny charges since he was ten. He was first to volunteer for the program and topped out on all the aptitude tests. In those giddy early days nobody dwelled too much on the irony of his choice of apothecarist for a transitional occupation.

It wasn't until after the Burleigh break-up that Cathy told David that he had been selling pot and black beauties and coke out of his small brick building from the day he first donned his leather apron. The cops knew about it but didn't bother him. They needed Lee as much as the stressed-out young bankers and partying college students did, Cathy explained. As long as the city's affluent young whites could get their recreational drugs from him they wouldn't have to wander into East Burleigh, where they ran the risk of giving the overstretched department more work when they were ripped off or blown away. No, Lee was safe. And expensive.

He noticed David as the tourists shuffled off.

'Well, look who it is,' he said, his swamp-mammal face puckering into a smile beneath his floppy Moravian hat. 'My guardian angel.'

'Hey, Lee.'

'So how have you been, man? You still working at the Fund?'

'Nah, I'm doing something else now.'

Lee nodded generic approval.

'And yourself?'

'Can't complain,' Lee said, dipping and feinting with his shoulders like a loosening boxer. 'Keepin' the customer satisfied.'

Professionally demure, he was waiting for David to make the first move.

'I need something,' David said finally.

'Candles? Herbs? Unguents?'

'Unguents? Come on, Lee, cut the shit. I know what you do here.'

Lee shrugged, locking the door and flipping over the 'Back in Five' sign.

'What is it you had in mind, Mr Webster?'

'Something for pain. Pain and nerves. Something very good.'

Lee considered this for a moment.

'Can you do it?' David asked impatiently.

'Well, I reckon this is your lucky day. Got just the thing. I know this guy, works for some psychiatrists. He'll have some stuff. High test shit. Pharmaceutical for the cuticle. How much you need?'

'I don't know. A lot.'

'What, a ton?' Lee asked, smiling.

'Enough for a few days.'

'No prob. Anything else? You want some blow? Herb? Crank?' He was warming to the task. 'Ecstasy? You tried that shit? Man, you'll see why those kids walk around with those smiley faces stuck on everything.'

'No, no. Just what we've said.'

'Awright.'

'What's the damage?'

Lee looked David up and down.

'One fifty. That's my cost. On account of you've always been so good to me.'

'I need it now.'

'Yeah, you look like it. Two hundred, then. Shipping and handling.'

David nodded. He was in no position to argue.

'Let me make a call,' Lee said. 'Come back in half an hour.'

He unlocked the door. A line had formed. Old people, eager for history.

There was a cash machine at the reception center. David got the money there, seriously depleting his checking account. Neither he nor Mary Beth would be paid until the end of the month and most of their savings were locked away in a CD with a thirty day notice on it. David suddenly wondered if that was going to be a problem in the next few days. The thought depressed him, like a glimpse of some great undone task. At least Mary Beth wouldn't discover this until after the drive. By then he would have thought of a way to explain everything, a way to set it all right.

With twenty-five minutes to kill, he found a free bench on the green, watching a fat woman put her hands and head through the stocks to have her picture taken. There was much hilarity and joshing from others in her group. But once everyone had clicked their shot they couldn't get the shackles off her. The stocks had somehow become jammed. David watched the panic grow in her eyes as she realized she truly was stuck. A security guard was called, but he didn't know what to do. It took the costumed blacksmith ten minutes to pry her loose with his traditional tools. When the drama was over David went back to the apothecary and handed Lee the money. He gave David a stack of candles in an Old Burleigh bag.

'Listen, my man says that's some state of the art shit there. They just invented them in Europe or France somewhere. Makes Valium look like Tic-Tacs. They chill you *all* the way out, OK? They could be about to fry your ass and you wouldn't care. All you need is a couple, two, three a day, max.'

David nodded numbly.

'Thanks.'

'Hey, do come back if thou needest something else,' Lee said, doffing his cap, chuckling at his wit.

David failed to see the humor.

Sara hadn't moved from the sofa. The tea cup lay on the floor, surrounded by a piss yellow puddle of camomile.

'What's that?' she asked.

'What you wanted.'

She looked quizzically at him as he unwrapped the package. The pills were in a labelless brown vial. He pried it open and shook one into her outstretched hand. She popped it into her mouth and sat back on the sofa, her eyes closed. He went for a glass of water from the dripping tap. When he came back she was swallowing a second.

'The guy I bought these from said go easy. No more than two a day.'

She didn't respond. He watched her take long, greedy gulps of water, her eyes shut firmly. They sat through two songs on the radio without speaking. The pills worked fast – he could see the first slight relaxation of her taut facial muscles.

'Who did you think they were?' he asked finally.

'Who who were?'

'The people this morning.'

'I don't know. Maybe they're . . . '

She opened her eyes and looked at him.

'Never mind. You're right. I was probably just imagining things. Paranoid.'

'You sure?'

'Look, David, don't worry. I'm all right now. I just needed some nerve candy.'

She noticed the brilliant blanket draped around her.

'I feel like a TV dinner in this,' she said.

He managed a smile.

'Could you help me take this off?' she asked, indicating the Ace bandage on her right hand. 'I think I'm beginning to rot under here.'

'Are you sure?'

'You know, I wish you wouldn't ask me that. Let's just as a matter of policy assume the answer is no and then let's go ahead and do it anyway.'

'Sounds like my kind of policy,' he said grimly.

He gently removed the two toothed clamps and began to unravel the dirty elastic. The odor of sweat and stale balm wafted between them.

'So what did you do yesterday?' she asked.

He completed three rotations of the bandage before answering.

'Me? Nothing really.'

'If you weren't doing anything you could have come to see me,' she said matter-of-factly.

He finally reached the end of the bandage, balling it up and tossing it to one side. The flesh beneath it was puffy and pale.

'How does it feel?'

She shook it experimentally.

'Stiff.'

He reached over and touched the bloodless skin.

'Does that hurt?' he asked.

'A little.'

He pushed harder.

'Ow, fuck,' she said, pulling her hand away.

Anger flashed in her eyes.

'Why did you do that?'

To bring you back to earth, he thought.

'That really hurt, David,' she said, cradling her hand.

'I'm sorry. I don't know what I was thinking.'

They sat in silence for a moment.

'You scared me in there, Sara,' he said finally.

'Yeah, well, join the club,' she said, resentment still in her voice.

She shivered a bit and the blanket fell off her shoulders. He replaced it, letting his hand linger on her back.

'Sara?'

'What?'

'Do you know who Will June is?'

For a moment he thought he could feel something play through her muscles. A tremor of fear or surprise. But he couldn't be sure. Not with the drugs she'd taken. Not with knowing her so little. He just couldn't be sure.

'No,' she said flatly.

He let go of her.

'He has a place up in the mountains. Not far from where you crashed.'

'So?'

'It's just that at the crash site you said something about getting back to Will's place.'

'So you said.'

'I just wondered if it was Will June you meant. Wilton June.'

She laughed impatiently, falling back on the sofa and staring at him.

'Since I don't know any Will, the answer's still gotta be no.'

'Then who was it? Who was it you were running away from?'

'Just this guy. You don't know him. And it's better you don't.' She cocked her head. 'Why?' she asked.

'He died.'

'Will June?'

136

David nodded.

'Well, I know lots of people who died, David,' she said. 'But he's not one of them. Why are you asking me this?'

'Just curious.'

Her eyes narrowed suspiciously.

'But now you're making it seem like you think—'

'No, Sara. I'm not saying that at all.'

'I mean it seems like you've taken one little imaginary delirious word and've been weaving this elaborate deal that has me connected to this dead—'

'Sara.'

She stopped talking.

'I'm not weaving anything. I was just curious. I won't mention it again.'

She sat up, her eyes suddenly resolute. She laughed bitterly and then her face grew somber.

'Listen, David – I have to go.'

'What do you mean?'

'You heard me. I have to get out of here.'

'Why? I mean, why now?'

She didn't bother to answer, as if the whole thing were beyond discussion. So there it is, David thought. Mission accomplished. More easily than you'd ever imagined. But for some reason he heard himself repeating his question.

'Why?'

'What do you mean why? Look at us here. This is crazy.'

'Sara, you can't go,' he said, his voice strained, not sounding like his voice at all.

'What do you mean, can't go? Am I under house arrest or something?'

'No, of course not. It's just, how far do you think you'll get, hurt and broke like this? A half-hour ago you couldn't even move from one room to another.'

'Yeah, well, I'm feeling a lot better.'

'For how long?' He rattled the pill bottle. 'Until these run out?'

They sat in silence for a minute. David wondered what he was doing, why he was suddenly trying to convince her to stay.

'So what do you suggest?' she asked.

'Just stay here for now. Get some strength back. In a few days, look, in a few days I'll help you go where you want.'

'Go where I want.'

'Where, Sara? There has to be somewhere.'

'Far away is all that matters.' She managed a wan smile. 'How about the moon? You know anybody on the moon? Buzz or Neil, either would do.'

David had a sudden, longshot idea as to how he could resolve this whole thing.

'How about Seattle?'

She looked at him.

'Seattle? What the hell are you talking about?'

'My brother lives there. Maybe, I don't know, maybe I can talk to him. He's cool about stuff. You could go stay with him. That's about as far away from here as you can get, right? Without a passport, anyway.'

'Seattle as in . . . '

'Yes.'

She nodded slowly, considering this.

'Just stay here a few more days,' David said, pressing home his advantage. 'Get your strength back, give me time to get it together, talk to him, arrange a flight. I mean, wouldn't that be better than just walking out the door and sticking out your thumb?'

She looked at her hands.

'I don't even think I could stick out my thumb.'

She looked up at David.

'Your brother, huh?'

'He's a great guy, believe it or not. A lot nicer than me. Richer, too.' David smiled. 'But he's my kid brother. He does what he's told.'

'Does he have a family or . . . '

'He lives with someone. Martin.'

'Ah, I see. Well, I guess I don't have much of a choice,' she said softly.

Neither do I, David was beginning to suspect.

'All right,' she said. 'You win. I'll hang.'

'Good.'

'But just a day or two, right? And then I'm outta here. The big fade.'

'Absolutely.'

She looked at him. David thought he could detect trust and affection seeping back into her eyes. Or maybe it was just the chemicals.

'So how did this June guy die, anyway?' she asked.

'Nobody knows yet. At least they're not saying. He was about to go to jail, it seems.'

'What for?'

'Taxes or something. He was rich.'

'How rich?'

'Rich like you wouldn't believe. Forty million plus.'

She laughed.

'Now you're making me sorry I didn't know him.'

'He's the guy I told you about who sold out the city. I always thought he was a pretty good guy for a capitalist pig. Patron of the arts, social conscience, all that. I mean, there was always something a bit different about him, something I couldn't put my finger on. Like he was doing all this corporate stuff with his tongue in his cheek. Like he had some other agenda. But then he caught that Reagan bug and went apeshit. I mean, he really gutted us, fucked us over but good. That's why this town's like it is. After that he just disappeared with his loot. People could never figure out why he did it, how anyone could be that greedy. Though now it's beginning to look like maybe he was leading anything but the high life.'

She nodded absently. Her eyelids seemed to be growing heavier. She looked up and caught him staring at her. A languid half-smile formed on her lips.

'Those are some drugs,' she said. 'You're a real life saver.'

He looked away, his eyes falling nervously on his watch.

'Are you going to go now?' she asked.

'Well no, not just yet.'

'Don't you have to be at work?'

'Not for a while.'

She stretched and settled back into the sofa.

'Man, you must really love this job.'

'I hate it, to be precise.'

'Join the club.'

139

He waited for her to elaborate but she remained silent. As he knew she would. A song came on the radio. She sat forward and turned it up.

'I used to hate this redneck shit but it's beginning to make all kinds of sense. They had this girl on a while ago called Suzy Bogguss. My kind of name.' She shrugged. 'I got tired of listening to that classical station you had it turned to. Those deejays drive me nuts. They're all so smug.'

She stretched again, her body uncoiling from the tension that had gripped it just a short while earlier. David was watching her eyes – her fractured irises seemed to have reassembled, glued by drugs and his promise of help. She met his gaze and smiled. He felt a jolt of desire for her. And then he remembered about June, about this morning's resolve.

'Look, Sara, the other night . . . '

'Yeah?'

'Maybe that wasn't such a great idea.'

Her smile collapsed.

'How do you mean?'

'It's just . . . look, you're going away.'

'Not today I'm not.'

He got up and walked to the window, looking out at the quiet street.

'Thing is, we don't know anything about each other.'

'And that's bad?'

'Well, yeah.'

She gathered the blanket protectively around herself.

'I always thought it's when people stop being mysterious to each other that the trouble starts.'

He said nothing.

'I don't understand you, David. I mean, first you practically beg me to stay, and now . . . '

'No, I guess I don't understand myself just now.'

'Well, when you do, let me know,' she said coolly. 'Just don't forget that we don't have lots of time here. As soon as I get mobile I'm out of here. You are still going to help me with that, aren't you?'

David nodded vaguely. The news came on the radio. June's death was the last item. Soon it would be history.

'You know, I do have to go.'

'I thought you said . . . '

He looked at her.

'All right. Go. Just don't forget about what you said. Don't forget about me here again.'

As if that's possible, David thought as he walked out the door.

Back at the Redwine Group, he locked himself in his office and puzzled over his inability to be done with her. It had all seemed so clear that morning. And now he was committed more deeply than ever, having offered to involve his brother as well as himself. Man, where had that come from? The news about June should have made him more eager to get rid of her, and yet it seemed to have just the opposite effect. He finally gave up trying to understand what was happening. There was nothing else to do but go ahead with what they'd decided. Keep her a few more days, then send her off. If people were looking for her he'd know by then.

He spent the rest of the afternoon trying to work. There was the insert to finish – it had to be at the paper the following morning. And in the evening he was scheduled to work the phones again. He didn't even get the chance to call his brother until ten minutes to six.

'Timbo.'

'David, how are you?'

'Not bad, not bad. Built any good ones recently?'

'Malls, man. Everybody wants fucking malls.'

'Welcome to the working week,' David said. 'Everything else going all right?'

'Somebody stole Martin's Wrangler.'

'No shit.'

'Yeah, we're telling everyone we're jeepless in Seattle.'

David laughed.

'So how's Mary Beth?' Tim asked. 'How's the drive going?'

'Slow.'

'She get our check?'

'Sure did. Many thanks.'

'Well, tell her fingers and toes are crossed out here.'

There was a pause.

'Listen, Timbo, I need a favor.'

141

'Sure, David. Anything.'

'There's this friend of mine, a woman. You don't know her, she's new in town. Anyway, she's having a bad time with this guy and the thing of it is, she has to get the fuck out of Dodge. What I was wondering is if you and Martin could put her up for a while.'

'Well, yeah, sure,' Tim said without hesitation. 'I mean, what, is she being abused?'

'Something like that.'

'You men. What's her name?'

'Sara. You'll like her.'

'Well, sure, that would be cool, David. I mean, we got all this room. You can send her any time. When did you have in mind?'

David had been twisting the phone's cord between his fingers.

'David?'

He released it.

'Might be a couple days yet.'

'Well, just give me the details when you got them. I'll talk to Martin but you know how he is. The more the merrier.'

'I'll be in touch. Oh, and Tim?'

'Yeah?'

'Listen, should you talk to Mary Beth, don't tell her about this.'

'You dog.'

'No, it's not like that. It's, well . . . complicated.'

'My lips are sealed.'

'Does Martin know that?'

Tim pretended to guffaw.

'Oh I do love straight humor . . . '

After hanging up he called the airline he normally used. He gave them his name and asked for his frequent flyer total. The woman worked the computer and then read out a distance.

'Will that get someone to Seattle?' he asked.

'Sure will, though it won't get them back again. Would you like to make a reservation?'

David was looking out the window.

'Sir?'

'Let me get back to you on that one.'

*

Later that night, sometime in the middle of all the darkness and silence, he woke up making love to Mary Beth. Her eyes were closed – she had been fast asleep as well. He knew he should stop but he kept on, thrusting hard into her dry vagina. He came quickly, the orgasm shuddering through his slumbering flesh. It was over before she was fully awake. They lay entwined for a few moments, breathing hard. When he finally opened his eyes she was staring at him in bitter confusion. He tried to say something but there were no words, so he got up and walked to the window. It had begun to rain, an insistent downpour that echoed through the big room.

'David, what was that? Why did you do that?'

He didn't answer.

'I didn't like that,' she said, close to tears. 'You shouldn't . . . I didn't like that. And plus I didn't have anything in, David.'

'I was asleep and . . . '

'And what?' she asked. 'What does that mean, you were asleep?'

'I don't know.'

But he did, of course. He looked out the window. The water washing over it made the world outside shimmer and dance. He knew he should say something to his wife but all he could do was wonder if it was raining like this on Locust Lane.

8

David sat on the porch until dawn, only vaguely aware of the rain sweating through the trees, the insinuating hiss of a nearby sewer. As hard as he tried, he couldn't make sense of what had happened with Mary Beth. He'd never done anything like that before. His brutality had shocked him almost as much as it had her. For a brief moment when he first woke it was as if he were standing beside his body, watching the whole grisly episode. Another inexplicable action to add to his growing catalogue.

With sunrise the house's alarm lights finally stopped flaring. They'd been going all night, strobing patches of yard where possums or raccoons wandered, where big branches shifted in the storm's breeze. The system was too sensitively calibrated. It should have registered only human intruders. Another thing he'd have to get adjusted. He let it run anyway, taking strange pleasure in the random light. He'd never really wanted to install an alarm, even after a string of burglaries hit the neighborhood in the bad days after the takeover. The house felt enough like a fortress as it was. But then, last summer, Mary Beth had brought home a roll of film that changed his mind. The first dozen pictures were of a weekend they'd spent on a houseboat on Lake Norman. The remainder were taken a month later, at his in-laws' fortieth anniversary. Separating the two bunches was a single, poorly focused photo of an erect penis, moments after ejaculation. Semen dribbled from its empurpled head like oatmeal from a baby's mouth. The hand gripping it was hairy and tattooed. It was taken from above, by the cock's owner. At first David thought it was some awful mistake, maybe a sick joke by someone at the lab. But then Mary Beth noticed her crumpled blouse in the background, the burnished wood floor. The photo had been taken with their camera, in their bedroom.

David tore through the house. Nothing was missing. The only thing different was the archipelago of formerly anonymous stains

Mary Beth found on the quilt covering the foot of their bed. It was an antique, passed down through the Covington family for generations. They burned it in the back yard. Two days later a man with thin sideburns came and sold them the state of the art alarm system that now flashed the night's intruders.

Morning rolled in, meager light and hungry birds and then the paper boy, who pitched the *Record* into the pachysandra. David pulled it from its plastic cocoon and read the lead story right there, while rainwater soaked his bare feet.

Former BT Head 'Took Own Life'

by Cathy L. Hunt

The death of N. Wilton June at his Ivanhoe County estate is being labeled a suicide by local authorities. June, former chairman of Burleigh Tobacco, was found dead at his remote house on Sunday morning, apparently from a massive overdose of insulin, which he had been taking for chronic diabetes. A note discovered at the scene by officers of the Internal Revenue Service's Criminal Investigations Unit has led police investigating his death to treat it as suicide. A source at the county coroner's office says June had been dead for approximately twenty-four hours before being discovered.

'There are no other suspects except the Devil and he's not in my jurisdiction,' Ivanhoe County Sheriff William 'Bob' Swisher claimed.

June, 57, gained national prominence five years ago when he instigated the leveraged buyout, or LBO, of Burleigh Tobacco by a group of Wall Street investors. Although the deal should have secured him upwards of $40 million, it is now known that subsequent reversals in share values greatly diminished that sum. Sources also claim that June had squandered most of his personal savings, though they could only speculate as to what became of the money.

145

It is now known that the former tobacco executive had recently begun to sell off a large portion of his property and assets, including his private airplane and New York apartment, as well as much of his art collection. Bankruptcy proceedings were initiated two months ago and an eight-part indictment naming June on tax fraud was unsealed last week, leading to Sunday's raid.

Borrowed Time

IRS investigator Ray Steadman would not comment on suggestions that June had been tipped off over the raid, though he conceded that the former tobacco boss knew he was under investigation. Steadman confirms that June's estate has now been seized by the IRS and will be auctioned to pay back taxes.

'He may have thought he had forty million,' a former associate said, 'but it wasn't worth the paper it was printed on. He was leveraged up to his eyeballs. The man was living on borrowed time.'

In addition to financial setbacks, June was known to have remained distraught over the death by cancer eight years ago of his wife Peggy. He was also stung by allegations that he had ruined the city of Burleigh, where he had lived and worked for over thirty years.

Remarkable Growth

Born in 1935 in Ivanhoe, June was the eldest son of a Pentecostal minister. After unsuccessfully trying to establish himself as an artist in New York City, he returned to North Carolina, working as a teacher, fire spotter and bartender.

In 1960 he became a sales representative for the Burleigh Tobacco Corporation, working his way up through the organization to become Vice President for Marketing in 1971 and Managing Director in 1977. In 1981, June took control of the company in a pitched boardroom battle with former chairman Eugene 'Bighouse' Cottle. His tenure at the helm was a time of remarkable growth for the company and prosperity for Burleigh.

Butcher of Burleigh

But in early 1988 June began secret negotiations with a group of Wall Street investors that led to the takeover of the company. Stocks and junk bonds were to be purchased at inflated prices, creating debt which, it was asserted, would be paid off by subsequent 'restructuring'. The deal went disastrously wrong when hostile investors entered the fray, pushing share prices higher than June and his management group had believed possible. Massive layoffs and the sale of assets ensued. June resigned, rich yet reviled, known to many as 'The Butcher of Burleigh'.

Little is known of his life since then. He became reclusive, spending most of his time at his remote Blue Ridge Mountain estate. He was spotted occasionally at the funerals of friends or art auctions, but otherwise became a shadowy figure. Lower than expected dividends on his complicated 'golden parachute' agreement with his former employer, government officials maintain, may have led to his systematic attempts to defraud the IRS, creating a tangled web of deceit that knowledgeable sources admit may never be fully unravelled.

David folded the paper. June's death was a suicide. Thank Christ. Even if Sara had been with him, at least she hadn't killed the man – he didn't even die until four days after David found her. And, after all, there were a lot of Wills out there. Maybe his hunch was wrong. Maybe she really did have nothing to do with June.

Powered by relief, he fixed breakfast for Mary Beth, serving it to her in bed. He apologized for the night before, saying he didn't know what had got into him. She seemed more confused than angry. Besides, she was in a rush to get to work. He knew he was lucky she had so much on her mind. She was a smart woman – this deception couldn't go on much longer, certainly not after the distraction of the drive was past. Something had to happen. Soon.

At the office David put the finishing touches on the Elk Run insert, noting ruefully that it was the best work he'd done since joining the Redwine Group. God, he thought, maybe this really is what I was made for. At ten o'clock he took the proofs over to the *Record*, dropping them off in the production department. After that the plan was to go back to Locust Lane and let Sara know that everything was set for her flight to Seattle. All they had to do now was decide when she felt strong enough to travel. It could be as early as that evening. And then it would be over. He could return to his normal life.

Before leaving the building, David had an idea how he might find out conclusively whether or not she had been with June. Just to be safe, before getting Tim involved with this. A way of making sure there wasn't something they'd left out of the paper. He went up to the newsroom on the second floor. The long chamber was alive with the low hum of implacable voices, the chatter of keyboards, the flicker of track lights over the sound baffles. Cathy was on the phone. She smiled and waved David over.

The youngest child in a family of Outer Banks shrimpers, Cathy was the first member of her clan to leave their coastal village, coming to college the same year as David. After graduation she'd taken a job at the *Record*, quickly developing a reputation as a fearless reporter who would confront redneck sheriffs and homicidal giants without batting an eye. When she married Rowdy the two couples had become inseparable. During their break-up David had tried to stay neutral, listening with patient equanimity to both of them, striving to keep them together. Mary Beth told him not to bother – the marriage was dead. But he persevered until the divorce proceedings had begun. Cathy had always appreciated what he tried to do and was forever reminding David how much she owed him for it.

'Well hey,' she said, hanging up the phone. 'This is a nice surprise.'

'I was just in the neighborhood.'

'Pull up a chair.'

He sat across from her.

'So how you been?' he asked.

'Still trying to break these chains. And yourself?'

David shrugged. He didn't want to go into himself.

'So, June bites the big one,' he said.

She shook her head.

'Weird, eh? Bet there aren't too many crocodile tears being shed on Main Street.'

'You been up there? To his place?'

'Sure have.'

'What's it like?'

'It's very, very weird. Like Xanadu or some such. I kid you not. Just stuffed with stuff. We're doing a feature on it for Saturday.'

'Stuff?'

'Hey, bub, pay your quarter.' She narrowed her eyes. 'Why do you ask?'

'Just curious. I mean, I was wondering if we'll ever know why he did it.'

She shrugged.

'They ain't let me see the note yet. Federal handwriting guys still have it to check it out. Though the fact that his demise directly preceded a multiple warrant raid sort of narrows the possibilities.'

'Any more light on why he put the company in play?'

'Greed, I guess.' Her eyes narrowed and she shook her head. 'Though I don't know. It's like that's almost too obvious.' She shrugged. 'We'll prolly just have to chalk that up to one of life's great mysteries.'

David resisted the temptation to ask her point blank if she knew about a woman being up there with him. There was no reason to get her curious. Besides, if there was a girl involved, it would be all over the paper. No, this was all he needed to know. It was a simple case of bankruptcy and suicide writ large. Sara was telling the truth, after all.

'Hey, David, could you do me a favor?'

David knew what was coming.

'I'll talk to him.'

'Thanks.' Her eyes misted. 'It's just . . . I really want to get on with the rest of my life.'

'Yeah, Cath. I know how you feel.'

He swung by work before going to Locust Lane, just to let Redwine know he'd be out for a while. Ginger stood in the hallway outside his office, bathed in the copier's reproductive light.

'There's someone to see you,' she said as he walked by her desk.

'Who is it?'

She shrugged.

'He says it's important.

David sighed loudly. He wanted to see Sara.

'All right.'

A man sat in the chair facing David's desk, reading the spread-open appointment calendar beside the blotter. He stood up quickly when he heard the door whisper against the pile carpet. He was tall, stick-thin, with a long, skull-like head. Black hair sprayed from his ears and nostrils. Despite the spring warmth he wore a formless raincoat that he showed no intention of removing.

'Hello, I'm David Webster.'

'David, my name is Ed Decker and I'd like to thank you for making time for me.'

His voice was deep, all coffee grounds and flicked ash. They shook hands. The man's bony grip was incredibly strong.

'Sure, no problem.'

David walked around behind his desk. Decker sat heavily, sighing, as if he'd just finished a great trek.

'Those are some storms you've been having around here,' he said, pulling the flaps of his raincoat tight, as if he expected one in the office.

'You get used to them.'

'Do you? Because I hate unpredictable weather. Bad, OK. Snow, sleet. I can handle it. As long as you know. But unpredictable? No thank you.'

They looked at each other.

'What can I do for you, Mr Decker?' David asked.

'Right, good. Cut right to the chase. I like that.'

He inhaled deeply and looked at the ceiling.

'David, I'm looking for a girl.'

'Aren't we all,' David joked feebly, trying to hide the sudden tremor of emotion he was experiencing.

'You just might have something there,' Decker said, rolling his head until his neck cracked. 'Fact is, I think you've had contact with the particular girl I'm looking for.'

'Contact?'

'You helped her after an accident to the northwest of the city last Tuesday.'

David gave a guarded nod.

'Sure, I remember. She'd hurt her hands. But I don't really know what help I can be.'

'Perhaps if you could tell me just what happened up there.'

'I've already told the police.'

'That you did. In fact, that's where I got your name. But, you see, the police might not have been after the same sort of thing that we are.'

'Can I first ask who you are? I mean, in what capacity . . . '

'Capacity. Of course. I thought we might skip the preliminaries, but, I'm the security director of a New York corporation.'

'What corporation?'

Decker rubbed at an eye for a moment, examined his fingertip for residue.

'We have diverse interests.'

'But no name?'

He looked at David, his expression souring.

'Yeah, we got a name, Mr Webster.'

'Could I see some sort of identification, Mr Decker?'

The man held David's gaze for a moment, then shrugged and reached into his back pocket, taking out a creased wallet. He removed a laminated card and handed it across the desk. David read. It was a New York State driver's license. Decker was forty-four. His middle name was Carl. He had blue eyes, an address on Staten Island. David handed it back. They looked at each other for a moment.

'And why are you looking for her?'

'She's a valued employee, David. We're concerned about her well-being.'

David knew he had to accept this. All of a sudden he was beginning to regret carding the man.

'Well, there's not much to say. I was driving along and we had a near collision and her car went off the road.'

'A *near* collision.'

'That's right. The road was slippery.'

'And you went back to help.'

David nodded.

'I asked her what I could do. She'd broken her hand, busted up her head, her ribs I think. So I went for help. When I came back . . .'

Decker was watching him closely.

'Go on.'

'And when I came back she was unconscious.'

'How did you know that?'

'Her eyes were shut. She didn't answer when I spoke to her.' David attempted levity. 'You know, the usual unconscious stuff.'

Decker didn't respond.

'And then the ambulance arrived and they took her to the hospital,' David continued.

'OK. Good.'

David brought his hands down on his blotter.

'Well, I'm glad I could be of—'

'Now, let's go back to when you first arrived on the scene,' Decker said, oblivious to the gesture. 'Can you remember specifically what was said? Between you and this woman.'

'Specifically? Well, no.'

'Well, let me put it this way. Did she say anything about where she was going?'

'It was pretty clear that was going to be the hospital.'

Decker grimaced and pulled his raincoat tight again.

'I meant in a more general sense, David.'

'It wasn't that sort of conversation. It was just, it was very matter-of-fact. It was over pretty quick.'

'I bet. How about where she'd been?'

David shook his head.

'Let me run one more thing by you,' Decker said. 'Did she have anything with her? A bag or . . . something that might be of use in locating her?'

'Not that I saw.'

'That's pretty strange, wouldn't you say?'

'I'm not saying she didn't have a bag. I just didn't see it. Like I said—'

'It all happened pretty fast.'

'Maybe you should check the car,' David offered.

'We did. There were some clothes but not . . . but nothing else.'

Decker began to roll his skeletal right hand.

'So she didn't, and I just gotta ask you this one thing, she didn't place anything into your possession?'

'What?'

'She didn't give you anything?'

'No. Of course not.'

Decker smiled.

'Of course not. Look at you. You're getting mad. Sometimes I think I have like zero couth at all. But these are the things you got to ask, David. I ask them once, boom, then we don't have to mess around with it.' He flattened his hand and started tilting it, riffing on scenarios. 'And there wasn't anybody else who came along?'

'No. It was just us.'

'And she was in the car the whole time?'

'Far as I can tell.'

'Can you remember where it happened, this accident?'

'Not really. It was on a detour. I could maybe guess.'

'NBD. I'll ask the cops.'

Decker slapped his bony hands against his bony thighs.

'David, thanks for your time. I'm going back to the hospital now to talk to some people there. Maybe they'll know something more.'

They stood.

'Well, good luck in finding her,' David said.

Decker exhaled and shook his head.

'With this girl I wish it was just a question of luck.'

David sat perfectly still at his desk after the man was gone, his suspicions that Sara had been fleeing more than just a domestic squabble blooming again. For some reason, something about Decker and the things he'd said made him once again suspect she'd been involved with June. Trusted employee, diverse interests. Something in her possession. What could that mean? And there were her words as well, uttered without calculation in the heat of the moment. *Maybe I should go back to Will's place first.* He remembered that tremor through her muscles when he'd mentioned June's name the day before. No, there was some connection there, something Cathy and the cops hadn't nosed out yet. If he only had some way to find out what it was, to see for himself before he put his name on her plane ticket and got his brother involved in this. Before he let her go.

And then it came to him. It was perfect. Inspired, he picked up the phone. Cathy was still at her desk.

'I have a request,' David said.

'I can be at Hyatt in eight minutes. Eight and a half if you want me to bring restraints or lubricants.'

'I was wondering if you could get me up there, Cath. To June's place.'

There was a short silence as she switched tack.

'To Ivanhoe? Why?'

'Redwine wants me to have a peek at June's crib so he can get an early bid in on this auction you mentioned in the paper. He figures if I can get a sense of what's going on before they go public he can get in a preemptive offer, cut a deal with the tax guys.'

'Not hardly.'

'You don't know Donnie. He has this way with authority.'

'Why doesn't he go up himself?'

'Doesn't want to raise suspicions among his competitors. You now how paranoid these guys are.'

'When?'

'As soon as possible.'

'I could, I guess. I mean . . .'

David could sense her deliberating.

'Let me think about it, make a few calls. I'll get back to you this afternoon.'

He arrived at Locust Lane a half-hour later, still undecided if he should tell Sara about Decker. The door was open so he let himself in. He stopped abruptly before he made it past the auction sign. She sat on the sofa holding a copy of that morning's *Record*. She was reading the article about June's death, so engrossed in it she hadn't noticed David enter.

'Sara?'

She clumsily folded the paper, tossing it to the floor as she looked

154

up at him.

'I didn't hear you come in,' she said without surprise.

'Sorry. It was open.'

He joined her on the sofa. She looked rested and calm, her amber eyes sparkling, her pale skin slightly flushed. Robert F. Lee's mystery drugs were still working their charms.

'Where'd you get the paper?' he asked.

'Oh, I went out for a short walk this morning and borrowed it from one of the neighbors. It's been a long time since I've seen one.'

'So what do you think?' he asked, watching her closely.

But she only shrugged indifferently.

'Same old same old.'

He stared at her for a moment longer before looking away. There was something else new on the floor – a tattered cardboard box.

'What's this?' he asked, nodding toward it.

'Ah. I found this in a closet in one of those bedrooms. Just some old stuff that got left behind. Family photos, books. A set of souvenir spoons. And look . . . '

She lifted out a box containing a jigsaw puzzle. The pieces were all blank, pure white.

'Something to do when you next abandon me,' she said.

'How are you feeling?' he asked.

'No pain,' she said, putting the box away. 'Those pills you got me are the real thing. You're a regular sandman.'

'You want some tea?'

'Sure.'

She watched him light the small flame.

'So how's it going?' she asked.

He looked up from the stove, thinking for a moment she was referring to his efforts to find out about her.

'Getting me out of here?' she explained. 'Seattle? Remember?'

'I'm still setting it up.'

She tilted her head dubiously.

'What does that mean?'

David looked back at the steady blue flame.

'No, it's just that Tim, my brother, he's away for a few days. He'll be back at the end of the week.'

'The end of the week?' she asked dubiously.

'It's not a problem, Sara. We've spoken. It'll be fine. Just be patient.'

'That's easy for you to say.'

The water boiled and he brewed the tea in silence. He was desperate to ask her about June again but didn't want to jeopardize her fragile mood. When the drink was ready he handed her a steaming mug and opened the bag of sandwiches he'd brought from the Bottomless Cup. They ate slowly, in near silence, their conversation bound by all the things they couldn't tell each other. Finally, just as they were finishing the food, she gave him a searching look.

'What is it, David?' she asked.

'What do you mean?'

'You seem weird today. Distracted.'

'No, it's just . . . something's bothering me.'

'Go on.'

'This guy you don't want to find you.'

'What about him?' she asked, suddenly wary.

'Just, you know, I'm wondering who he is. I mean, what he is to you.'

She sighed.

'All right, all right. You win. I'll tell you even though there's no good reason you should know.'

She sighed, her eyes narrowing as she dredged up the memories.

'Let's see, where do I start. We got, all right, we got involved when I was in pretty bad shape a while back. I mean, you thought I was in the wringer yesterday, you should have seen me then.' She was picking at the frayed edge of her cast, causing white plaster to powder her thigh. 'So he sort of took me under his wing. I hung out with him for a while. We became lovers. You know. And then I grew sick of it. It got to be like I was being smothered. Suffocated. He's got lots of money, you see. And this bad habit of controlling everything around him, everyone. At first all those extravagant gestures, all that doting, it was good. I used to mistake it for love. But then I figured out it was something other than that. So I bolted.'

She shook her head.

'Only he didn't see it like that. It was like he was supposed to own me. He's a collector of . . .'

She stopped suddenly and looked at David, her expression darkening.

'Why are you asking me all this now?'

'No reason.'

Her eyes narrowed.

'Has something happened?'

'No, of course not.'

She sat forward.

'Has someone been to see you about me? David?'

'No.'

'No one?'

'I said no.'

She accepted this.

'Would it matter?' he asked.

'Matter? If I knew they were here, if I knew they suspected where I was, I'd be out of here in a minute. Fuck Seattle, I'd go to Mexico or Tokyo or Hell. I don't care. Just get as far away as I could get.'

'They?' David asked. 'I thought we were talking about a he.'

She began picking at the cast again.

'Yeah, well, it's complicated. Real complicated.'

'I don't get it.'

'David, if I tell you then *you'll* know. You'll be involved. See what I mean?'

'Not really.'

'Well, trust me on this one. Put your curiosity on hold. It's better that way.'

She touched his arm with her good hand.

'But you have to tell me if anybody comes looking for me here, all right? You have to promise. Because that would be a whole new ball game.'

'All right.'

'I'm through with that shit. Before I go back I'll—'

'All right, Sara.'

'Promise? You have to promise.'

She leveled her eyes at him, giving him the same searching look she had at the hospital. David looked away. He knew the smart thing to do would be to tell her about Decker. Cash in those frequent flyer points and send her on her way. Then, that minute.

Like she said. Without delay. Whatever was frightening her was real and it was bad, he could see that on her face. All he had to do was put her in the car and take her to the airport. And then she'd be safe.

And gone.

The thought wrenched his guts with an unexpected severity. Yet another emotional ambush against his thinning defences. He met her expectant gaze and he suddenly knew he wasn't going to let her go. Not until he'd arrived at some sort of truth. About who she was, yes, but also about what he was feeling for her. This need to be near her, this desire he felt to make love to her again, this fear of letting her go. If it was the real thing or just some fleeting emotional eruption.

'David?'

Besides, Decker was gone. He didn't suspect anything. To tell her now would just cause needless panic. He'd had enough of that yesterday.

'Promise,' he said.

'Good.'

She sighed in relief. He stood up and walked to the window.

'David?'

'No, I was just . . . ' He made a show of looking at his watch. 'My boss is going to kill me.'

'All right. But come back tonight, then. After work. I can't stand all this being alone.'

He was scheduled to man the phones again that evening.

'OK,' he said.

'Maybe we could go out or something. I'd like to do something nice with you before I go. Something besides all this waiting and pain.'

'Yeah, that'd be good. I'll think of a place. Are you sure you'll be all right, now?'

She gave a thin smile and nodded to the box.

'I'll work on my puzzle.'

Me too, David thought.

There was a call from Cathy when he got back to the office.

'You wanna go see June's crib or what?' she asked.

He walked quickly over to the *Record*. She was in her car outside the main entrance, talking on a cellular phone. She gestured him in just as the conversation was ending.

'Look, sorry, David, but now it looks like you're going to have to take a rain check on Ivanhoe till tomorrow morning,' she said, punching down the antenna. 'I just found out I gotta bolt out to Peru.'

'What's up?'

'Little kid's missing. There's been a rash of them recently. I'm working on this theory that they're related. A ring of some sort.'

'Can I come?' David asked, wanting to pick Cathy's brain about June.

She looked at him for a second, then shrugged.

'Just keep your head down.'

Peru was a small town a few miles east of Burleigh. The police had set up a command center at the Free Will Baptist church. A preacher in his collar explained that the girl had last been seen playing in the church's playground at lunchtime. Her name was Rae, she was seven. Somebody thought they spotted her being led into the woods by a man in a dirty brown suit.

They formed the search line. Forty civilians and a few deputies, all armed with beating sticks. There were dogs as well, baying and pacing, blue tick hounds with their lugubrious eyes and slobber. Someone let them sniff a pair of Smurf sneakers. Xeroxed photos of little Rae were distributed. Cathy looked at one, then met David's eyes. He shook his head grimly.

'Tell me about it,' she whispered.

The searchers set off, Cathy and David trailing a few yards behind the line. Boots crunched loudly in the undergrowth. Flushed crows darted ahead, sounding to David like they were calling the girl's name. No one was saying anything except the preacher, who prayed quietly. Whipped branches danced before them.

'I finally got to read June's note, by the way,' Cathy said. 'The whole thing was pretty straightforward. He made some reckless investments and then panicked when they went belly-up. He'd counted on forty mill and when that shrank he was left up shit creek without a you know what. The tax guys had him dead to rights on a half-dozen conspiracy to defraud charges. Unless he got a change of venue he'd have been judged by a jury of his peers in his old stomping ground. And you know what the good people of Burleigh thought about Will June.'

'What happened to the money?'

'He was going to get a cut of the junk bond sales, you see. But all that do-ray-me went south with the recession. Looks like he would have barely cleared six mill from the deal once the dust settled. Which is serious jack to thee and me but he was deep in debt by then, having spent his savings and borrowed against the big figure. And not just from Chase Manhattan.'

'What do you mean?'

'My source at the IRS thinks there was some wiseguy interest in June of late.'

'So what was he spending it on?'

'Any and everything. You'll see when you get up there. Word is he was looking at a five year bid even with a change of venue. As well as enforced bankruptcy, and no cushy little Chapter Nine deal. I guess when you're his age, five years in the can looks not a lot unlike death. Especially when you're going to be released to a two-bedroom apartment near the railroad tracks with none of the amenities.'

The line stopped. Someone had found some clothes. But they were too old, the wrong size. The beaters moved on. David thought it was safe to ask his question now.

'And he was up there by himself?'

'At the end, yeah. He used to have a bodyguard, a faithful secretary, this nurse. But he got rid of them, one by one. There were lawyers too but you know those assholes, they're gone on the same wind as the fees. It was just him for about the past month.'

They reached a swollen creek. A heated debate broke out among the authorities as to whether to press on or start dragging its bottom.

'This is turning into a cluster fuck,' Cathy said, flipping her pad closed. 'Let's bolt.'

'Really?' David was surprised. There was still plenty of daylight left.

'They aren't going to find this kid. Not here. Not now.'

'You seem pretty sure.'

'They haven't found the other three yet, and they've been gone for many weeks.'

'Yikes.'

She held up the xeroxed photo.

'Think about it, David – if you had this and it's what you wanted more than anything, it's all you wanted in the world, wouldn't you hang on to it for more than just an afternoon?'

'Yes, I see what you mean,' David said. 'I see what you mean.'

9

There was no answer when he knocked. For a brief moment he experienced an echo of the previous morning's fear. He quickly let himself in and looked around. Light flickered beneath the bathroom door.

'Sara?'

'Be out in a minute.'

He sat on the sofa, still finding it hard to believe that he was here, that he was actually doing this. Taking her out to dinner. But what else could he do? She'd asked, and he didn't want a repeat of yesterday. So he'd called Mary Beth at the station after getting back from the search line, explaining that he had to work late. She'd accepted this without comment, lamenting that they could probably get by with two volunteers. David had wanted to cheer her up but there was another call for her before he could think what to say. After that he drove straight over to Locust Lane. Tonight he'd spend some time with Sara. And then, first thing tomorrow, he'd get up to June's place, see if he could discover who she was and what she was fleeing. And maybe after that he'd know what to do.

As he waited, he looked around the increasingly familiar room. She'd arranged things a bit – folded clothes, strategically located candles, placed the boom box on the mantle. He noticed something on the floor by the front window. At first he thought it was the newspaper but then he realized it was the pure white puzzle. She'd finished it. He stood and walked over to it. Christ, how did she do that in just a couple hours? There must have been two hundred pieces. David picked up the lid. Days of fun. Highest degree of difficulty.

'Well?'

He turned. She stood in the doorway, smiling uncertainly. She wore the cocktail dress they'd bought on Saturday – it couldn't have fit her better if it had been custom made. Her long hair fell over her pale shoulders. Time and the painkillers had swept the shadows and exhaustion from her face; her eyes were almost crystalline. She no longer wore the improvised sling, able now to carry the cast's weight.

'Look at you,' David said after a moment.

'This old thing?' she asked in a mock southern drawl.

They stared at each other, then David looked away, his gaze falling on the puzzle.

'You did this,' he said, pointing at it.

She shrugged.

'I'm familiar with the scene,' she said. 'Let's go.'

The White Hart Grill had once been the most fashionable restaurant in town, frequented for the better part of the century by Burleigh's elite. Black and white photos from those days lined the dimly lit lobby, group shots of well-dressed people, smiling broadly, stuffed with food and wealth. But nowadays it was a different story. The high ceiling was pocked by boils of herniated plaster, the simulated marble columns had turned the color of bad teeth and the picture window with the unrivaled view of downtown was webbed with small cracks. The salad bar's refrigeration system rattled like a pickup with a loose muffler; the cut glass chandelier had so many dud bulbs that it seemed to swallow light rather than emit it. Redwine had recently bought the place for a song, the idea being to refurbish it into a big screen sports bar. He kept it running for the time being for obscure tax reasons, staffed only by a skeletal crew of old-timers in their stiff red livery. David knew that if he came on a Tuesday night it would probably be empty. Which was precisely why he chose it for their dinner. Even if someone showed up, it was unlikely they'd know him. The Grill wasn't the sort of place his friends went. It was too shabby for a normal night out, too stuffy for slumming.

His heart sank when he pulled into the parking lot – it was nearly full. But, to his confusion, there was practically no one in the dining room when he went to check. Only a few old couples. He asked the teetering hostess what was going on but she just looked at him like he was speaking a foreign language. So he went back to the car and collected Sara. They were given a table beneath the big window.

'It's good to be out of that house,' she said as they settled in.

'I bet.'

'I can't wait to get out permanently.'

David said nothing as laminated menus were dispensed, as the bus boy sloshed ice water into their glasses. A cocktail waitress appeared. She was younger than the rest of the staff, not yet forty. She had a weary, defeated look on her face.

'Can I get you something to drink?' she asked, looking out the window.

'Vodka rocks,' Sara said.

'Ditto.'

Sara watched her retreat.

'What?' David asked, noticing a sudden intensity in her expression.

'My mom used to wait tables,' she said. 'When I was a kid. I'd sit in a booth with my crayons and milk shake, watching her move around, this smile plastered on her face.'

'Where was that?'

Music sounded suddenly behind swing doors on the other side of the room. There was a sign above them – Function Room.

'Delaware,' Sara said. 'That's where we ended up after our travels. Mom wanted to be a painter but it didn't happen. So she ended up working, you know, jobs.'

'What about your dad?'

'Never knew him. I thought his name was That Son of a Bitch until I was ten.'

The woman returned with their drinks. After she left the waiter appeared, an ancient man with a gnarled purple nose and watery eyes.

'Are y'all prepared to order?'

'Give us five,' David said.

The man stiffened, nodded once, disappeared.

'I think you hurt his feelings,' Sara said. 'So where were we?'

'Your mom wanted to be a painter.'

Sara rolled her eyes.

'I used to have some of her stuff but it got lost in one of my many moves. I thought it was like Leonardo, but I guess I would, right? Yeah, so that was us. Mom and me, I don't know, we were really close. That creepy kind of closeness. There was always some guy

164

around but it was like us against him. She tried to get her stuff shown, but everybody said it was too conventional. Too square. I didn't know it at the time but it really broke her up. I think she really wanted to be the next Georgia O'Keeffe or something. She finally quit and we settled down in Delaware, where she was from. We had this house with a yard and some cats and Mom got a housemate. Not some slob but a friend. Annie. Good old Annie. I went to school, I came home, I had friends. Mom was finally able to give up waiting when she got into the Eastern Stewardess Program. It was all right, you know? I mean compared with what someone like you grew up with it probably looked pretty slim, but, yeah, we were all right.'

Sara peered into the multicolored swirls of her vodka.

'But then she got sick. The big C. It just came out of nowhere. They cut off her left tit and then they cut off her right one. She used to sing this song. What did Delaware, boys? She wore a prosthetic bra, boys, that's what Delawore.' She managed a sad smile. 'Mom had this sense of humor, you see. She got better for a while but forget about being a stewardess. We had some insurance bucks, though, it was cool. Only then she got sick again. It was in her bones, the marrow. Marrow. One of those scary words they hit you with when you're a kid. Chemo. They sound like the bad guys in a cartoon. Chemo and Marrow versus Wonder Woman. I used to visit her after school. Spook city. People sitting around, waiting to die. And then the pain really came. And that meant morphine and . . .'

The song behind the Function Room door ended. There was applause, laughter.

'I see what you mean about hating hospitals,' David said eventually.

'Yeah. Finally they moved her into the dread auxiliary wing. But we could at least do stuff together. Painting, mostly. She started again. I mean, what did she have to lose? We did landscapes at first but, well, there's only so many times you can draw a lawn and parking lot. Then we'd paint each other but that got boring. So in the end we painted the other patients. The doomed, Mom called them. Man, they loved to have their portraits done. "Sara, paint me." "No, me, Sara, paint me." They'd sit there for hours and hours. They weren't going anywhere except the meat locker. We'd

165

never say that much. Just paint away. I could never really get the hang of it, never seem to conjure the person with lines. And then, well, one day we were just sitting around, watching soaps. Mom fell asleep and so I picked up a pencil and just sort of drew her. She looked so pretty, the way the light fell over her face. So peaceful. And guess what, it came out perfect. I was really excited, it was the first time I got it right. I wanted so bad to show her. So I shook her gently. Only she didn't wake up . . . '

Her voice caught.

'Sara . . . '

'No, it's just these pills. They make me maudlin every once in a while. It's just a side effect. It'll pass.'

She took a big sip.

'And so I just got up and ran out looking for a doctor or something. I finally found the guy who'd been treating her. Dr Singh. He wore one of those.' She idly twirled her hand above her head. '"What is it, he said? What is it?" I couldn't even talk but then I realized I'd carried the painting with me so I just gave it to him. And he took one look at it and, bingo, he knew. Knew she was dead. I really had got it right.'

'Sara . . . '

'After that Annie tried looking after me, but then the government found out and it was foster city. Most of them weren't too bad but a few, well, there are some stories I could tell.' She took a sip. 'Mr and Mrs Biggs and the punishment room. That's a good one. One little window, covered by a picture of Jesus. Little claws scraping inside the cinderblocks. You've been a bad girl. You've been . . . '

She stopped talking. David reached out for her.

'No, no,' she said. 'Don't worry. I'll be all right. Or whatever it is that passes for all right these days.'

The swing doors burst open. A woman in a peach-colored dress took a few drunken steps into the dining room, noticed where she was, said 'oh', retreated.

'What do you think that is in there?'

'I don't know,' David said. 'Wedding.'

'Let's go see,' Sara said, animated now.

'What about dinner?'

'I'm not so hungry all of a sudden. Come on, what do you say?'

She was walking across the room before he could answer. He threw some money on the table and followed her. The waiter watched them with eyes long immune to disappointment.

'I haven't been to a party in ages,' she said as she pushed open the swing doors.

The room was smaller than the main dining hall, more modern and featureless. The reception had been in progress for a while now. There was a disorganized knot of bodies on the small dance floor, moving in weary syncopation to the three-piece band. The Tony Troy Experience. The tables were strewn with toppled name cards and glasses. Some were abandoned, others overcrowded with clusters of laughing guests. Kids were sneaking drinks; a woman removed her laddered tights, laughing self-consciously, though no one else noticed. The big cake had already been cut – it reminded David of a construction site. An usher whose clip-on tie hung free from his collar stared darkly at a bridesmaid as she danced with someone else. Slightly above it all was a long elevated table where the bride and groom sat, stiff and formal, surrounded by shredded presents. Whorls of uninhaled cigar smoke moved above them as slowly as the cosmos. A photographer moved in suddenly and strobed them with his flash.

'Let's sit here,' Sara said, finding an empty table.

David snatched two glasses of champagne from a tray and they sat. Sara eyed the long table, sipping pensively, trying to figure something out.

'What?' David asked.

'What's wrong with that picture?' she asked eventually, nodding toward the dais.

David looked. At first he couldn't see anything. Just a couple of kids getting their picture taken. Ugly man, pretty girl. They were holding hands, a complicated lump of flesh on the white tablecloth. The bride appeared to be scared stiff – she held her head perfectly still, speaking out of the corner of her mouth. Then David saw it. She wasn't blinking her eyes when the flash went off.

'Jesus,' he said. 'She's blind.'

He looked at the crowd, noticing two clutches of blind people now, their heads frozen at oblique angles as they spoke into air. Then he looked back at the couple. The groom, beetle-browed, fat-lipped, was staring greedily at the bride. Another photo was taken.

'Creepy.'

'I don't know,' Sara answered. 'It's sort of nice.'

Another tray passed. David fetched two more glasses. Sara drank hers down in one gulp.

'Wow,' she said, pinching her nostrils. 'That's pretty bad champagne.'

'I could order . . . '

'No, it'll do.'

'Excuse me, lady?'

It was a boy. Eight, maybe nine, with freckles, sporadic teeth and a pencil neck dwarfed by his stiff collar.

'Hello,' Sara said.

'Can I sign you?'

'Can you . . . ? Oh yeah. Sure.'

He'd brought a felt pen with him. Sara placed her left arm flat on the table and the boy began to scribble, a bud of tongue emerging from his lips. Scott Todd. That was all, just his signature. When he was done he made to cap the pen but David took it from him, writing something on her cast as well. Sara read it and looked at him. Their eyes held.

'Can I have my pen back?' the kid asked finally.

David handed it over and the boy disappeared. Tony Troy finished a song, announced another. Sara's eyes grew playful.

'So?' she asked.

'What?'

'You gonna ask me to dance or am I going to have to ask Scott?'

David led her to the dance floor. People nodded and smiled as they passed. No one seemed to realize that they weren't invited.

'I think I better warn you . . . ' he said when they reached the square of scuffed wood.

'Forget about it,' she said. 'You're absolved. Anybody our age who can dance has something seriously wrong with their upbringing.'

The band launched into a slow song.

'Besides, I was sort of angling for just being held,' Sara said.

David gathered her in, his body immediately remembering hers from the crash, from Saturday night. They moved slowly, oblivious to the corny music, jostled occasionally by others. A simple sway, half-turns, that was all. David ran his hand over her thin back, her hips. The champagne moved through him and then he buried his face in the warmth of her long neck. He let his lips touch her skin and then he knew all his resolve of the past few days was gone. Her right hand gripped his shoulder, her left was a dull pressure against his spine. An amp screeched somewhere.

'This is nice,' Sara said.

'You move pretty good for a white girl.'

'It's called staggering, bub. That champagne did not pass go, did not collect two hundred dollars.'

He pulled her closer, losing himself in her long hair. It smelled vaguely of kerosene from the heater. He stroked it, carefully rolling strands between his fingers.

'If I could only stay like this . . . ' she said softly.

They danced until the music stopped and people applauded. David pulled back and looked at her. And then, because there was nothing else he could do, he kissed her, feeling the currents of cold drink on her lips and her tongue, the collapse of her breasts against his chest. Her good hand clutched at the back of his neck now, her cast pressed harder against his spine, almost painfully. They kissed until another song started.

'Do you want another dance or a . . . '

'Let's go back,' she said.

He drove home slowly, doing everything he was supposed to, not wanting to get pulled. Not now, not with her in the car. Not with where they were headed. They passed down the empty, over-lit streets of downtown, moving quietly among the few tall buildings and the shuttered shops. A patrol of hooded kids ran in front of their car at one intersection, hunters loping across a sierra. They were laughing and spinning. Beyond them a billboard had begun to burn, shedding multicolored leaves of ignited glue and paper on to the pavement.

'Such a strange town,' she said.

When they got to the house he lit the heater and some candles, found music on the radio. She watched him from the sofa. He sat beside her and they kissed for a long time. The cocktail dress slipped off as easily as he'd been imagining since he saw her in it earlier that evening. And then they were making love. It was different from Saturday. Despite the drink and the pills she was wide awake, responding to his touches, clutching him with her one good hand. For a few brief seconds he sensed there was a desperation there as well, a thirst for forgetting behind her passion. He found himself wishing he could sweep whatever it was away, if only for now. But all that soon passed and then they were just moving together.

'So here we are,' she said when they were finally lying still on the sofa.

He didn't answer, didn't open his eyes. He was trying not to think, knowing that once he did the moment might fall apart.

'Would it be too much to ask you to stay the night?' she asked. 'It gets pretty lonely around here.'

'That might not be such a good idea.'

'Why not?'

He said nothing.

'Look, David, there's no reason to . . . I mean, I know you're married.'

He looked at her. She smiled.

'It's not exactly a tough one to figure out.'

'No, I suppose it isn't,' he said, looking away.

'So are you going to tell me about her?'

'We've been married for over ten years now.'

'That's a long time to be anything.'

'Yes, it is.'

'What's her name?'

'We don't have to have this discussion, you know.'

'Priscilla? Daphne? Yeah, I think I'll call her Daphne.'

'Mary Beth.'

'So do you do this often?' she asked with playful malice.

'Do what?'

She tilted her head and squinted at him.

'No,' he said. 'Never, to be exact.'

'As in not even a quickie at the office Christmas party which you've regretted ever since?'

He shook his head.

170

'I'm flattered.'

'What's strange,' he said softly, almost as if he were talking to himself, 'and I know this is going to sound rotten, but what's strange is that this, that being here with you like this, it's like it has nothing to do with her. With us, Mary Beth and me. I don't know. It seems like nothing has anything to do with us these days. Except habit.'

'So you don't love her any more?'

'I don't know what I feel for her. Maybe it's love, maybe it isn't. We've been so close so long it's like . . . how can you know it's real if there's nothing to compare it to?'

'You used to, though? Love her?'

David nodded, then took a deep breath.

'It's just, you never expect things to get complicated, and when they do I guess sometimes you lose something. Or maybe you know it was never there in the first place. Shit, I don't know. It's not anything big that makes you finally realize all this, either. It's like, about a year ago I was telling her something that happened to me as a boy and her eyes sort of glazed over. I think maybe she checked her watch. Suddenly I remembered I'd told her this story before. More than once. And I got to thinking about it, going through my little inventory of memorable events, and realized I'd told them all to her. And vice-versa. We didn't have any more stories to tell each other. Except the stuff that happened to us together. And those aren't stories you tell each other. I was beginning to think maybe that's just the way things were meant to be.'

'So what do you think now?'

'I'm trying not to do too much thinking just now.'

'Smart boy.'

She repositioned her head on his chest.

'And so, what, is this Mary Beth individual why you're working at this job you hate?'

'No. I'm why.'

She waited for him to go on.

'It's funny,' he said. 'No way did I want to end up living like my parents did. My father, well, he had this corporate gig and it just wore him down. Year in and year out. I think he hated it but didn't know what to do about that. So I decided I was going to do something different. Avoid the whole mess. That's why the Social Fund was such a good thing.' He shook his head. 'And now here I am. Working for the man.'

'Well, surely you can get another foundation gig. I mean, how hard is it?'

'I'm jaded, remember?'

'Oh yeah.'

'The way June, the way one man could just sweep everything away. Makes you think that maybe the world is geared to that, and that everything else is just bullshit.' He laughed quietly. 'I'm beginning to suspect I've succumbed to the white boy's disease. Irony.'

'So where are your folks now?'

'Tucson. Dad doesn't do much, they gave him his watch two years ago. He just shouts at the tube and plays a lot of golf. Sends me Perot pamphlets with post-it notes attached saying things like "makes you think, huh?" Around four-thirty he starts prowling the carpets, waiting for happy hour. He has this grandfather clock even though he isn't one. When it chimes six he makes a beeline for the wet bar. He's collected so much static from the carpet by then that he always manages to shock himself on the ice thongs. This big blue spark you can see across the room. It seems to surprise him every time. By nine he's snoring.'

'And your mom?'

'She's a cheerleader.'

'As in . . .'

'That's right. Sixty-one years old. She didn't make the squad when she was in high school so now she's joined this team. The Senior Stompers. I don't think they have cuts, other than the ultimate one. They appear in parades, high school games. They performed at a Suns game once.'

'Jesus, what's that like?'

'Not pretty.'

They laughed.

'I laugh, but sometimes I wake up in the middle of the night and think that the only thing separating me from all that is thirty years of habit and toil.'

They lay in silence for a long time.

'David, listen . . .'

An urgency had crept into her voice.

'What is it?'

'Look, I want to make sure of something here.'

'Go on.'

She raised herself so she could look down at him, a strand of hair falling over her face.

'I can't help you, you know. Not like you've helped me. I don't have anything for you other than, you know, just what's here and now. Not anything real. I wish I did but I don't. Maybe if we'd met way back when . . . the thing is, I still have to go. You know that, don't you? This is unexpected and sorta wonderful but let's not kid ourselves.'

'Kid ourselves,' he said quietly.

'Look, I just want to make sure you don't think I'm something I'm not, that this is anything that's going to last much longer than one of these authentic make-believe candles you got yesterday. David?'

He sat up abruptly, rubbing his naked shoulders.

'Why are you so sure it has to be like that?'

'Because it does. Trust me. If you knew what was going on . . . '

'Sara, come on, this is nuts. What is it?'

She sighed.

'I really don't want to talk about all that, all right?'

'But . . . '

'David, really. Look, you have a life, I have a life. Let's just put both of those on hold for a few days. It's the only way this thing is going to work. That's not impossible, is it?'

'A few days isn't much.'

'It's a lot more than nothing. My experience has been that once you start talking about the future you have to start dealing with the past. And you definitely don't want to do that. Not where I'm concerned.'

'Don't sell me short, Sara.'

She sighed sadly.

'I'm not. It's just the opposite, in fact. I'm afraid of what will happen if you start to get involved.'

'Christ, how bad can it be?'

'David, you don't want to know. And you wouldn't even believe it if you did.' She looked away. 'Besides, if you knew then maybe you might not be so eager to help me.'

They lay in silence.

'After a while,' she said, her voice slow and steady, like a child reciting something hard learned, 'you learn to pick your spots. Play it as it lays until it's time to move on. That's the only way to keep going.'

'That's not how I see it.'

'Ah, but at the end of the evening you still have a life to go back to.'

He dropped back down to her side in frustration.

'I don't understand any of this, Sara.'

She nestled close to him.

'You don't have to understand. All you have to do is keep on doing what you're doing. Getting me better. Helping me out.' She shook him gently. 'And get hold of that damned brother of yours.'

10

The water's muddy surface wasn't reflecting anything but his thoughts. Though the flood had receded slightly, it still covered everything except the coop's undulant roof and the bent tree. Standing on the road's soft shoulder, her fading skidmarks at his feet, David couldn't get Decker's words out of his mind: *Did she place anything into your possession?* And there was Sara's eagerness to get back up here as well, the way she'd defied all of pain's logic by making her way to the shack. There was something more out there than a little cash and some plastic. He was sure of it. But the water was still too deep, still opaque with roiled mud. He'd have to swim to check the coop, dive down once he got there. Feel his way blindly. Besides, whatever was there would surely be long gone by now, ruined, carried away by invisible currents. As if to punctuate the impossibility of a search, a dark question mark of water moccasin slithered by, disappearing into a fissure in the tree.

He got back in his car and headed on. According to Cathy's directions, June's house was less than ten miles from the crash site. David drove hard, desperate now to see if she'd been there, see what she was trying to flee. If he just knew that, then maybe he could think of a way to keep her around, to have more nights like last night. He couldn't stop thinking about the taste of her flesh, its slight bitterness, the way it would cling to his lips for an instant when he pulled them away. Or how her upper lip would quiver with pleasure as he rose above her, as he moved into her. The cool pressure of her cast across his shoulder blades. Though it had been nine hours since he'd left her it was as if they were still lying together. There had to be some way to keep from losing all that.

The road soon began to climb a steep mountain. The Mustang pinged and coughed in complaint. David passed several trucks, their motors whining, bright blue smoke streaming from their chimneys. He had to downshift twice, floor the gas pedal just to keep moving. As he fought the hill he suddenly found himself thinking about the ones who got away. It was something that crowded into his mind often recently, this unexpectedly intense nostalgia for the women and girls who had for one reason or another slipped away from him. Such as Janet, the first girl he'd ever lusted after, a proud and dauntingly beautiful black girl who'd been bussed out to his junior high from Newark. He was thirteen at the time, a raging vortex of hormonal confusion. And she was a goddess – plaited hair and large, humid lips; astonishing breasts and a laugh which rang through the school's hallways like the morning bell. David had never spoken to her, the school's strong racial divide reinforcing his natural timidity. But he watched her every day, dreamed about her nightly for two months running. He'd learned her schedule, placing himself outside classrooms waiting for her to emerge. He'd sit near her in the cafeteria and find a window seat during algebra so he could watch her take gym. And then, near the end of their first semester together, she'd materialized in the seat next to him during an assembly. A few days after a near-riot the entire school had been summoned to watch *To Kill a Mockingbird*. He sat there, terrified, as she stared straight ahead, her chin high, suspended by pride. Waiting for him to speak. Just before the lights went out she looked over at him and David realized she'd been aware all along of the stares he thought were hidden, aware of his attraction to her. A smile full of dare crossed her lips and her eyes dilated for the briefest moment, inviting him to say something, maybe even to place his arm around her. But he didn't, he couldn't. The lights went down and she looked away, her chin rising a little higher. When David finally summoned the nerve to look back she was gone, sitting with her friends, her laughter rising above the soundtrack.

And then, during his senior year in high school, there was Carrie. Tall and thin, with long blonde hair and big dark eyes that always seemed latticed with Panama Red. Her perpetually black clothes were in stark contrast with the jeans and lumberjack shirts everyone else wore. She lived a few doors down from him, her parents feuding themselves into neighborhood lore, her one older brother vanishing into some sect, the Moonies or Children of God. She didn't date guys from their high, choosing instead older car freaks who'd wake up the quiet neighborhood as they sped triumphantly away from her house late at night. David drove her to school sometimes, when her mother was too hung over to get out of bed. She'd tell him about her secret trips to the Village, the burgeoning punk scene there, this professor at the New School who'd let kids crash on his floor. Sometimes he'd wander past her house late at night, hoping to catch a glimpse of her. But he never asked her out, unable to think where he could take her that she hadn't been before. Then, one evening, she knocked on his bedroom window. She explained that Television were playing CBGBs and asked David if he wanted to come, drive her into the city. He had a history test the next day – he needed to ace it to keep his grade average high enough to qualify for the Burleigh Scholarship for which he'd been shortlisted. They were good tickets, she said. His parents would never give permission. Television were hot, she said. The best thing going.

'Come on,' she said. 'Just sneak away.'

But he'd hesitated again and she was gone, leaving him with his books and his parents. Twenty minutes later he heard the unmuffled rattle of a car pulling away from her house.

And then, four years later, there was the hypnotist's daughter. A man called McStay had come to Burleigh to lecture at the medical school on hypnosis in anesthesia. Rowdy had gone along, spoken of his eccentric brilliance. So when David saw posters for a public demonstration at the campus theater he'd bought a ticket. The show was remarkable. McStay was a small, charismatic Scotsman who captivated the audience immediately. David had always been skeptical about hypnosis but when he saw Cathy on stage, utterly convinced her shoes were on fire, he'd been sold. Most striking, though, was the young woman assisting McStay. David couldn't take his eyes off her, the way she'd puff recalcitrant strands of hair from her brow as she carried some prop, how her long legs caused her tight gown to shimmer like a dark river when she moved. He went backstage after the performance but she was already gone. He thought he'd never see her again when, a few days later, he came upon her reading a magazine in the college library. He told her how much he liked the show and she invited him to sit. Her name was Margaret and the hypnotist was her father. She lived in Edinburgh, was going to attend the university there, get the medical degree her father's childhood poverty had denied him. But first she wanted to see something of America.

'Will you show me something of America?' she asked, her bottle green eyes widening.

They spent three days together. He drove her along the Blue Ridge Parkway, took her to Grandfather Mountain. There was a fiddler's convention in Galax where they spent the day, stopping at a redneck bar where the men asked to dance with her, one by one, each returning her to the table with a courtly bow. On their last night together David took her to the university gardens and she told him about Edinburgh, the Regency crescents and the erratic weather and the festival where she worked every year. They kissed for a long time and he asked her to come back to his place and she said yes. He could scarcely believe what was happening. They made love for a long time and then, with a strange matter-of-factness, she announced she had to leave. Her father was due in Florida. They agreed that David would come to Scotland that summer for the festival, stay in her flat, as she called it. They could see what happened. And then she was gone. They exchanged a few letters but when David met Mary Beth the letters stopped and that summer he stayed in Burleigh with the woman he was to marry, his mind far from festivals or cold cities across the ocean.

And then there were the women he'd encountered while working at the Fund, battered or strung-out, their eyes both wary and hopeful as they rehearsed their stories for him. One in particular he couldn't forget. Joy. He met her in a Tennessee halfway house whose funding was up for review. They'd spoken for a long time in the kitchen – she was on washing-up duty. He helped her dry. She'd just spent two years in prison for possession, but now she was through with drugs, ready to make a new start. As she handed David the dripping dishes their hands would sometimes touch. Later that night she knocked on his hotel room door. He never knew how she found out where he was, how she got away after curfew. He reluctantly asked her in. She sat on the edge of the bed and explained that her boyfriend was in trouble, he needed some money to pay a fine or they were going to send him back to prison. And he just couldn't do that, he couldn't make it in there. David asked how much and she said ten thousand dollars. He explained that wasn't what the Fund was for, that the money had to go to institutions, not individuals. She listened patiently.

'I'll fuck you for it,' she said when he was through.

Noticing his shocked look, she explained she'd do it more than once if that's what bothered him, she'd come to wherever he lived, stay there for a week or two, do whatever he wanted. She said she used to trick and knew things, things a man like him might like to find out about. But she needed that money. Ricky couldn't go back in. He'd die in there. He'd crossed some bikers and they were waiting for him. David, stunned into silence, had simply shown her the door. That night he barely slept. The next day, when he went back to the house for the financial review, she was gone, having never returned the night before.

There had been others, of course, one-night stands and longtime lovers. Relationships which had run their course. But those weren't the ones he remembered, those weren't the ones who inhabited his imagination these days. It was the ones who got away, the women he couldn't hold, that endured in his mind and his dreams. Now, as he neared June's place, he knew that he couldn't let Sara become one of them.

Finding it wasn't easy, even with Cathy's detailed directions. About a mile after the mountain crested there was a blind turnoff, leading to a road that eventually forked into two narrow lanes. The way David took was crowded by hedges, barely wide enough for his car. Rainwet branches clawed the roof; unseen potholes tested his suspension. He came to a stop when a dark blue sedan blocked the way. Two men stood talking by a gated driveway. David reckoned that the one dressed in a dark suit had to be his contact. The other, a security guard, was scraping something off his shoe on the split rail fence.

The man in the suit came up to the car.

'Webster?'

David shook the offered hand.

'Ray Steadman. Glad to know you. Listen, there are some agents up there taking inventory. They don't mind you coming up as long as you stay out of the way and don't touch anything.

'Fine.'

'Park here. You can ride with me.'

Though paved, the quarter-mile driveway was even narrower

than the one-lane road David had just travelled. Eight-inch speed bumps kept them at a crawl. Steadman pointed out a security camera hidden in the trees.

'Boy, he was really out of it up here,' David said.

'That he was. The outer edges of the property are hedged by an interlocking system of poisonous plants. Sumac, ivy, oak. Some stuff I never even heard of. Tell you what, it's better than any man-made fence I've ever encountered. Two of our boys needed medical attention after getting caught up in it. Some guys from the army are taking a look at it later today.'

He shook his head.

'Yeah, old June was hunkered down.'

'Why?'

'You'll see.'

They turned the final bend. The house was much smaller than David had anticipated. One storey, wooden, almost invisible amid the sheltering pines. A window near the front door had been broken and a section of gutter hung loose. Otherwise, the façade gave nothing away. It seemed perfectly normal. They parked behind three government cars clustered near the front door.

'So what is it exactly you have to see?' Steadman asked.

'Well, if you could just take me through the house, that would do it,' David said, following Cathy's instructions. 'I need to get some background for the story. Fill in the gaps.'

'Can do.'

A man with a clipboard answered the door, nodding glumly to Steadman, ignoring David. They stepped into a front hall crowded with a dozen statues, classical figures as well as emaciated modern works. They were haphazardly arranged, like people at a crowded cocktail party. A large *trompe-l'œil* depicting a mountain vista covered an entire side wall.

'Nice.'

'Just wait,' Steadman said.

They headed down a short hallway which ended in a room filled with leather-bound books. It seemed to David more like a store-room than a library, with thousands of volumes crammed into every available slot, overspilling on to tables and even the floor. The sweaty smell of aged paper hung in the air. Two men knelt near a hazardous-looking stack, one reading spines, the other writing in a ledger.

'Jefferson, Thomas.'

'Didn't he play for the Steelers?' the other guy said.

'Just write it down.'

David and Steadman passed into the next room, this one cluttered with ancient statuary, most of it erotic. Horny little gods; group sex friezes; gravity-defying couplings. There seemed to be no logic to the way the pieces were arranged, no attempt to sort or display them. It was all just stuffed in. Steadman stopped before a strutting bronze satyr with a hugely erect penis. Someone had placed a coded tag over the cock's swollen head.

'Guess how much that's worth,' Steadman said.

'What, the sculpture or a dick that size?'

The agent managed a lipless smile.

'A tool like that would be priceless, Mr Webster. The sculpture, on the other hand, should fetch forty large.'

David whistled and they pressed on. The next five rooms were devoted entirely to paintings. There was little furniture, almost nothing that made the house seem lived-in. Again, the emphasis seemed to be on quantity – the pictures were stacked three high in most places, none of them properly lit or adequately spaced. Some rested on the floor, leaning against the wall. Hundreds of sketches hung face-to-face in a storage rack. It was almost as if no one was supposed to see any of this. And there didn't seem to be a connecting theme to the work, no single era or style. There were portraits, landscapes, religious scenes. Many nudes, more porno-graphy. There were no identity plaques anywhere, though David thought he recognized the style of some of them from his Art 101 class. He puzzled out a few of the signatures, recognizing Hopper, Eakins, what he thought to be Whistler. In several places pictures had been recently removed – the dusted shadow of the absent frame still clung to the wall.

'All this stuff.'

'And just him to see it,' Steadman answered. 'It's the early innings yet but we figure there's about fifteen million worth of art in all. Minimum. Plus the property.'

'Holy shit,' David said.

Steadman pointed the way.

'And here's the bedroom. Where we found the corpse.'

There was a different clutter here than in the rest of the house. David could finally see evidence of human habitation, of Wilton June's decline and his death. Drawers had erupted their contents on to a carpet whose natural white had been darkened by a patina of fuzzy green mildew. Nearly every available surface was covered with crusted highball glasses, food wrappers, tipped liquor bottles. Letters and summonses and faxes lay crumpled on a roll-top desk. The bed had been stripped, revealing an indeterminate stain on the center of the mattress.

'That smell,' David remarked.

'Uh-huh.'

Despite the room's mess, there was only one work of art in it. A solitary painting which hung above the bed, toplit by a brass lamp. It was big, three feet high, perhaps four long. David walked up to get a better look at it, careful not to touch the mattress. It was crudely done, dense with two dimensional objects and flat figures. The setting looked like it could have been somewhere in the Blue Ridge Mountains, a half-dozen steeply overlapping peaks that surrounded a hardscrabble farmyard in the heart of a valley. Everything was centered on a shed where a mother nursed a baby among the grain-stuffed bags and poorly drawn animals. Three bearded men had gathered around them, chomping on straws, holding out jugs and whittled dolls. Outside, throngs of country people were making their way down perilous mountain paths, heading toward the mother and child. There were farmers leading donkeys overladen with baskets of food, soldiers gripping flared muskets, blacks with skin the color of aubergines. There was even a squad of plumed and painted Indians. All of them trudging resolutely toward the farmyard. The longer David looked the more he could see: the fiddler and dancers whirling behind a haystack, the midget angels floating among the crows in the mountain pass.

Steadman joined him.

'Jesus?' David asked, pointing at the newborn.

'That it is.'

'Who painted it?'

'Couldn't tell you. Some old-timer.'

'He wasn't very good, was he?'

'I don't know,' Steadman said. 'It sort of grows on you.'

David stared at it a moment longer, beginning to see what he meant.

'I never knew Christ came to America.'

'Yeah, well, the game ain't over yet, my friend.'

They looked at the painting a while longer. David noticed something in the bottom right corner, a solitary figure, a drunk with his back turned obliviously to the whole scene, liquor from a backhanded jug pouring over his slack jaw.

'Look at this guy,' he said, pointing.

'Yeah, there's always one joker who doesn't get the message. Come on. There's something else you got to see.'

They went into the next room, which wasn't much bigger than a walk-in closet. Near a heavily draped window there was a large stone cistern. It was free of design apart from the cracks time had made.

'Guess what this is.'

'Some sort of prehistoric trough?'

'Negative. It's an altar. They used to do human sacrifices in it.'

'Who did?'

'Mayans or Aztecs. One of those guys.'

'Who would want to own that?' David asked.

'Who'd want to inject a truckload of insulin into his veins?'

Steadman looked David over.

'Hey, how come you aren't writing any of this down?'

'I'll remember.'

They left the room.

'And he lived up here all by himself?' David asked.

'His wife died of cancer, what, eight years ago. They had a son but he died too, a few years before that.'

'How?'

'Dope, I think.'

'So it was just him?'

'Far as I could tell. He got rid of the help a couple months ago. Even his nurse.'

'No maid or gardener?'

'I think some people came in. Casual, you know.'

They entered the kitchen. There was a big oak table, a blue tile floor. Cast iron pots hung from the ceiling like cave bats. A vague smell of rot hung in the air.

'Did you read the note?' David asked.

'Yeah, I read it. The usual bull biscuits about being hounded and persecuted and not being able to go on any more. Guilty people are real good on the subject of how unfair life is.'

'No great love of his life or anything like that?' David asked in a joking tone.

'Nah, not this character. His wife maybe, though he didn't say as much.' Steadman formed another lipless smile. 'Will June wasn't what you'd call a people person. Tell you what, though. Near the end, things got pretty grim up here.'

'How so?'

'I came up here about, what, several weeks ago, back when it was still just a full-court press audit. You wouldn't believe the state of things.'

'Where was he?'

'In bed, watching cartoons. Tom and Jerry. Drunk as a skunk. Wouldn't even talk to his own lawyer.'

'All that money.'

'Yeah.' Steadman gave his head a rueful shake. 'I was that way until I got saved.'

'What way?'

'Had my own practice up in Alexandria, representing rich folk, looking for loopholes. Pulled down six serious figures, too.'

'So what happened?'

'Jesus came to me when I was stuck in a traffic jam on the Fourteenth Street Bridge and told me to knock it off.'

'Word is he's like that,' David said.

Steadman looked at him.

'You been saved?'

'Not that I've noticed.'

'Then we're gonna have to work on you, my friend.'

'Good luck,' David said.

'We don't call it luck, amigo. We call it grace.'

'This I've heard.'

The taxman shook his head.

184

'Yeah, you think if you can just get something that's all yours and hold on to it, then everything will be all right.'

'What's that saying?' David asked. '"He who dies with the most toys wins."'

Steadman placed an avuncular hand on David's elbow.

'Tell you something, Mr Webster. And you can take this to whatever bank you frequent. *We're* the ones who end up with the toys. We get the toys and the Lord gets the rest. Every darn time.'

With that, they stepped out on to the back patio and all of a sudden David realized why Will June had built his house here. Before him was a panoramic view of a long stretch of the Mud River, snaking its way through a valley five hundred feet below. The same river David had been detoured by the day he'd met her, the river that had flooded the crash site. If Redwine saw this he'd shit his pants, David thought. It made his vaunted Elk Run vista look like a peep hole into a ghetto garden. He stood there, staring. Birds hovered in the middle distance, riding thermals, waiting for something to kill.

'His own personal postcard.'

Steadman shook his head.

'Vanity, vanity, and more vanity.'

'What's that town there?' David asked, pointing to the brief human interruption in the mat of green.

'Ivanhoe.'

'Wasn't he born there?'

Steadman shrugged. They walked toward the edge of the property, passing a swimming pool, knee-deep with fetid, mossy water. Halfway down there was some motion in the trees. They stopped and looked. Two peacocks burst from cover, making guttural noises that sounded like reel-to-reel tapes rewinding. David stood his ground, transfixed, as they grew close. He'd never seen these birds up close. There was something obscene about the male's beauty, something both fake and frightening. The female seemed desperate. It started to peck at David's shoes.

'Hey,' he said, bounding away.

Steadman clapped his hands and the birds backed off.

'They're hungry. Those fellas up at the house won't feed them. They say it's not their responsibility.'

185

'Can't they forage anything for themselves?'

'They're domesticated, you see.'

The birds strutted just out of kicking range.

'Shoot, let me go find something,' Steadman said at last. 'I think I saw some feed in the back hall.'

He strode back to the house. The peacocks watched David forlornly, as if they knew he had nothing for them. He walked off toward the edge of the property, where he could take in the whole length and depth of the valley. Everything about this place was strange, stranger than he'd imagined. But there was no sign of Sara. Not even the smallest clue. He picked up a loose bit of brick and threw it into the unbroken canopy of pine below. It was swallowed without a sound. When he chucked another something caught his eye. A small cabin, nestled against the treeline. He checked to make sure there was no one around. Just the peacocks, watching him resentfully. So he walked down to it. The door was locked. He tested its weight – it was too heavy to force. There was a flower pot with nothing growing in it at his feet. The key was beneath that, surrounded by bloodless insects who began to writhe in the sudden light. Tough luck, guys, David thought. He opened the door and went in.

The cabin was simple. One large room with a kitchen divided off by a Formica counter. The ceiling was exposed beams, the walls scored wood. No art here. There was a big stone fireplace that looked like it had been used recently. The single bed was shoved up against a far wall, its mattress bare. A sturdy table rested next to it, beneath a picture window with a comprehensive view of the valley. David walked over, examining the only things on the table – a large mortar and pestle. They were made of marble, perfectly clean. As he went to put them back he saw that there was something beneath them. A single razor blade, an elongated steel triangle, the kind used in Exacto knives. It too was shining and clean.

David replaced the mortar and pestle and continued to look around, checking under the bed, opening the drawers of a small dresser. Nothing. The garbage can had been emptied and the only thing in the refrigerator was a small carton of spoiled milk, swollen to bursting. He checked the pull date – two weeks ago. He went up to the fireplace and rummaged through the char for a moment.

There was nothing but ashes.

He walked into the bathroom. The medicine chest was empty, the closet held only a stack of towels. David felt a sharp pang of disappointment. There's nothing for me here, he thought. The cops have been over this place; Cathy as well. If there was anything they'd have found it. You could have spent the morning in her arms and instead you've been up here, chasing phantoms.

He detected some movement in the tub as he turned to go. A spider. He watched it scramble across the porcelain and disappear down the drain, squeezing past a wiry strand that crossed the grid. Something clicked in the back of David's mind at the sight of that strand, some rogue synapse firing at will. He squatted down and touched it. Hair. It took a moment to yank it free – it was attached to a whole scummy clump that barely fit through the drain's filter. He rinsed off the tangle in the sink. Dozens of baby spiders fell from it, disappearing quickly in the swirling flood. When the water ran clear he held it up.

It was Sara's. He could tell by the look of it, the feel of it. His heart began to pound, his mouth dried suddenly. Christ, she had been here. He was right all along. A door slammed up at the main house and he remembered where he was. He flushed the wet clump down the toilet and went quickly back into the main room, where he began a more careful search. He sifted the ashes in the fireplace again, looking for something legible amid the gray and meaningless flakes. Finally, just as he was about to give up, he found a single fragment of paper, no bigger than a quarter. Small handwriting covered it. *the spirit of*. That was all it said. *the spirit of*.

Still on his knees, he looked around the room, noticing something he hadn't seen before, something on the floor a few feet from the big table. A splatter of red stains, several dozen of them. The same rusty color as the ones he'd seen on her shoes. He walked over, squatted, ran his fingers over them. They were dry, soaked into the porous wood.

He stood. Somehow he knew there was nothing else here. So he went outside, walking once around the cabin, finding a mound of ash out back. It was deep – someone had been doing a lot of burning. He began to poke through it with a stick. The ashes and charcoal were wet with all the recent rain, laced with mud and fallen leaves. After a few seconds his stick struck something. He knelt down and picked it out. It was a gnarled fist of celluloid. Melted black and whites, it looked like. Maybe negatives. As big as a billiard ball. He tried to peel a layer away but they'd all been glued together by the heat. When he held them up in the light all he could see were gray shadows.

'Webster?' Steadman called.

David slipped the clump into his pocket and walked quickly back to the front of the cabin. Steadman was having the time of his life feeding the peacocks. Like Christ with his loaves, David thought. As he started walking back up the lawn he passed a corrugated tool shed. A broken padlock hung loose on its door. He quietly opened it and looked inside. Garden equipment, a tool box, the sharp smell of chemical fertilizer. There was something on the tool box, a handwritten label.

> Property of:
> D. D. Jeter
> Onley, N.C.
> DO NOT MESS WITH THIS

David closed the door and walked back up the lawn, Jeter's imprecation sounding through his mind. The peacocks were eating with barely controlled fury.

'I wondered where you'd got to.'

'I had to tap a kidney.'

David took some of the food and helped feed the birds.

'So when you were up here before, last month, there wasn't anyone else living here with him, a girlfriend or something?'

'Not that I noticed.'

'Must have got pretty lonely,' David mused.

'Yeah, well, crime is a lonely profession.'

Steadman smiled and winked. This guy's all right for a born again IRS agent, David thought.

'Anything else you'd like to see?'

David placed a hand in his pocket, fingering the collapsed celluloid, the small slip of paper.

'I guess that should do it,' he said quietly.

*

188

He drove quickly back to Burleigh, convinced now that Sara had been with June for a time that lasted up until a few days before his death. Nothing else about the place made much sense, though. He was tempted to swing east to Onley, visit this gardener, this D. D. Jeter, to see what he knew. It wasn't far out of the way. But he had a noon meeting with Redwine that he couldn't miss. He couldn't risk getting him mad, not with Sara stowed in one of his houses. He made it to the office just in time, barely listening as Redwine droned on about targets and strategies and agendas. When he was finally able to be alone he put the stuff from the cabin on his desk. He examined the knot of celluloid, then looked at the charred slip of paper. *the spirit of*. That could mean anything. Or nothing.

Redwine popped his head in.

'Everything looking good?' he asked.

'Sure is,' David said, slipping the things into his desk drawer.

'When can I see those final proofs?'

'First thing tomorrow.'

'I was sort of hoping to see them today,' Redwine said, stroking his beard.

'First thing in the morning is the best they could do, Donnie. Sorry.'

He nodded and began to go, but poked his head back in.

'By the way, we might be needing that Locust Lane deal back pretty soon.'

'How soon?' David asked, feeling a swell of panic.

'Monday latest.'

David said nothing.

'That a problem?'

He shook his head slowly, though he suspected it might be.

She was reading the Flannery O'Connor stories when he got back, her long legs folded beneath her on the sofa. She smiled up at him as he came in, trust and affection in her eyes, and he was struck by a sudden guilt for what he'd been doing that morning. He immediately began to doubt what had seemed certain a few hours ago. After all, what did he really have? A clump of hair. Some melted photos and a cryptic note. They could have belonged to anyone, meant anything.

189

He sat beside her and they kissed, though he pulled away after a short while.

'What?' she asked, canting her head slightly.

He looked away.

'No, I was just wondering . . . '

'What, David?'

'How's that book?'

'*That's* what you were wondering?'

He nodded once, having realized there was no way he could ask her. Not here, not now. It would mean either calling her out on a lie or making himself look like a prying fool. Either way he'd risk losing her. No, he'd have to learn more before he could confront her.

'It's great,' she said, looking at its spread spine. 'She's one of my heroes. That black humor, there's nothing like it. She was an amazing character – do you know about her?'

'Not really.'

'A very strange cookie. She was crippled by polio. She lived on a peacock farm in Georgia.'

He looked up sharply.

'Peacocks?'

'Yes. You know, big feathers, beaks . . . David, what is it with you?'

'Nothing.'

She accepted this.

'So what did you do all morning?' she asked.

'Just working.'

'On my way out of here?'

David nodded.

'And when is it going to happen?'

He looked away.

'The end of the week,' he said after a short pause.

'Really?'

'I'm sorry it can't be sooner, Sara. It's just . . . '

'No, that's all right. I think I need this, a few days of this. Of last night.' She sighed. 'I mean, it's not like I'm looking forward to going. It's been a long time since I've been broke and alone and last time . . . well, last time I didn't really make it all that well.'

David began to shake his head.

'Look, Sara, I mean, why do you have to go at all? What I was thinking, why don't we find you another place nearby? A place you could stay in for real. I could maybe—'

'David,' she interrupted. 'Come on, we've talked about this. In a perfect world, I'd give it some thought. But not as things are. Not now. You have complications, I have them. Let's just stick to what we've decided. All right?'

'No, you're right,' he said quietly. 'I'm sorry.'

'When do you have to get back?' she asked, consolation in her voice.

'Not for a while.'

'Let's get out of here, then. Go for a walk or something.' She sat up, her eyes suddenly mischievous. 'I know. Let's have a picnic.'

'A picnic?'

'I know just the place.'

David went to Krogers while she dressed. He bought a bottle of wine and a generic cardboard basket with 'Picnic' stenciled across its lid. When he got back they set off. It was the warmest day since they'd met, the first that hadn't been menaced by storm clouds.

'Where to?'

'This way,' she said. 'I saw it when I was walking.'

They ambled to the end of Locust Lane, turning down a road that dead-ended against the Nowheresville fence.

'Ready?' she asked when they reached it.

'For what?'

'I've been dying to see this place ever since you told me about it. I almost went in earlier but I didn't want to get lost.'

'I don't know, Sara.'

'Oh, come on David, what are you afraid of?'

You don't want to know, he thought. But he reluctantly agreed. They walked along the perimeter for a long time, looking for a way in. No Trespassing signs were posted every few yards; vines ensnared the rusting links. Just when David was about to suggest giving up they found a spot where the bottom of the fence had been uprooted. It looked like a big, sneering lip. He lifted it high enough for her to duck under, then followed. Something in him expected

191

alarms to sound as they entered, tires of approaching cruisers to squeal. But there was only silence. They broke through the curtain of shade trees, emerging on a long, gently curving road.

'Wow,' Sara said.

It looked like a scene from post-war Europe. Utter desolation. All that's missing, David thought, are the headscarved women and hollow-eyed vets. Though this had once been a thriving community, from where they stood they could now see only one house that was still standing, and it was little more than a charred hulk of beams and brick. The others had either burned to the ground or been pulled out like bad teeth, leaving deep slots in the clay. There were a few rusted cars, listing and corroded satellite dishes. Meadows of crabgrass had overgrown the lawns.

'Still want to do this?' he asked.

'You kidding?'

'This way, then.'

He led her along what was once a sidewalk, its concrete fractured by roots. They passed a yellowed sign affixed to the creosote-stained trunk of a telephone pole asking if anyone had seen a parrot named Walt. Sara broke free from the path and approached one of the foundation holes.

'So where'd the house go?'

David joined her. Olive-colored water covered the bottom, a few bent pipes poking through its surface. A trash can lid floated in one corner, surrounded by an infinity of waterbugs.

'Just before they closed this place off,' he said, 'there was a house parade. It was amazing. A hundred of them on these giant flatbed trucks. They decided to move them all at once so they wouldn't be snarling up traffic. Everybody stopped work so we could watch them rumble down the interstate. House after house after house. You could feel the earth move as they passed. It shuddered right through the city, like a quake. One broke down and they just pushed it off the side of the road.'

'Where did they go?'

He shrugged.

'Away.'

They walked on, passing through several more streets of ruined houses and buildings, of useless road signs and weirdly intact mail

192

boxes. Nature encroached everywhere, the past week's storms multiplying the already riotous April growth. Moss coated the engines of rusted cars and the desultory tar roofs; vines pushed through the mortar of brick walls like the fingers of curious children. Nearly every road was spotted with hummocks of caked silt and long-burnt garbage. They walked on, marveling, saying nothing. Clouds of stuporous insects hovered above their heads like word balloons waiting to be filled in. Everything was uncannily silent, the only sounds the rustle of fat trees and the occasional call of birds.

'This is my kind of place,' Sara said, stepping over a tricycle half-buried in a dune of dirt.

They passed what had once been a car wash, its brushes and wires drooping like the innards of a gutted animal. They saw a diner whose walls and tables and counter had collapsed, leaving only the stools, rust-brown and swollen like just-sprouted mushrooms. At one point the roads stopped and they entered a small forest. Suddenly the silence gave way to a fusillade of bird and insect noise. Gobs of viscid cocoon hung from the trees above them. The ground grew swampy, sucking at their shoes. Sara stumbled, David took her hand. Unseen animals broke for deeper cover as they passed. When they emerged he stopped abruptly. One of the bird calls had sounded distinctly human.

'What?' Sara asked.

'Did you hear something?'

'Of course I heard something. It was like Doctor Dolittle on acid in there.'

'No, I meant . . . a human something. A shout.'

She looked around.

'There's no one else here, David.' She tugged at his hand. 'Come on, don't freak me out. I'm paranoid enough as is.'

They rejoined a road, passing a dog's skeleton lying in a grassless yard. A cracked leather collar hung loosely around its neckbone, the rusted chain connected to a metal hook that was buried in a concrete slab. A half-dozen smaller skeletons were arranged neatly at the bottom of the big dog's ribcage.

'Somebody got left behind,' he said.

'David . . . ' she said.

He led her away, joining what appeared to have been a main road. They followed it. The ruins here were larger than the houses they'd been seeing. Shops, schools, churches. Signs and billboards lined the way, most of them erased by time and weather. They passed a huge plastic cow that stood resolutely outside a demolished steak house, a cloud of wasps flying in and out of a puncture on its bulging neck. Their buzz echoed inside it like static from a distant radio. David and Sara turned on to a narrow street that dead-ended at a burned-out church. There was a blank bulletin board out front, the words North Burleigh Methodist Church barely visible on its brick housing.

'Hold on,' he said. 'These are the people who were supposed to look after the stretch of road where we had our accident.'

'I guess this is our spot, then,' Sara said.

They entered the building, stepping over the charred rubble of its collapsed front wall. The remaining three walls still stood, having somehow dodged the flames. A canopy of stretched ivy formed an impromptu roof. The floor had been scavenged, leaving just soft grass and a dusting of trapped dandelion seeds. They spread out the blanket. Sara dropped down on it, weary from the long walk. David opened the basket and the wine and they began to eat. Most of the food was bland, almost stale. Cheese and crackers, bread, dried fruit. They ate sparsely, speaking little. Sara seemed preoccupied by something, as if she were trying to solve a problem, make up her mind. She kept on giving him searching looks, turning away when he asked her what. Halfway through the meal a feral-looking cat appeared and she tried to earn its trust, slowly making her way back to the front of the church to feed it. David lay on his back and watched her, sucking on a frond of grass, his head propped on the basket. Thoughts of June and Decker and his wife were suddenly far from his mind. The cat watched Sara as well, seeming gradually to decide that, despite all the potential dangers, this woman was to be trusted. I know how you feel, David thought. But then it fled, just as it was about to take the food she offered. Something had spooked it. David stood and looked around, remembering the call he'd heard, worried again that there was someone else nearby. But everything seemed quiet. He looked at Sara – she had begun to collect the plastic letters that had fallen from the church's bulletin board, slotting them back into the black grid. 'Dv and Sra wer her' was the closest she could come. When she finished she came back to him, dropping to her knees, smiling at him.

'There,' she said, replacing a strand of hair behind her ear. 'Now we're immortal.'

He gently pulled her down to him.

David stared up through the roof of vines, watching a vapor trail slowly seam the sky. Sara's head lay on his chest, the spray of her hair covering his torso like a blanket.

'This is so strange,' he said.

She didn't answer.

'I mean, it feels so right, so real. And yet I know it can't be.'

'How do you know that?' she asked.

'I just can't get over the fact we know so little about each other. That I still have a thousand questions about you.'

'You know,' she said after a moment. 'We could be given big fat files on each other, slide shows, fingerprints, report cards, home movies – all the data in the world, and we wouldn't know any more than this. Words and pictures, those are for lying. The body's how we know.'

'In that case I think I'm on the way to being an expert.'

She laughed a little. David was still staring at the sky. The jet was gone, its trail dissipating already.

'So how would it work, anyway?' she asked.

'What?'

'You know, what you were talking about earlier. Me staying around here.'

He looked at her.

'You serious?'

She nodded. He pulled the blanket up over her shoulder to protect her from the late afternoon chill.

'Easy. I mean, there are plenty of places around. We could get something through my company, your name wouldn't even have to be on it.' He stared up into the canopy of tangled vine above them, working it out. 'And, you know, I could maybe get you a job, once you feel like it, once you're well. I have lots of friends. You'd just be this person.'

'I could make up a new name.'

'Yeah. Though I like Sara. You should keep that.'

He sat up.

'You're serious about this?'

She held his eyes for a moment, then turned away.

'I don't know. Maybe. Let me think about it.'

A cool breeze whipped up the dandelion seeds around them. She shivered.

'We should go.'

'Yeah, all right.'

They dressed in silence, both still a bit overwhelmed by her suggestion.

'What are we going to do with this?' she asked, pointing to the basket.

'Leave it for your friend.'

They walked back the way they'd come, passing the plastic cow, the dog skeletons, the car wash and the diner. At one point David thought he saw some movement in the trees up ahead, thought he heard another human call. But he couldn't be sure. He picked up the pace anyway.

'You know,' Sara said as they approached the border of trees by the fence, 'there's something I better tell you.'

David looked at her.

'I mean, about what's going on with me. If we are going to do something together you should know. But you have to promise to believe me. Because it's a really strange story.'

'Promise.'

'Well, about this Will thing.'

She sighed and smiled wryly.

'It's so fucked up, I don't even know where to start.'

'I've found the beginning always helps.'

Before Sara could speak again there was a sudden coughing noise from the solitary charred house they'd seen when they first entered. She stopped and looked at her stomach. Her white sweater was suddenly a vivid red. She touched her good hand to it and then that was red as well. There was another coughing sound and David felt something sting his neck.

'You're history!' a familiar voice shouted.

A man dressed in military fatigues, goggles and a wool cap stepped from the house. He brandished a large pistol.

'Hey, you guys aren't blue team,' he said.

'What the fuck?' David asked, his voice clotted with anger.

The man raised his goggles. It was Rowdy.

'David?'

His disbelieving eyes fell on Sara. He stared at her quizzically for a moment before recognition dawned.

'Hold on. What is she—?'

'Damn it, Rowdy,' David said. 'You scared the shit out of me.'

But he was still looking at Sara.

'Are you all right?' he asked.

'David,' she said quietly, drawing close to him.

David looked at her. Panic and fear filled her eyes. She'd placed Rowdy's voice. He looked back at his friend, who had taken a few steps toward them. Without another word Sara turned and ran.

'No wait,' Rowdy said. 'Look, let me have a . . . '

David stepped in front of him, his hands held at chest level.

'Rowdy, don't.'

'David, the fuck's going on here?'

More mock soldiers appeared a few hundred yards away. They spotted Rowdy and began to run toward him, whooping, priming their weapons. Their colors were different from his. They were the enemy.

'Look, just let us go,' David said. 'I'll call you. Please.'

'But—'

'Rowdy, trust me. I'll call.'

A paintball whizzed between them. Rowdy nodded confused agreement and David took off after Sara. She had disappeared into the ring of shade trees. He couldn't see her, could barely hear her. He moved fast, twigs whipping his face, branches tearing at his clothes. He finally caught her just a few yards from the fence. She'd stumbled on to her knees.

'Get me out of here,' she said.

'Yes, yes, all right.'

He helped her to her feet and led her toward the fence, escaping through the section shaped like a sneering lip.

*

197

Back at the house, she tore off her stained sweater, then collapsed on to the sofa.

'Damn, damn, damn.'

'Hey, quiet now,' David said, stroking her back, her hair.

'Now he knows I'm here. I'm fucked. I got to go, David. It's . . . '

Her skin was very pale and she seemed to be having a hard time breathing.

'No, he won't say anything,' David said. 'Not until I talk to him. OK?'

She didn't answer.

'Sara, you have to believe me. I can handle Rowdy. It'll be all right.'

She still didn't respond, her face buried in the cushions. After a while he gently rolled her over. Her eyes were closed. Red dye stained her stomach and her breasts and streaked her face. Not knowing what else to do, David picked up the WBRR shirt from the floor and began gently trying to wipe the color away, though all he managed to do was smear it around.

'I got to get out of here,' she said, shaking her head furiously, her eyes still shut. 'What the fuck was I thinking? I can't stay around here. They'll . . . '

She looked up at him.

'You have to get me out of here.'

'All right.'

'Now.'

'Listen, I'll take care of Rowdy. He won't do a thing unless I tell him. You have to trust me on this, Sara. We should stick to the original plan.'

She sat up, allowing him to hold her close. This seemed to calm her a little.

'You have to trust me on this,' he said.

She pulled back from him and looked into his eyes.

'When, then?'

'Tomorrow. I'll arrange it.'

'And he won't come for me, this doctor? He won't tell anyone?'

'No.'

She closed her eyes and dropped her head.

'Sara?'

She nodded, then looked up at the mantle.

'I could really use one of those pills. I'm feeling very straight all of a sudden. Very Sara.'

She began to stand but he gently stopped her.

'Before you do I want you to tell me – what were you going to say to me? You know, before he showed up.'

'It doesn't matter now.'

'You said something about Will . . . '

She looked back at him.

'It doesn't matter, David. Not now.' Her voice was resolute. 'I'm going away tomorrow. It's decided.'

'I think you should tell me anyway,' he said.

She noticed the dye on his neck.

'God, you're a mess, too,' she said, ignoring his insistence.

'Sara . . . '

'Let me clean you up,' she continued.

She started to remove his shirt. He rolled his shoulders to help her, though he was still staring at her expectantly. She refused to meet his eyes as she began rubbing his neck with the T-shirt.

'Sara, come on . . . '

She continued to ignore him. After a few more futile attempts she dropped the shirt and touched her good hand to the stain.

'Sara . . . '

'This is a strange color.' She was examining the residue on her palm and fingers. 'It's just like . . . '

And then, without a word, she spread her hand wide and pressed it to his naked chest, leaving its print there. When she pulled her hand away her eyes were fixed on the mark.

'It's just like . . . '

David remained perfectly still, waiting for her to explain. But she simply made another handprint, beside the first. Her eyes were strange, gripped by something he didn't understand. Then she looked up at him and shook her head, twice, slowly. He knew she wouldn't tell him now and suddenly that didn't matter. Nothing mattered but being here with her now, touching her. He put his hands on her and then they were making love, wildly, thoughtlessly, streaking the color across each other every time they touched.

When they were through, when his muscles uncoiled and his

breathing slowed, he looked at her. She lay perfectly still beneath him, her head averted, her eyes as distant as a nameless star.

'Sara, listen to me. I love you.'

She didn't answer for a long time.

'If that's true then you'll stop trying to make me tell,' she said finally. 'If that's true then you'll help me go.'

He looked away, his eyes coming to rest on the handprints on his chest.

'Yes, all right. All right.'

It was nearly five o'clock by the time he got away, after she'd taken her pills and fallen into a restless sleep. He hurried home, having promised to cook Mary Beth dinner tonight. Once again, he stopped by Krogers, this time picking up some shrimp and angel hair pasta to make her favorite dish, some wine and a double chocolate cake for dessert. In the back of his mind he knew it was a shitty thing to do, pretend like everything was normal with his wife while he was getting more deliriously involved with Sara. But it was all moving too fast for him to try anything else. He couldn't let things with Mary Beth get out of control as well. He stumbled through the supermarket like a sleepwalker, exhausted and depressed, enduring the curious stares of people who noticed his stained clothes and neck and hands. He was still unable to believe what had happened in Nowheresville. He'd almost had her, almost found out about her, almost convinced her to stay.

There was a message for him at home from Rowdy. A simple and ominous 'Call me'. David tried reaching him at the hospital but had no luck. He got the machine at his condo, instructing him not to talk to anyone until they spoke. Then he quickly changed clothes. There was no time for a shower – he could only wash what was left of the red dye from his neck and hands. Mary Beth got in just as he was finishing with the cooking. For some reason her mood was better than it had been for days, her mouth folded into an impish smile. He poured her a glass of wine and she drank it right down.

'So how are things at work?'

'Next topic,' she said, though she kept smiling.

'Sorry. Dinner'll be ready in about fifteen.'

'That gives us time.'

'For what?'

She motioned with her head for him to follow her into the living room.

'I'll show you.'

He followed her, experiencing a vague sense of dread as they passed through the house.

'So what's up?' he asked when she turned to face him.

'You, I hope.'

'What do you mean?'

She began to undress.

'I mean, I know you've been acting crazy of late and in many ways I don't approve but on the other hand it's kind of turned me on.'

She dropped her blouse to the floor, peeled off her skirt.

'Mary Beth . . . '

She tossed aside her bra and took a deep breath, her breasts rising expectantly.

'Let's do it, is my point.'

David thought of his Sara's handprints on his body.

'Now?'

Before he could say anything else she'd cupped his neck with her warm hands and begun kissing him. Deep, hungry kisses.

'Mary Beth . . . '

'Hmmm?'

He could feel her stepping out of her underwear.

'Look, I can't.'

She pulled back, one leg of her panties still shackling her ankle.

'You can't what?'

'You know.'

'Why not?'

Because I've given her everything. Because I don't have anything left for you.

'I don't know. It's just . . . I don't know what to say.'

She backed away and he found himself staring at the thin scar on her abdomen.

'What do you mean, you don't know what to say? I want to make love. Nobody's asking you to *say* anything.'

He was lost for words.

'What is with you, David?' she asked angrily. 'You've been all over me for the past week and now you're acting like you don't want me.'

'I don't know what to say.'

'Will you shut up about say?' She placed a hand on her forehead, spiking up her hair, staring wide-eyed at him. 'I don't get this. First you want to hump me on one of the biggest nights of my working life. Then you make a fool of yourself in front of all those people at the concert. Then you rape me in my sleep. And now when I finally say let's, you know, you make me feel like some piece of whale blubber.'

She was waiting for an answer.

'I'm sorry,' was the best he could do.

'Sorry? Who gives a damn about sorry?'

He shook his head.

'Do you want me to leave you alone?' she asked. 'Take a rain check?'

He didn't answer.

'All right, then,' she said angrily.

She picked up her bra.

'Mary Beth, look . . . '

'What's the smell?' she asked.

Dinner. He turned to see smoke and flickering light through the kitchen door. He ran in. The French bread had caught fire in the toaster oven. He speared it with a knife, tossed it in the sink and jerked on the faucet. As it came apart in the water the front door slammed. Shit, David thought, hurrying out of the kitchen. But by the time he got to the porch her Honda was pulling quickly away. He watched her disappear, standing there until the wind whipped up and an alarm light flared. David waited until it stopped its manic strobe, then went upstairs to wash himself clean.

11

There was a car parked in David's space. A long, chocolate brown sedan with a constellation of rusting dinks and a collapsed back bumper. One man behind the wheel, another slouched in the back seat. David honked. The driver's only response was to adjust the rearview mirror. The passenger remained perfectly still. David leaned on the horn, motioned impatiently. Nothing. So he pulled up and blocked them in. I don't need this, he thought as he got out of the Mustang. Last night had been his worst since meeting Sara. He'd been tempted to go back to Locust Lane after Mary Beth fled but he had to speak with Rowdy first, make sure he knew to keep quiet. And yet his friend was nowhere to be found. After leaving several messages at the hospital he decided to visit himself. But he still had no luck. The receptionist couldn't answer his questions – the place was a madhouse, some sort of emergency was in progress, stretchers and anxious relatives everywhere. By the time David gave up it was almost midnight, too late to see Sara. To make matters worse, Mary Beth never even made it up to the bedroom, choosing to spend the night in one of their guest rooms. She was gone when he woke, her outline still visible on the sheets of the bed where she'd slept.

He walked angrily up to the interloper, stopping abruptly when he saw it was Ed Decker behind the wheel.

'Morning,' he said cheerily.

David nodded distractedly. This wasn't good. He thought he'd seen the last of this guy. He tried to get a look at the man in the back, but Decker's smirking skull blocked the way.

'You're in my place.'

'Why don't you hop in for a moment? Then, boom, we're out of here.'

David looked at his watch.

'It'll only take a sec,' Decker said.

David walked around to the far door and got in, sneaking a look at the passenger as he did. He seemed to be in his late thirties, with thin violet lips and heavily lidded eyes. His dark blond hair was pulled into a nub ponytail. The skin on his face was smooth, baby soft, as if it had never been shaved. There was no shirt beneath his expensive suit – his chest was pale and hairless. He was staring out the window, making a show of ignoring David.

'You want one a these?' Decker asked, partially lifting a greasy Biscuitville bag from the console.

'No thanks.'

'They had a two-for-one special. I sorta went nuts.'

David noticed the small flecks of dough involved in the unshaven stubble of Decker's chin. One piece clung to the end of a long nose hair.

'I'm still looking for that girl.'

'No luck, huh?'

'Luck,' Decker complained generally. 'He keeps on talking about luck.'

The passenger didn't respond.

'I talked with the people at the hospital yesterday morning. This muscle man doctor and a nurse something-or-other. Interesting developments – they're of the opinion our girl was faking that coma.'

David performed a terse, appreciative nod. Decker rolled his neck until it cracked loudly.

'How about you?' he asked. 'What do you think?'

'I wouldn't know.'

'But you went to see her.'

'Well, if you'd been in an accident you'd be concerned about her . . .'

Decker held up two greasy fingers. David stopped talking.

'Twice. The first one, right after the wreck, that's a gimme. You can have that. What about the second time, at five the next morning?'

David felt a pulse of fear.

'I was worried about her,' he said. 'Like I said, I felt responsible.'

'That's a lot of worry for someone you don't even know. Wouldn't a phone call have sufficed?'

David didn't say anything.

'You still feel responsible about her?'

'In a general sense.'

'How general?'

David tried to hold the man's gaze, but wound up looking out the window. A bird had just taken a shit on the hood, an omelette of smooth white and chunky gray that spread slowly across the warm metal.

'Look, I don't understand where we're going with this,' he said. 'I told you everything I know about this woman.'

'This night duty nurse said she heard you two talking.'

'What?'

'She said you were there with the doctor and then he left and you guys started yapping.'

'It was just me talking. I was asking her . . . I wanted to see if she really was in a coma.'

'Why?'

The car rocked gently as the passenger shifted.

'Look,' David said, deciding to go on the offensive. 'I'll tell you why. It's no big mystery. I was worried about a lawsuit. And I spoke to her because I figured if Sara really was awake then we might come to some sort of—'

'You said—'

'—understanding without getting the insur . . . '

'You said—'

David stopped talking. Decker raised his thick eyebrows.

'You just said Sara.'

Somehow, David knew that the man in the back seat was looking at him now.

'Well, that's what she told me her name was.'

'When?'

'When? Up at the crash site.'

Decker slapped his skeletal hand against the dashboard, leaving a spread of greasy fingerprints there.

'You see, that's exactly what I mean when I say that one discussion on these matters is never sufficient. There's always some little nodule of information that will come dislodged in subsequent conversations.'

He smiled triumphantly. The crumb of biscuit finally fell from his nose.

'So, Mr Webster, David, let's start all over again – how was it she came to tell you her name was Sara? Because, I got to tell you, this girl, she's not the sort to go disclosing things.'

Tell me about it, David thought. He found himself looking at the deodorizing figure that hung from the rearview mirror. A small man with a big head. Some cartoon character, the guy who always tried to bag Bugs Bunny. David couldn't remember his name and for some reason that bothered him. 'I'll Get that Wabbit!' his word bubble promised.

'I don't know. I guess I was just thinking, you know how they say you're supposed to keep people awake.'

'That's what they say.'

'And so I was just making small talk with her. You know. What's your name, stuff like that.'

'And she said it was . . . ' He spread his hands. 'Sara?'

'That's right. Just Sara.'

Decker adjusted the rearview mirror so he could see the passenger.

'That's an interesting choice,' he said into it.

There was no reply.

'Why, isn't that her name?' David asked.

Decker ignored the question.

'So did she say anything else during this small talk of yours? Anything at all would sure be of use. 'Cause I gotta tell you, we're playing some serious catch-up ball here.'

'She said something . . . ' David snapped his fingers, a cheap theatrical gesture he immediately regretted. 'She said something about Florida.'

'Florida?'

'I can't be sure, but I think she said that's where she was trying to go. Things happened . . . '

'So fast, yeah.' Decker became pensive. 'Florida. That's good. That's useful. And is there anything else?'

'Not that I can remember.'

'Hey, don't worry. You've been more help than you know.'

He patted David reassuringly on the shoulder with his greasy fingers.

'And you can rest easy, chief – nobody's going to be suing you.'

Decker looked in the mirror and chuckled. 'Am I right?'

'You most assuredly are,' the man said in an English accent.

David wanted to turn to look at him, but for some reason thought that would only further compromise him.

'Can I ask you something?'

Decker nodded.

'What did she do?' David asked. 'Why are you looking for her?'

'David, all I can say at this juncture is that, wherever she is, she's confused. She needs our help. Hence our concern.'

David stared out the window at the Redwine Group building.

'Well,' he said after a moment. 'I'd better get to work.'

'Me too.'

'Good luck in your search.'

Decker shook his head.

'There's that word again.'

David managed a smile and finally looked in the back seat. The passenger ignored him, blowing condensation against the tempered glass, drawing shapes in the steam and then rubbing them away. His hands were small and pale. David got out and started to walk toward the building.

'David,' Decker called, his voice lilting with mockery. 'Would you come back here, please?'

He froze.

'I don't think we're through just yet.'

David turned. The moment he saw Decker's eyes he could tell that the man knew he was lying. He strode warily back to the car. The passenger had just beaten himself at tic-tac-toe.

'Yeah?'

'Your 'stang,' Decker said, tossing a jutting thumb over his shoulder. 'It's blocking me in here.'

David drove fast down back roads, checking his rearview mirror every few seconds to be sure there was no one there. He'd left the office soon after they disappeared, his immediate plan being to go over to Locust Lane, warn Sara what was happening and pack her off on the next flight. After all, it was what he'd promised her. Decker was supposed to be gone. He'd counted on that when he broke his promise to her the other day. Saying her name to him was a major fuck-up. And the look in his eyes when he'd called David back to the car – the guy knew that something was up. Before leaving the office, David had grabbed the clump of melted photos from his desk to take with him in case she didn't believe he'd been to June's. There was no time to try to find the slip of paper with its cryptic message amid the chaos of his drawer.

But before he'd even left downtown he realized he couldn't do it. He couldn't just send her away. Not now, after the last two days. There had to be a better way to help her than to simply pack her off into the unknown. If only he knew what was going on, what these men were after, then maybe he could figure out how to get rid of them. And so, despite his promise to her, he turned north, driving fast into the countryside. He would see this D. D. Jeter, find out what he knew about Sara. Figure out if she really had been with June, figure out what had happened above Ivanhoe.

Onley was one of few remaining all-black enclaves still surrounding Burleigh. David knew the way – he'd been up here several years ago to assess a teen pregnancy program. For some reason he couldn't remember if they'd been funded. Strange, he thought, how all those good works had a habit of slipping away from his memory, his life. He stopped at the Exxon station that provided the town's hub. Four men of various ages and hues stood around a paint-stripped Camaro, looking at it with the forlorn patience of pall bearers who really didn't know the deceased that well. David asked if anybody knew a D. D. Jeter.

'What's your bidness with Dallas?'

'I got something for him.'

There were bemused smiles, muttered curses.

'Man come here says he got something for Dallas.'

'Shee.'

'What you got?'

'His tools.'

This silenced them.

'Leave 'em here.'

'No,' David said evenly. 'I'm supposed to give them to D. D. Jeter and no one else.'

The men nodded. Tools were currency out here, David knew, maybe better than cash. After a short conference in which David wondered if his death was being mooted the leader broke free and showed him the way. It wasn't far. Jeter lived in a small clapboard house surrounded by a billowing, maze-like garden. David knocked on the tattered screen door. There was no answer. He knocked again.

'What you want, white?'

A small man with bandy legs stood at the corner of the house. A shotgun dangled in his hand like an afterthought. Its barrel was the same color as his skin.

'Are you Mr D. D. Jeter?'

'I'm him, yeah.'

David stepped down off the porch and walked over to him, one eye on the gun.

'And you worked for Will June?'

'I did his garden some, that's right. You the law?'

'No.'

'You the bank?'

'No.'

'Then what the hell you want to be on my property fo', white?'

'I was wondering if I could ask you a few questions.'

He stared dubiously at David.

'You see, I saw your tools up there and . . . '

'My tools?'

David nodded.

'You gone help me get my tools back?'

'That's right,' David said, grasping the opening he'd been offered.

Jeter shook his head.

'I was beginning to think they wouldn't never let me have 'em,' he said bitterly.

'Who?'

'The govment. I went on up after Mr June died and they wouldn't let me on the property. I told them I had five hundert dollar worth of tools up there but they said it's the tax man's now. I said I paid the tax man for every dollar I ever earned. They said if I wanted to make a claim I could go see the judge. The judge. I said man why you wanna law me like this but they just ran me off. You believe that shit?'

'I'm sorry.'

209

'Not as sorry as I am, white. Come on, you comin'.'

He led David around the side of the house, leaning his gun against a blistered wall. Out back was a large vegetable garden, rich with the odors of chlorophyl and dung.

'Picking these snap peas,' he explained. 'All this rain they ripe up too fast.'

He handed David a dented colander, then headed down the path. David followed, using it to catch the peapods tossed in his direction.

'I just have to ask you a few questions,' David said.

'Go on,' Jeter said. 'I know them tools like they was my own flesh.'

'I'm sure you do. Um, how often did you go up to June's place?'

'Three days a week, usually.'

'Did you build his fence?'

Jeter turned and smiled.

'Pretty good, huh? Bet some of those police got caught up in it.'

'Two had to see a doctor.'

'Hot damn,' Jeter said. 'Don't know why they had to go all the way to a doctor, though. Cure always grows right alongside the poison. That's a simple fact of nature.'

'So why did June want to keep people out so bad?'

'Never asked.'

'It must have been strange, near the end.'

'Strange all along.'

'How so?'

Jeter didn't answer. David stared at the intermittent wires of gray hair on the back of the old man's neck. Just ask, he told himself.

'Was there, did you see a young woman there a week ago, couple weeks ago? Tall, thin lady, with dark red hair. Strange colored eyes. Amber.'

Jeter kept picking and tossing, his craggy fingers moving with surprising agility.

'She lived in that cabin by the treeline,' David continued.

'I know where she stayed.'

David stopped in his tracks. So there it was. My God. He'd been right after all. A tossed peapod landed silently on the tilled ground in front of him.

'So you saw her? You knew her?'

Jeter turned and looked David in the eye for the first time.

'You for sure gone help me get my tools back, white?'

'Yes, I will. I just need to get some background. You know.'

Jeter brushed his hands together. He was through picking. The colander was full.

'Yeah, I know that girl. Never did tell me her name, though.'

'How long was she there?'

'Lessee. A good month before Mr June died.'

'A month?'

'*Good* month. Closer to two.'

'Do you know what she was doing there?'

Jeter shook his head.

'Alls I know is that just after New Year Mr June said there'd be somebody comin'. Made it seem real important. I was sposed to do what she said, help her out if she needed it.'

Jeter's eyes narrowed in memory. A faint smile crossed his face.

'Yeah, I remember that girl. Quiet, real quiet. Pretty girl. Too skinny, though. I was forever leaving her things to eat.'

He shrugged.

'First I thought she was fambly but I don't think so.'

'Was she, you know, involved with June?' David heard himself ask.

Jeter gave David a dark look.

'In-what?'

'Were they lovers?'

'Now how am I supposed to know that, white? Just who the hell are you?'

'I'm just trying to sort out June's estate. If you don't want to cooperate then . . . '

Jeter held up his hands.

'Look, I don't know *what* they were,' he said. 'When she first come he was like to be fussin' over her all the time. They passed a lot of time together up at the house or specially down where she was staying. Mr June seemed excited, like some fool kid. Talked about how she was going to save him or some such shit. Used to always be bringing her thangs in that little cabin of hers.'

'Like what?'

Jeter shrugged.

211

'Just thangs. I'd see him in the morning, going down to the cabin, carryin' packages. Couple three times he had me pick her flowers. Not just a bunch but a whole damn barrel full. Cornflowers, snapdragons. Once – never forget this – one day this truck pulled up and it was two peacocks. You believe that? I said, "Mr June what you doin' get them nasty birds for, tear up my garden, foul up the place." Alls he said was she wanted them.' Jeter scowled. 'Hated those birds.'

'They're still up there.'

'Well, they can have it.' Jeter shook his head. 'But then it changed.'

He looked around, uncertain whether or not to proceed.

'Go ahead.'

'Mr June started drinking real heavy. I mean *real* heavy. Stumblin' about. Yellin'.'

'And when was this?'

'Three weeks ago, anyway. Didn't see them together too much after that. She spent just about all her time down in the cabin. All locked up. He'd come down but wouldn't stay long. Couple times she wouldn't even let him in. Once I heard them fussin', she was telling him to git, let her alone. My shed was right there, you see. She said she was gonna go if he didn't leave her be. And then he started beggin' her, sayin' she had to help him. "You got to help me with this," he said. "You got to finish what we started."'

'Help him do with what?'

Jeter shrugged.

'You askin' the wrong man, white. And then I didn't hear nuthin' for a few days. She was in her cabin, June in his house. And then he sent me off.'

'Sent you off?' David asked sharply. 'What do you mean? When?'

'Lessee. Friday 'fore last. Got to work and there was a note on my shed from Mr June, saying he wouldn't be needin' me for the next week. Well, he might not a needed me but his garden did, all that rain. I went up to the house but he didn't answer when I knocked. So I went down talked to that girl. She said she didn't know nothing about it. Seemed real nervous, would hardly open the door. Then I saw there was a check from Mr June in the envelope, too. Signed up and everything. Week's pay, in advance. My experience is folks pay

212

you in advance you take the money. So I went down to Myrtle Beach to see my son Claude. He got a club down there. Got them wet T-shirt contests. You ever seen that shit?'

David nodded.

'Then come Monday week I show up and the govment man's there. Say June's dead. Say I can't have my tools.'

'You tell them about her?'

'Didn't tell them jack. They best give me my tools 'fore they can talk to me 'bout what I know.'

'How about the newspaper?'

'Ran her off too. She ain got nuthin' for me.'

He looked at David.

'So when's it gonna be?'

'What?'

'My tools.'

David didn't answer. Jeter's eyes narrowed.

'You gone help me get them tools back, right, white?'

'I'm doing what I can,' David said.

Which, considering there was nothing he could do, was, in a way, true.

It began to rain as David pulled away, a fine spring drizzle that would only last long enough to rainbow the oil on the roads, to glisten the trees. So that was it, then. What started out as a longshot suspicion on Monday morning was in fact true. Sara had been with June. And they had been lovers. June was the man she had talked about, the one who had helped her, the one she'd fled. The one who expected so much from her. He'd helped her when she was in a bad way, fallen in love with her. That must have been what he meant about finishing what they'd started. David could certainly understand that. He'd lavished gifts on her, trying to hold on to her. She'd mentioned Flannery and her birds; June bought peacocks. It was good, then it got bad, and then she was gone. She'd taken something from him as well, one of the houseful of artefacts he'd acquired. He'd gone off the rails after that, after she'd left him with nothing but his financial ruin. So he killed himself. No wonder she was in such bad shape Monday morning. She must have heard it on the radio.

David's mind raced on. And Decker? He must be one of the shady creditors Cathy had mentioned. Hunting whatever it was Sara had taken, maybe one of those paintings June had bought with borrowed money. How did he know about her, though? It took David several miles of thought before it came to him. June had told him. Of course. The last bitter act of a ruined man. That was why there was no mention of her in his note. And why everything in her cabin had been burned. He wanted to obliterate every trace of her.

As he drove back to Burleigh he began to feel exhilarated by his discovery. Of course, there were still unexplained things. Those rust-colored stains, for instance. But those could be anything. A nosebleed, ketchup, nail polish. The simple truth was that now, at the end of his search, David knew there was no reason for her to go. He could tell her what he'd discovered. She'd understand why he hadn't believed her, forgive him for it. He could assuage whatever guilt she felt over June's death. After all, it had happened days after she was gone. She wasn't to blame for a sick man's actions. David knew he could convince her that she didn't have to leave. And as for her theft – well, he'd meet this Decker, tell him that whatever they were looking for was under eight feet of Mud River water. They'd have no choice but to give up their search for her. It was the truth, after all. He pulled off the highway at the North Burleigh exit, heading for Locust Lane, powered by the knowledge that everything was going to be all right now.

But then, just a mile from the house, he suddenly remembered that he had yet to speak with Rowdy. He could be telling anyone that he'd seen her. David turned abruptly back toward town. He didn't need any complications. Not now, not before he'd spoken with Sara. Not when everything was on the verge of being all right.

Rowdy was still at the hospital, taking a break in the staff cafeteria. Last night's emergency had passed. David found him sitting alone at a corner table engrossed in *Kickboxer!* magazine. He looked up as David dropped into the chair opposite him.

'Fuck, there you are,' he said, tossing the magazine on the table. 'I've been trying to get hold of you all morning. Nobody at your office knew where you were.'

'No, I've been out. I called about a thousand times last night. I even came by.'

'Didn't you hear? Bus crashed outside of town yesterday afternoon. It went into a swollen river. I was up to my ass in hypothermia and shock all night. By the time I was able to call you it was like three in the morning.'

He lowered his voice.

'I didn't, you know, want to call you at home, with Mary Beth and . . .'

'No, no, I understand.'

'So David, the fuck is going on here? I almost shit my pants when I saw you guys yesterday. I mean, that was the Mystery Date, right?'

David nodded once. Rowdy shook his head.

'What the hell are you doing with her?'

David looked around the cafeteria, wondering where to start.

'I . . . when was it, it was last Thursday that I saw her.' He began to ruffle an edge of the magazine. 'Outside my office. She was just standing there, dazed and confused. I went out and talked to her. She was in real bad shape.'

'You're telling me.'

'She needed help. My help. She thought her stuff was still up at the crash site. She wanted to take a cab up there, right? I mean she was clueless. So I drove her. Only it was flooded out, everything was gone. I asked her where she wanted to go, who she could call. The usual questions. But she wouldn't say. I couldn't just turn her loose on the street, you know? So I put her up in a hotel but that was no good and so I found her . . . someplace else.'

'In Nowheresville?'

'No, we were just . . . it's hard to explain.'

'Why the fuck didn't you bring her to me, man? She's still my patient, you know. I haven't discharged her yet.'

'She wouldn't let me.'

'Wouldn't *let* you?'

'You don't know her. She's very determined.'

'I reckon so.'

'She's trying to get away from this guy and so I'm just helping her until, you know, she's ready to move again.'

'What do you mean, this guy?'

215

'Boyfriend or something.'

'Is that what she told you?'

David looked up.

'Yeah. Why?'

'Because a cop came around yesterday morning asking questions about her. That's what I wanted to tell you when I saw you guys.'

David stopped ruffling the magazine.

'A cop? What did he look like?'

'A real ectomorph. About six-two, one fifty. Big hands, hair coming out of his ears.'

'His name's Decker.'

'Something like that.'

'What makes you think he's a cop?'

'I just presumed. I mean, he sure seemed like a cop. Otherwise I wouldn't have even talked to him.'

'I don't think that he's a cop.'

'Yeah and I don't think he's just some boyfriend.'

'What did he say?'

'Just that he wanted to ask her some questions. He wasn't very specific, though I got the impression that it was something very heavy.'

'What did you tell him?' David asked.

'What do you mean, what did I tell him? I told him the truth. That I knew zip.'

'Well, if you see him again you have to keep quiet about . . . '

'Yo, David,' Rowdy said, waving his hands, calling time out. 'It's me, remember? I'm not going to say anything to anyone you don't want me to. But listen up, if I were you I'd find out what this babe is running from before you get any more involved with her. Because it looks a tad more serious than boy trouble.'

David nodded impatiently. He knew all this. He had this covered.

'Now, you got to let me to ask you a few things, all right?' Rowdy asked.

'Go on.'

'Has she been vomiting or having dizzy spells?'

'No.'

'How about her eyes? Do they seem dilated?'

'No, her eyes are fine.'

216

'And her wrist? Is it swollen or throbbing, you know, anything more than just the usual pain?'

'It's getting better.'

They sat in silence for a moment. A tray dropped somewhere, there was jeering applause.

'So, what, are you guys, you know . . .'

David nodded. Rowdy ran a big hand through the brush of his hair.

'Holy shit. You mean you're really having, like, an affair with this babe?'

'If that's what you call it.'

'Hey, compadre, if you're having sexual congress while married to another woman, well, that's the accepted terminology. Believe me.'

David remained silent.

'So what are you going to do, David? Because – and I know you didn't ask – I got to tell you some things here. I mean, first of all, and I doubt I need to say this, but this guy, cop or not, I wouldn't play around with him. His interest in your girl there seems a notch or two above the casual.'

David nodded impatiently. He could handle Decker now that he knew the truth.

'And, secondly, I mean, David, what the fuck are you doing? You know me, I'm not going to get all sanctimonious on you, but I never pegged you for sailing into the Bermuda Triangle of Love.'

'Look who's talking,' David said, regretting it immediately.

Rowdy pulled back, stung.

'Yeah, right, I *know* who's talking. I *know* I fucked up.'

David nodded an apology.

'Look, you're still sitting here, so I might as well tell you this,' Rowdy continued. 'You should kick back for a minute and analyze this thing. Take a serious reality check. All right, I don't know, maybe it's not so great with you and Mary Beth now, all right? But at least it's real. It'll come around, it'll get better. I kick myself morning noon and night for not staying with Cath.'

David shook his head with slow obstinacy.

'I don't know that what I have with Mary Beth is real.'

'What does that mean?'

'It means that maybe what I have with Mary Beth is just this, this, I don't know, this safe house I've been hiding out in. To keep the real world at bay. I'm feeling things for this woman I can't even begin to get my mind around.'

Rowdy grabbed David's wrist, his big hand incongruously gentle.

'I know what you're thinking, David, I really do. I've been there, you *know* I've been there. But here's the thing – how do you know this girl isn't just this brush fire that's going to blow out in a few days, weeks? Believe me, ninety-nine times, that's all it is.'

'It isn't. Not with her. I know it isn't.'

'How?'

David couldn't find the words. Rowdy leaned forward.

'David, this is your marriage you're fucking up here. This is your *life*, not some fake house or whatever you called it.' He released David's arm. 'Look, you wanna tear yourself off a piece, let me fix you up with somebody. Come on.'

'That's not what this is about, Rowdy.'

'Then what is it?'

'A chance.'

'For what?'

'For what. For . . . look, since day one I've played it by the book. Married the right girl, worked the right job. Big house, friends. And it's all had nothing to do with real life. With how things really are. With June and Redwine and her.'

'June? What are you talking about?'

David laughed.

'I'm talking about two boats and a helicopter.'

'Two . . . ' Rowdy held up his hands. 'David, I don't want to get official on you here, but you're losing it. You are making zero sense. You should see your eyes, man. Come on upstairs and let me give you the once over, write you something for your nerves. Just a pinch between the cheek and gums. And then you me can go over and see this girl, wherever you got her stashed. Sort this whole fucking mess out.'

He placed a hand on his heart.

'Strictest confidence straight down the line. You can trust me.'

David looked at his friend.

'I can't do it, Rowdy.'

'Why the hell not?' he pleaded.

'I promised her I wouldn't.'

Rowdy canted his head like a bull.

'David, I can't let you do this, man. It's like giving you the keys to your car when you're drunk.'

'I know I'm right. If you knew all the facts then you would, too.'

Rowdy shook his head.

'Man, I just can't—'

'Mind if I join you?'

They both looked up. It was another doctor, a plump woman with thick glasses. Her tray was stacked with jello and chocolate milk.

'Jane, we're sort of in the middle of . . .'

But she'd already sat.

'Heard you had a bad night,' she said, oblivious to the tension between the two men. 'How many you send down?'

'Two, though there's one more who probably won't make it.'

'Thanks a lot,' she said, her voice thick with sarcasm.

'Jane here's a forensic pathologist,' Rowdy explained.

David stood. He didn't care what Jane was. He had to see Sara. Tell her what he knew. Tell her it was going to be all right.

'Well, at least I don't have to travel up to Ivanhoe for this one,' she continued, dissolving a cube of jello in her mouth.

'Listen, Jane, no kidding, we—'

'What were you doing up in Ivanhoe?' David interrupted.

Jane looked David over as she took a sip of her chocolate milk.

'Working my ass off on Will June's autopsy, that's what,' she said, tabling her drink.

'I thought that was all set,' Rowdy said, looking at her now as well.

'Nah. There were some discrepancies.'

'What kind of discrepancies?' David asked, dropping slowly back into his chair.

Jane smiled toothlessly, basking in the attention. There was a little brown moustache above her upper lip.

'Well, the coroner up there is about ninety years old. The guy isn't even really a pathologist. Just a family practitioner who moonlights. Anyway, he was *technically* right about the time of death. From the body temperature and state of rigor it was clear June had died thirty-some hours before he was discovered. But one of the paramedics at the scene had a hunch that something was funny, that June had been gone longer than just one day. So he told Swisher, who called us in for a consultation.'

Her mouth twisted into a rictus of self-satisfaction.

'Well, we confirmed the Ivanhoe coroner's verdict, no sweat, but something did seem fishy. I measured blood sugar, insulin levels, but that was all inconclusive. I mean, everything I tried came up weird, like there were two times of death, like he'd died twice. And then I noticed something on his coccyx. At first I thought it was just a bruise or a scrape but then I realized it was a nascent sacral decubitus, just a little sucker, about as big as a dime.'

'Bed sore,' Rowdy explained to David.

'Well, corpses don't develop sores, as you know. And then I got it. Clear as day. June *had* died twice.'

'Say what?' Rowdy asked.

'You see, what happened was, even though he died on Saturday, he actually killed himself considerably earlier.'

Rowdy was nodding his head, finally getting it.

'I don't understand,' David said.

'He used insulin,' Rowdy said.

'Which sends the system straight into hypoglycemic shock,' Jane continued. 'In a nutshell, he put himself into a coma.'

'Claus and Sunny,' Rowdy said.

'You got it. Only Sunny had people looking after her. But since June was on his own, he died after just a few days. Of thirst. His metabolism was like zilch which is why he lasted so long.'

'Jane, you're a star,' Rowdy said.

'So when did he do it?' David asked, his voice almost inaudible.

'Shoot up? Well, I wouldn't go to court with this, but given the size of the sore and all the other evidence, my guesstimate is that he'd been out four days, minimum. Maybe even five.'

'So he was injected on Tuesday,' David said quietly.

Jane chomped another jello cube.

'Maybe late Monday,' she said. 'But certainly early Tuesday morning at the latest.'

David stood up abruptly, pulling his keys from his pocket. As he did the melted clump of photographs tumbled to the floor. He reached down for them but Rowdy had already picked them up. While bent over, David could see his friend's shoes. They were covered with dim red drops from his long night's work with the bloodied and the dying.

'Look, I got to go,' David said, standing quickly. 'I got to . . .'

'Hey, the fuck are you doing with a bunch of burned-up X-rays?' Rowdy asked, examining the gnarled cluster.

'X-rays?' David asked.

Rowdy held them up for Jane to see. She nodded agreement. But David didn't wait around for her confirmation. He was already moving across the cafeteria.

12

She was asleep when he got to the house, curled on the sofa, her body partially covered by the survival blanket. The radio was tuned to the country station, its volume low. David stared down at her for a long time. She was there when he died. She was there. The words kept running through his mind until they began to cease meaning anything. An hour ago he thought he'd understood and now he knew nothing. Finally, he touched her shoulder, just as he had that first day at the crash. Her eyes opened.

'I was just dreaming,' she said, stretching her arms above her head.

'What about?'

'The one where you're in a plane that can't seem to get any altitude.' She rubbed at her eyes. 'I must be anxious about the flight.'

David nodded distantly as she sat up.

'So, right. OK. I'm packed. I'm ready.'

'Sara . . .'

'Not that there's that much to take.'

'Sara, listen . . .'

She noticed his expression.

'What is it? David, are you all right?'

He sat beside her.

'David? Come on, you're scaring me.'

'I know,' he said finally.

She slotted a strand of hair behind her ear.

'Know what? What do you mean? David, what's happened?'

'I know you were with June.'

She looked away.

'What makes you think you know that?' she asked quietly.

He told her about going to Ivanhoe and what he'd found at the cabin, told her about visiting Jeter.

'All right, stop,' she interrupted. 'You know but you don't

understand. Just listen.'

She licked her lips once, quickly.

'OK, yeah, I was up there for a while. I knew June from back in New York, when I worked for this art dealer. I just needed a place to hang out for a while. It was cool at first, but then he flipped out and so I got out of there. And I took a couple things, yeah, but he wouldn't have missed them. They were just . . . I mean, you saw the place. It was like buried treasure. Now, him dying, that happened long after I was gone.'

'No, it didn't.'

She looked at him.

'What do you mean?'

'He killed himself late Monday, early Tuesday morning. Before you left. That's why you were running.'

'But the papers . . . '

'They've done another autopsy, Sara. It took June several days to die. But he'd shot himself up before you left.'

She looked away.

'Damn,' she said softly. 'Damn.'

'Sara . . . '

She looked back at him, shaking her head angrily.

'You just couldn't leave it alone, could you?' she said. 'I told you it was better that you didn't know. Why did you have to go prying into it? Why couldn't you trust me?'

'Come on, Sara. What do you expect? We've gone a bit too far to play make-believe.'

She laughed.

'And here I was thinking that was exactly what this was. A few days of make-believe before we got back to our real lives. I thought that was the deal, David. Not asking questions. Having a little faith.'

'You were lovers, weren't you?' he persisted. 'He was the one you've been talking about.'

'Lovers? With Will June? Is that what you think?'

'Yes,' he said softly.

'Lovers,' she said, shaking her head bitterly. 'My God. Will June couldn't love anything. Not anything alive.'

'What, then?'

She took a deep breath and looked him in the eye.

'Please, David. Let's just forget it. Can't I just leave and . . . '

She stopped talking, recognizing the grim determination in his expression.

'No, I guess not.' She looked away. 'All right. You win. Look, when you were up there – did you go into his bedroom?'

David nodded. She sighed and shook her head, seemingly beset by second thoughts.

'Sara . . . '

'Remember the bed?'

David just stared at her.

'There was a painting above it. It's called *The Adoration on the Shacktown Road*. By an artist named Thomas Apostle.'

'I saw it.'

She smiled bitterly.

'No you didn't.'

'What do you mean? I stood right there. I could've touched it.'

'What I mean is that the one you saw was a copy. A fake.'

'A fake? How do you know?'

'Because I painted it, David. That's what I was doing up there.'

He stared into her angry eyes.

'But if that's a copy then where's . . . ?'

He'd guessed the answer before he could even finish the question.

'That's what I stowed back there at the crash. That's why I was running. I'd switched them, taken the real painting. Stolen it. That's why I had to find you, David. Why I had to go back.' She began to pick at the frayed edge of her cast. 'And that's why I have to get away. Because he'll think I still have it.'

'Who?'

'The man I work for. He'll know what I've done. He'll think I have the real painting. And he'll want it back.'

'I don't get this, Sara.'

'Look, it's not that hard to figure out. I was hired to make a copy of that painting for June. That's what I do, David. That's what I am.'

'But why? I mean, if he had it already, why would he make a copy?'

'To keep from losing it. Think about it. You take a collector like June, they have to get rid of a painting they love, maybe more than one. Taxes or insurance or divorce or bankruptcy – the usual reasons. Before they can put it on the market they get a call from this dealer who offers to sell it for them. With an added benefit.'

'You make copies for them to keep.'

'No. David. Come on – I make a copy for them to *sell*. They get to keep the original.'

David was gripping at his forehead.

'So let me get this straight. What I saw at June's was a fake. And the original . . .'

'I had with me in the car. And that's what Ant will want.'

'Ant?'

'Anthony.' She smiled wryly. 'He's English. *He's* the one I've been telling you about.'

David remembered the passenger's accent. He stared at her for a moment.

'You're a forger? That's what this is all about?'

'Not my preferred term, but yes, that's me.'

'Jesus.' He sat in silence for a moment. 'So what happened up there, Sara?'

'June killed himself. That's what happened. Things were, well, getting pretty heavy near the end. When I first got there he was all right, a bit edgy but then most of the people I work for are. I guess he still thought he could keep the wolves from the door. All he had to do was get liquid, pay them off. We got along all right. He'd watch me work sometimes, help when I needed it, get me things. But after a while he began to get weird. Drinking, sitting in his room all day, leafing through old Sotheby's catalogues. Things went from bad to worse. He kept pushing me to hurry up and finish. I think he knew they were going to charge him, knew time was running out. I was tempted to just bag it but, well, Ant wouldn't have allowed that. Not with six serious figures coming his way. Besides, I'd fallen in love with the painting by then. I was hooked, I had to crack it. So I just holed myself up in that cabin where I was working. And then, last Tuesday, I finished. But when I went up to the house to tell him . . . he'd done it. Topped himself. I guess he'd heard he was going to jail, that he wouldn't even get to have his precious painting. I didn't know what to do.'

She looked up suddenly.

'I couldn't believe when I read in the paper the other day that he hadn't died till Saturday. Because he sure looked dead to me. He was whiter than his sheets and the needle was still there, hanging out of his arm. At first I was going to call Ant and tell him to send in the cavalry but then . . . '

Her eyes glazed over in memory.

'You see, while I was working on *The Adoration*, I don't know. Maybe because it was so hard, so good, so honest – it made me realize I didn't want to do this any more.' Sara smiled, as if she were remembering an old troublesome friend. 'I don't know how long it took Apostle to paint, but it was a real bastard to copy. My hardest job ever. I suppose you could say it was my masterpiece. You see, Apostle didn't know what he was doing, not in any technical sense. That was his genius. He just made it up as he went along. With most painters, there's a system you can pick up on. Tricks they've borrowed, techniques they've learned. But with a primitive it's different. Apostle had no formal training, he was just this uneducated preacher. He painted *The Adoration* just before he died, sometime in the eighteen-nineties. He had this vision of Christ coming to the Appalachians . . . '

She was looking toward the window, though her eyes were full of the painting.

'Anyway, copying it, facing its honesty every day, I realized I'd had enough of the lies. Problem was, how was I going to get out of the game? Ant is, well – Ant's a dealer. In every sense of the word. It's not like I could just turn in a letter of resignation.'

David pictured him in the back of the car, drawing those designs in the steam.

'But now that June was dead I thought – what if I just took the original myself? Sold it straight to a buyer. Left the copy in its place, destroyed all traces of what I'd been doing there. Even if Jeter talked no one would ever guess what I was doing. They'd think what you thought – that I was some bimbo. And, as far as they could see, nothing was missing. I knew just the guy, this private collector in New Orleans I'd done a job for, an oil guy who'd always wanted to own an Apostle. There are only a couple of his works out there and they're very hot. I'd tell him the story, make him pay cash on the barrel. He would have, too. He knows me. And no one would ever know except him. And Ant, of course. But there would be nothing he could do once it was sold. After that he'd never find me. Not where I was going with all the money I got, with the tracks I was going to cover. You see, he wouldn't have even known I'd gone until after they found June. Which I figured would be days. Weeks, maybe. Nobody ever came up there. So I went back to my cabin and framed the copy. God, that was a bastard, I had to work so fast and yet be so careful. But I did it. Then I hung it. And after that I burned everything, threw the original in my car and split.'

She shook her head.

'Only what I didn't figure on was wrecking. Even then, though, I thought it would be all right. When you came back to the hospital and I heard where you worked I thought I'd had my break. I could get you to show me where it was and grab the painting. Still make it to the buyer. But then there was that damn flood.'

'So that's why you faked the coma.'

'You can see why I didn't want to explain who I was, what I was doing. Especially since I didn't know if they'd found what I'd stashed. God, it was murder getting it back to that shack after you'd gone for the cops. The last thing I remember was hiding the painting. I didn't have the right packing stuff, you see. It was just rolled up in a cardboard canister.' She shook her head. 'And then I was in the hospital. I almost said something to you when you came the next morning. It was weird – I had a feeling I could trust you. Something about the tone of your voice, the look in your eyes when I saw you for that brief moment. But then that fucking nurse showed. If she hadn't maybe we could have made it in time.'

She looked up.

'So now you can see why I have to go,' she said. 'Ant isn't stupid. He thinks I have this painting which he could get millions for.'

'Millions?'

'Primitives are in, David. That's why he decided to take the job in the end.' She shook her head ruefully. 'No, Ant is not to be fucked with. And then there's this other guy, Decker; he's worse. He used to be a detective. He came to arrest Ant on fraud charges a couple years ago. Two hours later he was an ex-cop working for us. Not a nice guy. And if he finds me it's not going to be so easy convincing him that the painting's a goner.'

'You could show him the crash site, explain . . . '

'And what's to stop them from thinking that isn't faked as well? They know me, David. They know how good I am.'

They sat in silence for a while.

'How did you ever get into this, Sara?' David finally asked.

'God, you tell me.' Her eyes narrowed. 'You see, after Mom died, it was a fucking nightmare. Luckily, I found out in high school I really *could* draw. I guess all that scribbling with her paid off. I started working hard at it and ended up getting a scholarship to the Rhode Island School of Design. Man, that was like another world. David Byrne was there, all of them, though they were a few years ahead of me. I was good at life classes but that wasn't exactly in vogue then. It was all installations, conceptual stuff, performance art. Everybody forming bands. This one guy shot himself in the arm and got a fucking Guggenheim for it. Problem was, I didn't really have the disposition for any of that. I was just this quiet girl drawing her faces and her peaches and her apples. Just a wrist. They let me go after the second year. They were nice about it and everything, tracked me into this restoration gig. I had a definite flair for that. I started out filling in cracks on third-rate oils some stockbroker'd want to hang in his co-op. It was backbreaking work but it really taught me how a painting is put together. I got better, got a bit of a rep, travelled some. Spent six months in Venice, which is sort of the Mecca of restoration. But things there got real bad and then . . . '

She flaked more dried plaster off the serrated edge of her cast. She was lost in the story now, propelled by its momentum.

'And after I came back I got messed up. There was this guy in Italy and, well, he lied to me. I couldn't handle that and I guess I went off the rails. Thought the world was made of lies. Started using everything I could get my hands on. Pills, weed, crank. I was like in a Lou Reed song most of the time. And then Ant found me. He was a hot shit dealer, he hired me to touch up stuff he'd bought. And not just restoration work, either. I'd add things to make paintings sexier, as he put it. Hot air balloons, horses, the odd tit. Or maybe slap on a different signature. We became, you know.'

'You were lovers.'

'Well, I think your verb tense there might be news to our

Anthony. So there I was, sitting pretty in the West Seventies. Ant was really smooth the way he got me into the game. My first few jobs were totally legit. Rich people who'd splashed out on Picassos or whatever and couldn't afford the insurance to keep them in their homes. I'd knock off a copy which they'd hang above the sofa and then they'd stuff the real thing in their safe deposit box. All perfectly above board. And then . . . '

She shook her head.

'You don't know what it was like the first time I saw one of my works sell. *My* work, right? The reserve on it was three something and it ended up going for four-forty. Ant and I were watching the board from an anteroom and we were, we were like kids. And suddenly everything was right with the world. I didn't need dope, didn't need anything except a primed canvas, a couple weeks and a place to hide away. And I could copy *anything*. I got to hand it to Ant in that regard. He got me straight by giving me the chance to be crooked.'

'How many have you done?'

'Thirty-one all told. And I can tell you where every single copy now is. Most of the originals, as well.'

'I don't see how someone doesn't catch on.'

She shook her head.

'You don't understand, David. It's foolproof. Look, let's say you got – all right, let's say it's a Constable you have to copy. Well, you don't just go in and start slapping acrylic on a synthetic canvas. First you got to get the materials. This is where Ant's so good. Because of his contacts he can pick up some piece of shit from that era with the right carbon-fourteen, watermarks, whatever. He has this guy, a chemist we call Poindexter, who strips that painting down, emulsifies the paints, sizes the blank canvas. Then, once he gets the materials all righteous, I'll spend a few days rehearsing, weeks if I have to. Over and over, sketch after sketch. Until I get the lines right, until I get the artist's flow right. Until I *am* the artist. Because you only get one chance with a primed canvas. It's like a perform-ance. It's amazing the things you have to think of.'

She smiled.

'Did you happen to see any peacocks up there?'

David nodded.

'I'd asked June to get me some of their feathers. Because that's what they say Apostle used for his fine quill work. So June went and got a couple of live ones. They weren't so happy when it came time to contribute to the cause.'

She looked at him.

'You see how careful we are? I mean, just getting the paint mix right was a real bastard. At first I brewed up a standard thick impasto thinking that would be all right, but then I discovered it was really this bizarre gouache—'

'Whoa, hold on, you're losing me here, Sara.'

'The paint, David. Our people up in New York had done up a batch for me but it wasn't right. There was something a bit off. I ended up having to make it myself. Apostle used a clay saturate in his mix, you see. Clay and gum. That's how he got those reds, those amazing ochres. And I had to boil down cornflowers for that Carolina sky, hunt out oak galls to use for that inky black. Dallas was helpful, though he didn't know it. He'd find me resin for the varnish, flowers for the color. But it was that clay mixture that was the key.'

'Your shoes . . .'

'My shoes? What about them?'

'They were covered with these red drops. I thought it was . . .'

'What, blood?'

He nodded and she gave a brief laugh.

'Put a leash on that imagination, bub,' she said. 'It was paint.'

'And what about the X-rays? I found them ruined in the fire. I thought . . .'

'They were for the pentimenti.'

David gave a taut, helpless shake of his head.

'You see,' Sara said, 'there's more to a painting than meets the eye. One sure way of telling a copy is that there's nothing beneath it. Most are just painted directly on the canvas. Real works will have all sorts of false starts and fuck-ups beneath them. Pentimenti. Changes of mind, it means. So before you copy a painting you have to X-ray it to see what's underneath. I do exact replicas of them because you never know if someone has a record. Especially now that the Japs are in the market in a big way. They're pretty meticulous about keeping records.'

'Man, you have it all figured out.'

'You don't know the half of it.'

'But I still don't understand. I mean, couldn't people tell the copy's new?'

She shook her head.

'Once it's done, you distress it to make it look old. Bake it, chuck on some phenoformaldehyde, leave it out in the rain. Whatever. You even have to duplicate the major cracks, just in case there's a real accurate photo somewhere. Then you slap on some varnish, distress that, and you're done.'

'And no one can tell the difference.'

She shrugged.

'Well, even if they could, they probably wouldn't look.'

'Why not?'

'Because the provenance is unbroken. You see, that's Ant's *real* genius.'

David gestured helplessly.

'The provenance,' she explained. 'The ownership. If a painting is missing for decades or a new work suddenly appears on the market from a dead artist, then doubts are inevitably raised. Especially after some of the scandals of the past few years, Hebborn and Keating, guys like that. People will feel like they have to check it out. They'll call in so-called experts, but that's no problem, they're easy to scam. It's the scientists you got to worry about. They keep getting better all the time at dating and chemical analysis. But the way Ant sets it up, it's perfect. He just keeps his eyes open until he sees a collector who's in deep shit. Then he approaches him with our little shell game. As far as anyone knows, what's then sold is perfectly legit. The provenance is unbroken. Its whereabouts are always accounted for. I mean, calling in scientists and experts is expensive and besides, most people would rather believe something's real than be told the bitter truth.'

'But I don't get it. I mean, once you've sold the copy, the person who has the original, they have to keep it under wraps, right? Or else the whole deal's blown.'

Sara nodded slowly.

'But what's the use of that?' David asked.

'It makes them love it even more.'

'I don't see it.'

She smiled wryly.

'There are private collections out there you wouldn't believe. A whole alternative tradition. There's this one Caravaggio, *The Nativity of San Lorenzo*. It was stolen in the sixties and now it's gone underground in Sicily. The mafia families pass it among themselves, using it as collateral on their deals. And then there's this guy, this Jap. A couple years ago he spent like a hundred and sixty million dollars on *two* paintings. Count 'em. Two. A Van Gogh and a Renoir. And you know where they are now? Locked away in a safe in Tokyo. And only he has the combo. The most expensive paintings ever sold and there is exactly one set of eyes that can behold them.'

'Hold on,' David said. 'Isn't this the guy who said he's going to have them cremated with him when he dies?'

'You see now?'

He nodded. He did.

'But how did you find June?'

'It wasn't exactly hard. He was a perfect candidate for Ant's scam. Overextended but passionate. Collectors who just see art as an investment are no good for us – why should they part with five or ten points and risk getting busted for fraud just to keep hold of something they don't care about in the first place? Something which has no resale value? But there are others who can't bear parting with this thing they love, who don't care about investments or money. Who just have to have the thing itself, at any cost. Real collectors, not just bankers in oil and watercolor. They're the ones Ant ropes in. He has a real nose for them.'

She rolled her eyes.

'June was the worst I've ever seen. He was utterly obsessed with collecting. Especially the Apostle. That was his baby. He gave Ant an amazing cut so he could keep it. I don't know, it's like he couldn't love it unless he owned it.'

'Didn't I read that he wanted to be a painter?'

'Yeah, he said something about that, though that was a long time ago. I think he had some sort of conflict with his dad, this hard-ass minister. Or maybe he just couldn't cut it. They way he explained it, his collection was his way of revenging himself on the old man, on

232

the world that wouldn't appreciate him as an artist. I sorta knew how he felt, you know? I once asked him if I could see some of his own stuff. He said – you do, my dear. Every day.'

'That's why he sold the company, then,' David said. 'Jesus. So he could have the money to build his own private collection.'

Sara shook her head ruefully.

'He thought he could buy and trade his way up to Guggenheim or Getty level once he had that seed money. But he didn't have what it takes, what people like Ant have. That cold eye. He was something of a legend up in Manhattan, ol' June. He'd just lose it in the auction room. People really saw him coming. Nobody can pull it off when they're bidding for things they crave. That's how Ant spots his prey.'

David looked at her and smiled.

'I just can't believe you thought I wouldn't want to help you if I knew all this.'

'Really?' she asked, her voice suddenly quiet.

'I think it's sort of great, actually.'

She smiled uncertainly, picking at her cast again, sending flakes of plaster to the floor.

'But you're done with all that now,' he said after a while.

'That was the plan.'

'Will you miss doing it?' David asked.

'I'm not going to lie to you,' she said. 'For a while there, it was perfect. But spending so much time with that *Adoration*, seeing the way Apostle worked, without guile, on instinct . . . it's hard to explain. I mean, I'm not going to be doing this until I'm seventy, right? I've got to stop some time. One day somebody's going to slip up, die or get busted, and an original is going to be found in their possession after a copy is hung somewhere else. Two and two will be added and after that happens the party is definitely over. My skills will go toward making license plates. And plus, now Ed's trying to convince Ant to get into artnapping as well.'

'Artnapping?'

'Decker gets someone to steal a painting. They hold it for ransom. And while they do I'd copy it. Then the owner pays up, thinking he's getting back the original. Only the joke's on him. And Ant, meanwhile, has sold it to one of his private clients.'

233

'Jesus, Sara.'

'You see now? You see why I want to get out? So when June killed himself, I figured, why not bolt now, when fate sort of shows up and says, well, sweetie, here's a fortune for the taking.'

'Two boats and a helicopter.'

'What?'

'Do you remember that joke I told you? Back at the hotel?'

It took her a moment, but she remembered. She gave a brief, sardonic laugh.

'I'd settle for just the helicopter.' She looked at him. 'So now you know. You can see why I have to go. Decker's going to come looking. Tomorrow, the next day, whenever. We've been lucky so far but eventually he'll figure out I'm still in town. And he *will* find me.'

'I still don't see why you can't explain about the crash and the flood and . . . '

She was shaking her head.

'You still don't get it. The painting isn't the main consideration here. It's *me* that really matters. What I can do, yeah, but also what I know. Man, I could take you through some museums and collections . . . no, Ant will never cut me loose. Never.'

She looked at him.

'That's why I didn't want you to know, David. Because with these people, knowing is everything. All they have are their secrets and once you mess with those, well, they can be pretty unforgiving.'

'Yeah, I can see that.'

'And so you also can see why I have to get out of here.'

He began to rub his right thumb into his left palm, scrolling up thin strands of oil and dirt from the pores.

'Look, Sara, maybe . . . come on, there's got to be another way than just you going.'

She shook her head obstinately.

'No, listen. What if I found you somewhere else in town to stay? Like we were talking about yesterday. Or maybe I could get you somewhere in the mountains.'

'And what would I do for money?'

'You could find a job. I know graphics people through work. Shit, I don't know. You could change your name or something. Like

234

you said.'

'David—'

'Find a birth certificate of some kid who died, make up a whole new identity. Like in the movies—'

'David—'

'I'm just trying to think of a way to keep helping you.'

'You already have. Getting me out of here. I mean, that was always the point, wasn't it? Helping me get right away. That's why you put me up in the hotel and then here. That's why, right?'

'Things have changed since then.'

'Not for me they haven't. Not in reality. I'm sorry, but that's how it is.'

He stood and walked to the window, looking out at the dark, quiet street.

'I told you from the start how it had to be,' she continued. 'I told you that anything good that was going to happen here was just temporary.'

'I know.'

'Maybe, maybe once I'm wherever I am then you can come see me or . . . God, I don't know, David. Don't make me think about this now. It's hard enough as it is.'

He turned around. Their eyes met.

'Are you still going to get me out of here?'

She was right. When it had just been a broken love affair and a simple theft there was a way. But not now. This was too much for him.

'Yes, Sara. Of course I will. But it's getting too late to do anything today. I haven't been able to . . . look, give me one more night. I know that isn't what we agreed but, just, give me that.'

'But that's all. All right?'

He nodded his agreement, unable for some reason to say the words.

13

Mary Beth's car wouldn't start. David could hear it as he lay in bed, churning over like a great machine digging through the recalcitrant earth. By the time he'd roused himself and stumbled downstairs she already had the keys to the Mustang.

'My car . . . ' she whispered, her voice hoarse.

'I heard.'

'I'm taking yours, all right?'

He hesitated.

'David?' she asked impatiently.

'No problem,' he said, though for some reason he couldn't shake the feeling that it might be.

He called the garage after she left. The wrecker arrived a half-hour later.

'Don't you service this?' the mechanic asked after popping the Honda's hood, his voice tinged with a native disgust of automotive civilians.

'It's my wife's.'

'Ain't you never heard of chivalry?' he shot back.

He diagnosed for a while longer.

'OK, try cuttin' her on now.'

David turned the key. There was a groan, a lurch, then nothing.

'Nope,' the mechanic said. 'Gotta pull her.'

'How long?'

'Tomorrow morning.'

David watched in frustration as the Honda was hoisted. He'd hoped he could get this fixed right away. Now he'd have to call Mary Beth, arrange to get the Mustang from her in order to take Sara to the airport. Resulting, no doubt, in another lie. At least it would be the last one.

After the car was towed he showered, dressed and walked the mile to his office. He took his time. It was a beautiful morning, warm and clear, the sky a perfect, vaporous blue. All the recent rain had left the city violently green. Spore and flying seeds hovered in the air like a light snow; pollen dusted the windshields of parked cars. People had written things on them, the usual obscenities.

When David arrived at work there was no sign of Decker's battered sedan. For a moment he tried to convince himself they had believed him yesterday after all, that their threat had passed. But he knew the odds of that were slim, especially after what Sara had told him last night. No, Decker and Ant were still around. They weren't going to give up on her that easily. David knew he still had to be smart for a few more hours for her to be free.

A specimen of the insert was delivered just after he got to the office, still warm to the touch. He spent a few minutes looking it over. It really was the best thing he'd ever done for Redwine. He leafed through the photos and drawings, his own lively and vapid prose. The shape of things to come, he thought. He took it up to his boss's office.

'Here you go,' David said. 'My masterpiece.'

Redwine's eyes narrowed in satisfaction as he leafed through it.

'This is just fine, David. Just fine.' He began to stroke his beard. 'You done good, son. We really are going to have to look for more for you to do around here.'

David nodded sourly.

'Maybe after the Elk's up and running you me could have a look at how we can get you into the selling end of things. In fact, I got something big in the works you might be just the man for.'

'That would be great, Donnie.'

He started to go.

'Oh, David?'

'Yes?'

'I am going to need that home back on Monday, after all.'

'Yes, all right.'

'Everything worked out over there? Your friend, uh, back on her feet?'

'She's doing great. I'll be helping her move to a new place this weekend.'

Redwine grunted and returned to his work. He didn't care about the details. He just wanted his property back.

David went back downstairs and called the airline. He was

moving robotically now, doing the things he knew he had to do. There was a flight at five that evening. He made a reservation and was told there was a possibility of an upgrade. It was too early to call Tim, though that wasn't a problem. He could be reached later. Tim was set. David checked his watch. Seven hours until her flight. He wanted desperately to spend that time with her, make love to her once more. But that would be too risky, place too much strain on the brittle will he'd summoned to let her go. Best to simply wait until it was time, pick up his car, then head over to Locust Lane. Take her to the airport, put her on the plane.

And then she would be gone.

After that there was just the morning to get through. As he sat in his office, surrounded by the chatter and squawk of the salesmen, he began to wonder if he really could go ahead with this. But the more he thought about it, the more he realized he had no choice. He couldn't keep her around. They'd find her here, he knew that now. They wouldn't give up. They needed her. And he couldn't go with her. There was no way he could simply walk out on his wife without a word of explanation. Besides, if he were to disappear abruptly then Decker and Ant would know what had happened, would be able to follow them. For him to accompany her would place her in greater jeopardy than she was already in. Maybe after she was gone, after Decker and Ant had moved on, he could disentangle himself from this dead town and follow her to wherever she ended up. For now, though, he knew he had to send her on her way. It was time to keep the promise he'd made to her.

Mary Beth called midmorning.

'We're not going to make it,' she said hoarsely.

'What? Who?' David could hear a slight echo of panic in his voice.

'Us. The drive. Who did you think?'

'No, sorry. I didn't . . . '

There was an awkward pause and then he began to speak normally, explaining about her car, telling her he'd need his back for a while later in the day. No problem, she said. They talked for a few moments about his work, she gave him some numbers on the drive. Her anger with him seemed to be passing. David's heart sank as they spoke about these daily things, as he caught a glimpse of the vast plain of drudgery and normality lying ahead of him. Mary Beth said she was going out to lunch with an emergency sponsor, a guy from a local CBS affiliate who might want to talk about a deal that would allow WBRR to stay on the air in an altered format. Which would mean the end of listener supported radio in the greater Burleigh area.

'Shit,' David said.

'Yeah,' she rasped. 'Anway, I'll be back by two.'

'I'll be over after. And hey . . . '

'Yes?'

'Keep the faith.'

If she answered, he didn't hear it.

At noon he popped out for lunch at the drug store down the street where there had been Civil Rights demonstrations in the early sixties. Twenty impossibly mature black kids getting spit on, kicked and beaten by dough-faced rednecks in their letterman sweaters. Framed pictures of them hung on the walls. Their discipline and selfless courage heartened David, giving him some small faith that he really would be able to let Sara go. He looked at the menu. A generation ago people had been risking death over the right to consume weak coffee and starchy grits and now they served International Cuisine, enchiladas and tandoori chicken and tiramisu. Times change, David mused over his chili dog. Change hard and fast.

On the way back he passed the Burleigh Swap. He had an idea. He stepped in, nodding to the big security guard.

'Jewelry?'

'Top floor.'

He walked slowly up the steps, passing tambourines and rocking chairs, microwaves and shotguns. A scratchy record played on the PA. Before the break-up the Swap had been a dingy little pawn shop, its sole window filled with clarinets kids had given up on, china sets nobody wanted to inherit. Since then, however, it had grown to department store dimensions, doing better business than Penneys or Sears out at the mausoleum-like mall.

The third floor was smaller than the lower two, more dimly lit. Four banks of glass cabinets reflected the wan light. David walked up to the clock section, watched by the wiry man who stood behind the counter, his hands locked behind his back, his bushy eyebrows raised in expectation. David slowly removed the watch from his wrist.

'You interested in this?'

The man took it from him, raising his craggy chin as he surveyed it through the lower half of his bifocals.

'Would this be real?'

'The person who gave it to me said so. And she'd know.'

His big eyebrows danced.

'We shall see, we shall see.'

The man removed his spectacles and reached for a magnifying glass. He took his time examining the watch, looking at its face, at the inscripted serial number on its back, the authenticating stamps. As he worked David's attention wandered to his glasses, lying on the counter. A half-dozen strands of yanked eyebrow hair were entangled in the noseguard, their bulbous white roots dewy in the reflected light. David looked back at the man, who was staring at the watch's face now, explaining that the final test for authenticity was to see if the maker's mark was encrypted on the seven o'clock stripe. He let David look with the glass. It was there, invisible to the naked eye.

'Mind if I open it?' the man asked, giving the dial a probationary twist.

'Be my guest.'

He picked up a toy-sized screwdriver and gently levered up the back. He blew gently into its works, grunted, then snapped closed the housing.

'Your friend knows of what she speaks.'

'That she does.'

'One moment, please.'

He disappeared into the back room. David could hear him speaking on the phone. He looked idly down at the display case, crammed with dozens of watches. Something familiar caught his eye. His watch, the one that had been stolen two weeks earlier. It was still ticking, still telling the right time.

'I can give you eighteen hundred dollars for this watch, sir,' the man said when he returned.

'Fine.'

At least she'd have that much.

'How would you like it?'

'Cash, if that's possible.'

'Oh yes, oh yes. That's always possible.'

'Yeah, and how much is this one?' David asked, tapping the glass above his old watch.

'I can let you have that for fifty dollars, sir.'

'Fine. Just deduct it from the total.'

He was about to call Tim when Redwine buzzed him.

'David, can you come up here?'

'Can we make it in about ten?'

He could hear the rustle of his boss's beard against the receiver as he smiled.

'What do you say we make it right now?'

David trudged wearily up the steps, hoping this wasn't important. Working this afternoon wasn't part of the plan. He'd have to get going soon if Sara was to make her flight.

He stopped abruptly as he entered the office. There were two men with Redwine, both sitting with their backs to the door. David immediately recognized the nub of pony tail on the left, the raincoat on the right.

'Ah, here he is.'

Ant and Decker turned.

'I believe you know these guys,' Redwine said, all innocent bonhomie.

Ant stood.

'David. It's been such a very long time. Too long.'

He instinctively took the dealer's outstretched hand. It was small and cold. David tried not to think about it touching Sara.

'Good to see you.'

Decker was standing as well.

'You remember Ed,' Ant said.

Decker didn't extend his hand.

'Your friends and I were just talking property,' Redwine said.

David's heart was pounding.

'Donnie has some quite remarkable things on offer,' Ant said. 'We were admiring your work on the Elk Run development. In fact, we were thinking perhaps of nipping up there and taking a look around for ourselves. As per your suggestion.'

'Tell you one thing,' Redwine intoned. 'We got to get ol' David here on the A Team, he keeps scaring up business.'

Ant laughed heartily, patting David on the shoulder.

'Yes, David has always been something of a go-getter. Well, shall we go? I've made reservations at your Hyatt's half-star restaurant. The manager there was quite unforthcoming this morning as to what a grit is and I was hoping perhaps with your help we could coax the truth out of him.'

David nodded once. Decker was already at the door, rolling his neck. Ant turned to Redwine.

'Well, then. Donnie. It was nice meeting you. I'll speak with my principals and then get back to you.'

'Keep in mind what I said about those points.'

'We'll call.'

'Hey, we'll *deal*,' Redwine said, cocking a finger at Ant.

David walked numbly to the chocolate brown sedan, sandwiched between Ant and Decker, too stunned to do anything else. All he could think was that he wanted them to be far away from Redwine and what he knew. Decker opened the back door and David slid obediently in. The other two got up front, Decker behind the wheel. The deodorizing figure dangled from the rearview mirror. They'd driven a few blocks before Ant turned in his seat.

'Now, David, let's dispense with all the nonsense,' he said. 'Where is she?'

'I don't know what you're talking about.'

'Yes you do,' Decker said, angling the rearview mirror to look at David. 'You soup-sucking little fuck.'

'The woman from the crash?' David's voice sounded small and phony.

'Yes,' Ant said with theatrical weariness. 'That very one.'

'What makes you think I'd know where she is?'

Ant stared at him for several seconds, a vague smile playing over his violet lips. Then he turned to Decker.

'All right, Ed. Carry on.'

Decker sped up, turned abruptly a few times. They wound up on the street of empty shops where he'd found her just over a week ago.

David glanced at the sign with its two kissing silhouettes, thinking for a moment how different things would have been if he hadn't followed her there. If he'd taken her to the hospital or just sent her on her way. At the end of the street they pulled into the parking lot of an abandoned tobacco warehouse, driving across it and through some unhinged bay doors, right into the sun-crossed heart of the ruined building. Curing vats, empty and ruptured, surrounded them. The air was putrid with the smell of rotting wood and rust. A flock of small birds, flushed by the sound of the car, escaped through a jagged hole in the roof.

Decker parked, pulled up the emergency brake and turned around.

'Motel Six,' he said.

David didn't say anything.

'Two nights, our girl, your plastic. Case fucking closed.'

'Now, David,' Ant said. 'Please.'

David sat perfectly still. Decker sighed and got out of the car. He took off his raincoat, folded it carefully into a square, then sat back down in the driver's seat.

'David?' Ant asked.

'All right, look,' David said. 'There's no need for any of this.'

'Agreed. But none the less, here we are.'

'Ant?' Decker was pleading. 'Thirty seconds, max. Personal best. Clock me.'

His mind focused by the threat of imminent violence, David suddenly knew what he had to say.

'She's gone.'

Ant's eyes narrowed.

'Now what makes you say that?'

'Because I helped her go.'

'You did.'

David looked into the vast, dead space around them, his mind racing now.

'OK, listen. Two days after the crash I did see her walking around town. She'd left the hospital, she was in real bad shape. I knew something was wrong but . . . but I helped her for a few days anyway, paid for that hotel room, got her something for the pain. What you have to understand is that she said she was alone, that she

243

was broke. And she said there was some reason she couldn't go back to the hospital. We drove up to where the crash had been, she thought maybe all her stuff was there. But it was flooded out.'

'What stuff?' Decker asked.

'She never said. I assumed it was just her purse. Money, i.d., stuff like that.'

'This is a steaming pile of horseshit,' Decker protested. 'You could pick the straw out of this.'

'Go on, David,' Ant said.

'I told her she could use my phone but she said there was no one to call. It wasn't hard to see she didn't want anyone to know where she was. Maybe I should've called the cops or something but . . . '

'But?'

'But I decided to help her out. She was so . . . I gave her some money so she could recover for a few days. I looked after her, brought her food and medicine. Then I put her on a plane.'

'Where?'

'Atlanta. The nearest hub. She said she'd decide where she was going when she got there.'

'How come I can't find any record of this?' Decker asked.

'I paid with cash,' David said, his confidence growing. 'My company card was maxed out and . . . well, I didn't want to use my personal one.'

'Do you know what she was calling herself when she made this flight to freedom?'

'Sara something. I don't remember.'

'Why the fuck didn't you tell me this on Tuesday?' Decker asked, a rogue vein squirming on his temple.

'Because she asked me not to,' David said sharply. 'She said some people might be coming after her who she didn't want to see. Creeps, I think was the term she used. So when you show up I'm thinking, I don't know this guy. That's why I carded you. If you'd have been a cop maybe I would have told you, I don't know.'

'Do you know that she had something of mine with her?' Ant said. 'Do you know you've helped a thief?'

'The last time I saw her she didn't have anything with her but some second-hand clothes.'

'So why were you so fucking generous?' Decker asked.

244

'How many times do I have to say it. I felt responsible.'

'And so there was nothing in it for you?' Ant asked. 'She didn't promise you anything?'

David shook his head.

'This is a crock,' Decker moaned. 'Let me tune this douche bag up, we got him here.'

'Look', David said, 'if you don't believe me why don't you go up there, where the crash was. I'll draw you a map. I'm sure you'll find whatever it is you're looking for under five feet of the Mud River. Just bring along some flippers and a blow dryer.'

'Where were you the last few days?' Ant asked, his voice less edgy. 'We tried to follow you but you kept on disappearing into the great unknown.'

'Working,' David said. 'Redwine's been busting my balls. You've met him.'

'So why'd you ditch the 'stang?' Decker asked.

'My wife's borrowing it today,' David said in cool triumph. 'Her car's in the shop.'

They sat in silence for a long time. The roused birds were returning to their roosts.

'All right,' Ant said finally. 'I believe you. I'm sorry for the melodrama, David. We're not violent people. Just anxious. You did what you thought you had to do and I respect that. You weren't to know the facts of the matter, otherwise you would have no doubt done something else. As far as you're concerned you helped a pretty woman in trouble, helped her get away from a couple of, um, creeps.' His violet lips formed a wan smile. 'It's just a shame there aren't more people like you out there.'

He turned to Decker.

'Ed?'

'Yeah, sure, the story holds, but I still think this prick should answer for what he did to us.'

Ant smiled at David.

'You'll have to forgive Ed. He's an enthusiast. No, David's intentions were pure.' He laughed grimly. 'I guess that's why we found his behavior so confusing.'

Decker started the car, gunning the engine, swearing to himself. The vein on his temple was writhing like a bagged snake beneath his skin. He whipped the car through the warehouse, trying to flatten a landed bird, just missing it. They drove the short distance back to the Redwine Group in silence. When they got there Ant turned and offered David his small, cold hand.

'Look, Mr Webster, sorry to take up so much of your time. You can see how this thing looked to us. No hard feelings, all right?'

David shook hands with the man, wanting to make everything seem normal.

'We won't be troubling you again,' he said.

'No problem.'

He started to get out of the car.

'Hey, fuckface,' Decker said. 'Aren't you going to wish us good luck?'

'I don't think so,' David said quietly.

Decker's laughter followed him as he crossed the street. He stepped on what was left of the dead pigeon. It was road smooth, as hard as rock.

'Oh, and David?'

He turned. Ant was smiling at him, gesturing with a crooked finger for him to return.

'One more thing.'

David walked warily back to the car.

'Look, I'm sorry about this, but in our eagerness this morning I'm afraid we paid your wife a visit. You see, when Ed saw that she was driving the Mustang and you were late to work, well, we feared the worst. So we went over, thinking she might have a clue to your whereabouts.'

'What did you say to her?' David asked.

Decker was giggling uncontrollably.

'Nothing but the truth,' Ant explained with mock innocence. 'Just that you'd put a young woman up in a cheap hotel for a few nights. She seemed dubious at first, bless her cotton socks, but your signature on the receipts Ed had secured brought her around.'

Decker was pounding the steering wheel, gnawing a bony knuckle, gasping for air.

'Of course,' Ant continued, '*we* know you're innocent of any wrongdoing, but I still think you might want to have a word with her. Looked at the wrong way this . . . '

David was already running. It took less than five minutes to get to WBRR. The 'Ten Days of Giving' banner sagged above the front door, its words folded into near-illegibility. The big cardboard thermometer still registered several feet below the goal. The receptionist buzzed him through the inner security doors. Nearly a dozen people sat around the pledge table, most of them speaking on phones. Their voices were tense, irritable. The drive would be over at noon the next day. Then would come the reckoning. He looked beyond the pledge-takers to the soundproof broadcasting booth where Mary Beth sat. She was on air. David could hear her muted, rasping voice on the loudspeaker. He waited until she was finished before knocking gently on the window. When she looked at him her eyes seemed blank. He let himself in. In the next room two men in headphones watched them.

'Mary Beth?'

She didn't answer. There were two small bulbs on her panel, red and green. The red was lit. He sat beside her, looking at the panel in front of them, its buttons and meters and dials. The microphone's bent arm hovered in front of her face, like it was about to choke her.

'Look, I can explain those guys . . . '

She swallowed. It seemed to hurt her. The men in headphones continued to stare. David wondered if they could hear this.

'It's just, God, I don't know where to start . . . '

And then he could see in her eyes that she knew everything. All the pieces had finally fallen into place. The story he'd just told Ant and Decker would be no use here.

'Go on,' she said, her voice a hoarse whisper.

David looked at the red light. It was nearly a minute before he could say anything.

'It, I just wanted to help her. That's the thing you have to understand here. Everything else stems from that. I mean, she was hurt, you know? I saw her walking around the street after she left the hospital. She had nothing. Nothing. And so I got her that hotel room. She couldn't really stay there so I got a house for her, this empty place. And—'

'You've been fucking her there.'

'Mary Beth, that isn't what I'd planned.

'That's why you wouldn't touch me the other night.'

David didn't say anything. Her voice sounded awful. He just wished she'd stop talking.

'Who is she?'

'Mary Beth, look, just stop hurting your voice. It's no use. I can't explain any of this.'

She laughed bitterly.

'As if that's what I want. An explanation.' She was speaking so softly he could barely hear her. 'You're pathetic, you know? You've always had this pathetic streak in you. I'm sure you think it's some dark corner of your soul but it's just . . . pathetic.'

'She's going away,' he said. 'I'm sending her away. Today. It's all arranged.'

She was staring at the panel.

'Look, Mary Beth, I've made a mistake. She's going to leave. I won't even see her again. I'll get Rowdy to do it, pick her up and take her to the airport. She's going to be out of our life.'

'Our life?'

'We got about sixty seconds here,' one of the men announced over the PA.

She took a sharp breath, summoning words from some deep verbal well.

'Oh, I get it. So now you've had your fling and you're going to come home and things are going to be strained between us for a while but eventually we'll be all right. Just like before.'

The words came through her throat like scraping fingernails.

'But they won't,' she continued. 'Not really. Not this time. We'll be like those couples you see who have this, this thing between them. Like Rowdy and Cath. And everyone can see it and everyone knows what it is and that means that somebody has to live in this state of perpetual humiliation.'

She shook her head.

'Remember, David? How we were going to be different? Have something real, not some compromise, not some deal—'

'Mary Beth, stop,' David said.

'About thirty here.'

Her eyes flashed.

'Just go. You've humiliated me. Not just physically. You've humiliated me by saying that everything I can give, every iota of my

248

heart and mind, my best years, isn't enough for you. It's just what you did while you were waiting for your grand passion to rumble down the highway.'

The music ended. The light above the mike remained red.

'Dead air, Mary Beth,' the technician said. 'I'm not going to switch over to you until you say.'

'Get out of here,' she said. 'Just . . . '

And then she gave a brief, keening screech. Her voice was gone. She buried her face in her hands and she was crying. David reached out to touch her heaving shoulder but before he could there was someone sitting between them, another deejay, his mouth close to the mike. The small light turned from red to green.

'OK, we're back,' he said, his voice mellow, liquid. 'Sorry about that pause, folks . . . '

David got up and left the booth. He headed quickly for the nearest door, passing the storage room where they had come the week before to make love. He eased open the emergency exit and stepped into an alley. The door slammed just as he realized he'd forgotten to get the keys to the Mustang. He tried it. Locked. He would have to go around front to get back in, have to face his wife again. And he knew he couldn't do that.

He looked around the alley. Its brick walls were covered with the illegible hieroglyphics of young vandals. Out front, someone began to lean on a horn. It seemed to go on forever. And then it stopped, its echo dying quickly. When it was quiet again David started to run. He sprinted to the end of the alleyway and then began heading northwest, toward Locust Lane. He moved as fast as he could, jumping fences, walking through the lobbies of underpopulated hotels, cutting across parking lots, bolting over empty streets. He was soon out of downtown, charting a course through the mowed lawns of some residential district. Dogs barked or gave brief chase, people working their gardens looked up in alarm. He had to stop once to ask directions, another time to drink from a hose. Halfway there, he walked for a stretch, kneading his cramped side. He made it in the end, though. All five miles to Locust Lane.

'Look what the cat dragged in,' Sara said when he staggered through the door. 'Where have you been?'

He collapsed on the sofa, exhausted and elated.

'David?'

'There's a new plan.'

Her smile wavered.

'Oh yeah? What now?'

'We're going to spend the night here and then in the morning I'm going to get us a car. And then we'll go.'

'We?' she said.

'That's right.'

'As in . . . ?'

'You and me.'

The idea had come to him while he was running. There would be no flight, no Tim. He would go with her. There was no longer any reason to stay now that Mary Beth knew. It was all so simple. They'd spend the night at Locust Lane, and then, in the morning, he'd collect the Honda from the garage and they'd slip quietly out of town. Even if Decker and Ant were still around they'd have no way of tracking him. He'd take nothing with him but the clothes on his back. He'd leave everything else. At some point, when they were far enough way, they could dump the car, buy a new one.

And then there would be no tracing them. They could start over. Everything would be new, there would be no past left to chase them, to haunt them. They could give themselves different names. Recreate themselves. Forge a new life together. A real life, not some compromise.

'Sara?'

'Where would we go?' she asked uncertainly.

'Anywhere. We'll just drive until we get there.'

'And what about your wife and your job and . . . '

David just shook his head. She stared at him for a long time, then looked away.

'Are you sure you want to do this?' she asked.

'I am.'

'All right,' she said. 'Yes. All right.'

She smiled.

'I didn't want to say anything but . . . '

'But what?' he asked.

'Well, I hate flying.'

*

He woke up in a quiet hour, somewhere in the middle of the night. Sara was sleeping beside him – they had wound up on the floor, on a loose bed of clothes and blankets and cushions. He felt a momentary jolt of panic, thinking that he had to get dressed, hurry home. But then the day's events came back to him. There was nowhere to go. This was where he was supposed to be.

He looked at her for a long time in the weak light, at her occasionally quivering eyes and half-open mouth. Her right arm was resting across his naked abdomen. He stroked it gently, remembering how swollen and pale it had been when he'd unwrapped it a few days earlier. His touch woke her.

'Your wrist seems better,' he said.

She closed her eyes and nestled closer.

'It is. I'm going to stop taking those pills when we get where we're going.'

'Really?'

'Yeah, I think I'm going to take a permanent vacation from chemicals.'

'So it was bad.'

She sighed and shook her head.

'We don't have to talk about—'

'No, it's all right,' she said. 'Yeah, it was always bad. Though I didn't begin to use heavily until after Venice. Before then it was just, you know, party time. I'd have some of whatever was being passed around. But when I was in Italy somebody hurt me and I guess I just sort of came off the rails.'

'What happened?'

Her eyes were open now.

'What happened. Well, there was this guy. Marcantonio. Marco. He was a painter, a good one too. Had some stuff at the Biennale. We met, you know, however people meet. He wasn't your typical *ragazzo*, he didn't have all the blustery bullshit about him. He was quiet, sorta shy. This is what I thought. We became lovers, we got a place together, out on the Giudecca, away from all the tourists, from everything. I was twenty-one, old in some ways but real young in others. I was working long hours during the day, and at night . . . well, let's just say the nights were good. Like these. It was just us. This was in the winter, when you can take Venice.'

251

She was silent for a while.

'I guess he was the first, I mean who was something more than just a simple boyfriend or a roll in the hay. It sort of sneaks up on you and then, wow, you're a goner. But don't get me wrong, it was good for a while there. He said he loved me, all that. We went everywhere together, couldn't keep our hands off each other. And then he lied to me. I mean, here I was, this supposedly street-smart girl, and I fell for his bullshit like some shitkicker from Peoria. I used to laugh at all those *turisti* chicks who would be conned and yet . . . I guess he was just dealing me a more refined line. So some people told me I should open my eyes and I didn't listen to them at first but then one night I decided to follow him. It was a real dark night, foggy. Following him wasn't easy. But I did. And sure enough. What made it really galling was that she was an American too, this rich babe I'd seen around, a collector who bought for some museum out in LA. She opened the door and pulled him into the light and I knew. I knew. And what was worse was that in that instant she could see me, too. And there was no surprise in her eyes. Just this smirk. She knew all about me. I was their little joke.'

She shook her head.

'I started to walk, I don't even know where. It was so spooky, foggy and quiet, like only Venice can be. And I turned this corner and there were these strange lights and voices and this dull ugly sound, like waves slapping against rocks. It wasn't until I came right upon them that I saw what these guys were doing. They had these big flashlights pointed down into the water, waiting for squid to surface. They were attracted to the light, the poor suckers. They'd just pop right up. And then the men would reach in real quick and grab them, not even using nets. And in the same quick motion they'd swing them against the stones. Real hard, so the heads would explode. They did one just as I was passing – I'll never forget the sound, never forget how the ink splattered all over my legs.

'The guys looked up at me and started to talk their talk and for a moment I thought why the fuck not. But then I just turned around and ran. I didn't run home, no way was I going back there. Instead I went to where I worked. I let myself in, it was just me. I'd been restoring a Pontormo that had been damaged in a flood and I was just about finished with it. Man, I must have been really crazy because I just took a knife and went after it. I mean it was like *Psycho*. Demolished it. And then I just bolted. I was on the Lido when the carabinieri finally caught up with me the next day. They put me in a hospital out there. Leather restraints, Librium, the whole nine yards. Shaved my head. Yeah, we had a blast. I used to lie there and watch the lizards on the walls, the ceiling. They're good at staring matches, those lizards.'

Her eyes narrowed.

'That's where I learned to play possum so well. After a while I could beat anything they had. Smelling salts, pin pricks. Nothing could wake me unless I wanted to. Because people kept coming with their questions. My boss, sweet old Dottore Pignatti, I broke his heart for sure. A priest, psychiatrists. People from our own beloved embassy, who, by the way, were the only ones who treated me shitty in the whole deal. Finally this prosecutor came to see me, this young guy with long lashes. I talked to him, he looked all right. He said, "What are we going to do with you, signorina? Why did you do it?" So I told him the truth. The whole story. When I was done he just nodded and closed his folder. Made perfect sense to him. You gotta hand it to the Italians. Three days later I was on a flight home. Deported.

'Only when I got there it wasn't like there was a reception committee at JFK. The people back in Venice had kept what I'd done out of the papers but you can believe I wasn't going to find work again. The word was out. I started hanging around SoHo, living with guys, terrible guys, Warhol holdovers, Eurotrash. Doing lots of dope. Another ghost in the city. Then I ran into Ant, or I guess I should say he ran into me. We'd known each other a little, he'd heard my story. So we got together.'

She laughed bitterly.

'You know why I did it? Went with him?'

'Why?'

'Because of the work, yeah, but more because of something he told me. He said he'd never lie to me. And you know what? He never has. Ironic, isn't it?'

They lay still for a long time.

'Sara . . .'

'Hmmm.'

He sat up and looked down at her, tempted for a moment to tell her about Ant and Decker, confess that he'd broken his promise. Tell her that he'd done it to be with her, to make this possible. Protect her. But that would be foolish. It didn't matter now. Ant was history. They were free.

'What is it, David?'

'No, it's just, I almost forgot.'

He found his jacket amid the scrum of discarded clothes and took the money from its pocket.

'What's that?'

'Two thousand bucks, just about.'

'Jesus, where'd you get that?' she asked.

'I sold the watch.' He smiled. 'You were right. It was the real thing.'

14

David walked quickly through the unfamiliar neighborhoods. He was going the long way, avoiding places where he might run into someone he knew, orienting himself on the small cluster of downtown towers. It was a normal Saturday morning in Burleigh, busy but languid, as if people didn't really care whether or not they reached their destinations. Kids joked their way to Little League games, yard sales were being laid out on driveways and lawns, recycling trucks made halting progress down quiet streets. David barely noticed any of this, though. He might as well have been in Miami or Calcutta. All he could think about was Sara, about the way it felt to wake up with her next to him, about the fact that they would soon be going away together. The city was a mirage – it was like he was already gone.

It took him almost an hour to reach the garage, only to find that the car was still on the rack. His irritation quickly passed when he realized there was no hurry. Sara wasn't going anywhere without him. Not now. A few minutes wouldn't make any difference. He went into the shabby little reception room, pouring himself a cup of coffee and taking a seat. There was a copy of that morning's *Record* on the cluttered table at his knee. Cathy's feature dominated the front page. David smiled to himself – there was nothing she could tell him about Will June. Nothing anyone could tell him. Not now. Only the odd line registered as he skimmed the type. 'Lonely soul surrounded by wealth he could never enjoy.' 'A death witnessed only by unblinking eyes of paint and clay.' Typical Cathy, David thought. Apostle's *Adoration* was visible in the background of the poorly separated color photo on the front page. Man, if only they knew, he thought.

The receptionist interrupted him with the invoice. He paid it out of the money from the watch, then opened the paper to see the rest of the June photos. There was the sacrificial urn, the peacocks, the view. The last photo was typical Cathy – she'd managed to convince the Ivanhoe sheriff to let her reproduce part of June's suicide note. David shook his head, marveling at her ability to wrangle stories out of thin air. He read the fragment they'd printed.

And so I have decided to end my own life rather than let my detractors and persecutors achieve the satisfaction of seeing me wind up in the one place I never dreamed I'd be – behind bars. If I am a criminal then we are all criminals together. What I have done was well within the law, written and especially unwritten, of our times.

David stared at the note for a long time, trying to picture June writing it, trying to imagine what kind of despair would drive a man to kill himself. Especially when he was so close to getting away with the thing he loved most. Then, something clicked in David's mind. June's small handwriting. It looked familiar. Where had he seen it before? He racked his brain, trying to place that scrawl. Pressurized air sighed in the garage. David looked up. The Honda began its slow progress back to earth. It was time to go.

He took one last look at the photo and that's when it hit him. He jumped to his feet, knocking over a gumball machine as he backed away from the newspaper. It shattered loudly, sending colored balls everywhere. But David's eyes were locked on the note. Jesus Christ, he thought. Jesus Christ.

'Hey, buddy?'

It was the mechanic. He looked at David, at the spilled gum, back at David.

'She's all set.'

'Who?'

'The Honda.'

David nodded.

'What was the problem in the end?' he asked numbly.

The man lifted a carburetor. With the dangling wires and viscid black grease it looked like a severed head. David snatched the keys from the mechanic's free hand and ran to the garage.

'Hey, what about all this gum?'

He drove quickly to the newspaper, parking illegally, explaining at reception that he was going to the production department to check on the insert. They nodded him through, accustomed to his presence. No one paid him any attention downstairs – they had the Sunday edition to put together. He walked quickly past the sloping graphics desks and the colorized computer screens, stopping at the bin where the photographs from that day's edition were kept for filing. Let it still be here, he thought. He looked through the pile. A three-car crash, a forlorn young woman watching a deformed child play, two men cradling a giant squash. Something from the flood – a snapping turtle dozing in a recliner chair. And then he saw the June pictures. Peacocks, the urn, and, at the very bottom, the note.

'David, what can I do you for?'

It was Coy Wilkes, the photo editor. They'd been fighting about the color separations on the insert and Wilkes sounded like he wasn't about to do anyone any favors, least of all David.

'I was just looking for some of our pictures,' David said, slipping the photo under his jacket before he turned. 'Donnie wants them for a display.'

'Can't it wait until Monday?' Wilkes asked peevishly.

'No prob,' David said. 'I was just in the neighborhood.'

He walked quickly for the exit before anyone could notice the stolen photo. It was a thirty second drive to the Redwine Group. He locked himself in his office, tearing out his desk drawer and dumping its contents on to the desk. Pens, schedules, letters. As he rooted through the mess he remembered what Sara had said about how she copied pictures. How she did sketch after sketch, again and again, until they were perfect. Until she lived the lines. Until she was the other person.

He finally found it, wedged inside the carry-out menu from the Bottomless Cup. *the spirit of.* He placed the fragment of charred paper next to the photo. They had only printed one of the six paragraphs from the note in the paper – it was boxed off on the photo by blue pencil. David began to read the parts they hadn't printed. What he was looking for was right there at the top of the page.

I do not understand why I am being hounded like this. I am simply a businessman who behaved in keeping with the spirit of the times. If what I've done is a crime then . . .

David moved the fragment to the top line, placing it flush with the words it echoed. They were a perfect match.

She was pacing the front room, ready to go.

'I was beginning to think you'd had second thoughts,' she said when he came through the door. 'It's been hours.'

'They were late fixing the car,' he said softly.

'But it's all right now?'

He sat on the sofa without answering. Her face froze in concern as she perched beside him.

'David?'

He couldn't say the words. In the end he simply placed the charred fragment and the photo of the note beside her on the sofa.

'What's all this?' she asked, staring down at his evidence. 'What have you been doing?'

'You did it, didn't you?'

She looked up at him.

'What do you mean?'

'You killed June.'

She looked away. Her right hand started worrying the edge of her cast.

'You killed June,' David repeated. 'You shot him up with insulin while he was drunk or asleep, I don't know. You knew all about needles from your junkie days, didn't you? You'd already forged a check to get rid of Jeter. And then you faked the suicide note. As only you can. It took you several tries to get it right. To live the lines. This,' he said, holding up the fragment, 'is from one of the dry runs.'

She looked at him, shaking her head slowly.

'You fool,' she said quietly.

'What?'

She smiled sadly.

'Of course I killed Will June. What do you think? That he just up and died at the right moment? That's not how things work, David. Not in my experience.' She looked away, her eyes narrowing. 'He was a goner, anyway. You saw the place. Fucking greedy pig. I hated him. And it was so . . . it was so easy.'

'But why didn't you tell me?'

'Why do you think? So you'd keep helping me. My lie, David, made all this possible. And when we became lovers I wanted to protect you. In case they found out, in case everything went wrong. You could honestly say that you didn't know. And then when you said we'd go away together . . . ' She shook her head bitterly. 'God, it would have been so perfect if you hadn't pressed, if we could have spent this morning just driving. If only you'd believed me, we'd have been all right.'

'But it wasn't true,' he said quietly.

'So what?'

He was beginning to realize the mistake he'd made.

'Look, what if I said it doesn't matter,' he tried.

'Then you'd be lying, too. I know you, David. That's why I tried to hide it from you. You like to be close to it but you could never last once you were in it. I know you.'

He looked down at the sofa. White plaster now covered the photo. He gently brushed it away. What have you done? he thought. What have you done? His mind raced wildly, looking for a way to put this right.

'No,' she said, the bitterness in her voice replaced by fear.

David looked up. Sara's face was blank, her stunned eyes fixed on the front door. Before he could turn to see what it was something else grabbed his attention. Ed Decker, stepping in from the kitchen.

'Hey, it was open,' he explained.

David turned. Ant stood by the auction sign, smiling at Sara.

'Hello, um, what is it we're calling ourselves these days?'

'Sara,' Decker answered.

'Ah yes. Sara.'

David stood up quickly, uncertain what to do. Decker moved closer.

'Just try it, fuckwad,' he said, rolling his neck until it cracked.

'So where is it you two were thinking of going?' Ant asked, taking a few steps into the room. 'Because we can give Sara a lift. I'll just *bet* we're heading in her direction.'

No one said anything. Ant looked at David.

'I just came from a meeting with your boss, David. It was quite an ordeal – four cups of piss-poor coffee and an hour of bloody racing stories. I really thought I had him, though. It dawned on me not long after we dropped you off yesterday, you see. As plain as day. You work for a property developer. Where else would you hide her? So after you so cunningly gave us the slip at your wife's radio station I thought, why not just inquire of Mr Donnie Redwine?'

Sara looked up sharply at David. He took a few instinctive steps away from her.

'But we couldn't pin him down until this morning,' Ant continued. 'Imagine how nervous that made us, especially since you'd apparently vanished. But when the time came to pop the question, ever so subtly, to explain there had been a change in our plans and we had to go early, that we just *couldn't* leave without saying goodbye to our old friend – he wouldn't tell. Oh, he was quite sympathetic but he said he'd given you his word that he wouldn't disclose, what did he call it, your little deal. That he couldn't break a confidence.' Ant shook his head quizzically. 'Funny where you find integrity these days, eh? We thought that was it, you'd done it, got away. We were just getting in the car to leave when who should we see but our Mr Webster himself racing into his office, looking ever so anxious. So much so that he didn't even notice us. We waited until you came out and we followed you in your funny new car and, well, here we all are. Together at last.'

'Me, I'd a kept the 'stang,' Decker offered. 'Those are some serious wheels.'

'Actually, your story about having sent her away was pretty good, David,' Ant continued. 'I should have believed it. But then I guess I understand how these things work. I could see that covetous glint in your eye. I'm an expert at that look. After all, it's how I keep body and soul together. You never were going to let her go, were you? Not from the minute you had her spirited away. The minute you knew she was yours.'

'You know him?' Sara finally asked. 'David?'

'We've been having discussions with Mr Webster for quite a while now. Four days.'

'Five,' Decker said.

David looked down at her, shaking his head, unable to think what to say. He'd taken a few more steps back, so that he was almost in a corner of the room.

'You bastard,' she said. 'You fucking promised me.'

'I thought . . .' He didn't know the end of the sentence.

'David should take some lessons from Donnie Redwine on keeping promises, it would seem,' Ant said.

'You've been lying all along,' she said coldly, her eyes still on

David. 'You come in here all bent out of shape and now, Jesus, five fucking days. That means all the time we were . . . '

Ant moved over to the sofa, sitting beside her. David flinched and Decker moved closer.

'Easy, you yuppie fuck.'

'Can I look at your arm?' Ant asked her.

She let him take her cast gently in his hands, the anger she'd just shown David dissipating rapidly.

'Does it hurt?' he asked softly.

'Not so much any more.'

'I can't tell you how relieved I am to see it's your left arm. When I heard you'd broken a wrist I thought it might be your drawing hand.'

'No, that's fine,' she said, her voice barely audible now. 'All healed.'

'That's marvelous news.'

He read what David had written on the cast and gave a brief, dismissive laugh.

'How touching.'

He read the other inscription, then looked at Sara.

'And who is this Scott Todd?'

'Just . . . never mind.'

'Ed?' he asked.

Decker shrugged.

'Sara, what the hell are you doing here?' Ant asked, his voice still gentle.

She cast a sidelong glance at him, nervously replacing a strand of hair behind her ear.

'I just, look Ant, I was just sick of it. I just wanted out.'

'I can understand that. June's death must have been a shock for you.'

Decker gave a brief, sneering laugh. Ant silenced him with a look.

'You weren't thinking straight, I know that,' he continued. 'Look, maybe we can take a little break or something. We'll go down to the place on St Thomas.'

'A break is not what I meant.'

'But Sara, even if you did get away from us – what were you going to do?'

'I don't know. Something else. Anything.'

'I see. And how long do you think it would be before you had your twentieth nervous breakdown, eh? How long do you think it would be before you started poking things into yourself again, scorching that pretty little nose?'

'I was . . . ' She was looking confused. 'He was going to help me.'

Decker snorted again, unrestrained by Ant this time.

'Him?' Ant asked, pointing a thin finger at David without taking his eyes from her. 'He doesn't know you, Sara. He doesn't know what you need to keep going. He doesn't know what you love, like I do.'

He put one of his small hands on her good arm.

'I told you, didn't I? They'll all lie to you. Except me. I was right, Sara, wasn't I?'

She nodded faintly. He looked around.

'Now I suppose we should sort out where my painting is, and then we can vacate the premises.'

'There is no painting,' David said from his corner. 'It was destroyed in the flood.'

'Gimme a shovel,' Decker said. 'Oh man, gimme a fucking shovel.'

He began to look through the things she'd packed, kicking around the camping gear.

'He's right,' Sara said. 'There is no painting. It's ruined.'

'Now how am I supposed to believe that?' Ant asked.

'If it wasn't do you think I'd still be here?' she asked, her voice barren of emotion. 'With him?'

Decker stopped his search.

'Ouch,' he said.

'No,' Ant said, smiling up at David. 'I imagine you're right.'

Sara was looking at David now as well, with the same clinical glare he'd seen those first few days. Though this time there was no question in it, no curiosity. Just total knowledge and utter contempt.

'Sara . . . ' David said.

'That's not my name,' she said flatly.

Ant took a deep breath.

'Well, it would seem Mr Apostle's masterpiece is a write off. Pity.

262

It's quite fashionable. Not to worry. There's always plenty of work for the industrious.' He stood. 'Now then – shall we go? Sara? Don't worry, love. You can take all the time you need to get over your little adventure. We'll start you back slowly. Maybe find a Mondrian or a Rothko for you to do.'

To David's horror, she managed a thin smile.

'Tell her about the slope,' Decker said.

'Ah, I almost forgot – my sources on the Ginza tell me the sublime Mr Saito is about to be arrested. Bribery or something like that. I'm going to make a preliminary approach to his people next week, see if he might be interested in our services. You've always wanted a crack at our Vincent, Sara. Only this time I think Ed should come along to make sure you don't have any more accidents.'

'Yeah, I already got me a set of chopsticks,' Decker said.

Ant noticed something on the mantle. The pills. He picked up the brown vial and looked at Sara, rattling them.

'Now what the hell is this?' he said, anger in his voice for the first time.

Sara nodded to David.

'He got me those. For the pain. I've been tranked out all week. That must be why . . . '

She didn't finish the sentence. Ant looked at David, tipping his head.

'You're good, Mr Webster,' he said coldly. 'A fast study.'

'You can leave them,' Sara said. 'I won't need them any more.'

Ant put them back.

'No, I imagine you won't.'

He offered her a hand. She took it and stood. David knew he had to do something.

'I'm not going to let you do this,' he said. 'I'll call the cops or . . . '

Decker stepped closer, nodding enthusiastically, his hands held flat.

'Or what, asswipe? You gonna go for it? Come on, Ant. Let me organize this guy.'

'Ed, please. David's on our side in this thing, whether he knows it or not. He won't be telling anyone anything. He's as guilty as the rest of us. Besides, I don't think he really wants to send Sara to prison. And even if he were so inclined – where's his proof?' Ant flashed his sickly smile. 'Look, David, I really do want to thank you. For a moment there yesterday I was frightened you'd done the decent thing, that you really had helped her go. And that would have made our job a lot more difficult. Impossible, perhaps. But now—'

'Let's go, if we're going,' Sara interrupted. 'I'm sick of this fucking place.'

And then she simply left, walking toward the door, passing by David without even glancing at him. Ant followed a step behind her.

'Sara,' David said. 'Wait, you can't go now.'

'Listen to this,' Decker said.

She kept walking.

'No, wait . . . '

'David, please, the show's over,' Ant said, pausing by the auction sign. 'Take your very little car and go home.'

They disappeared out the door. David started to follow them but then Decker was there, something small and black in his hand. David took another step and there was a noise like a gas stove being switched on. The next thing he knew he was lying amid the scattered pieces of the blank puzzle. His nerves hummed and his brain's synapses fired crazily, images and voices flashing by like rapidly switching channels. Somehow he found the energy to raise himself to his knees. But, before he could stand, there was that click again. And then there were no voices, no images. Just a long slope of darkness for him to roll down.

When he finally woke he could hear someone talking. It took him a few moments to realize that the radio was on. He listened without moving. It was the deejay who'd stepped between him and Mary Beth the previous day.

'Come on, we're still a bit, well, we're down on our goal here with just, look, just an hour to go. Come on, now. This is important, people.'

David struggled to his knees, the sudden elevation making him dizzy. He remained still for a moment, gradually feeling something wet on his face. He touched it. Blood stained his fingertips, sourced by an inch-long gash beside his right eye. He picked up one of the abandoned shirts and pressed it to the wound, which responded with a sharp, waking pain. He stood and walked woozily to the door, the taser's jolts still flickering through his body's electrical system. He'd been out for a while – a fresh layer of pollen coated the Honda, the sun was approaching its apex. He briefly contemplated driving after them but he wouldn't have known where to start looking, wouldn't have known what he was going to do in the one-in-a-million chance he found her.

He turned back into the house, realizing that there was something sticking to his blood-wet face. A piece of the white puzzle. He peeled it off and threw it on the floor, then collapsed on the sofa, still holding the shirt to his cut. The radio began to crackle and fade – the batteries were running down. Rogue spasms played through his muscles, his head was a matrix of random pain. He listened to the dying music for several minutes before he could summon enough energy to stand. Slowly, meticulously, he gathered every-thing they'd used, everything they'd touched, piling it all on the old sofa. The clothes, the camping gear, the brilliant blanket. The photo and the bit of paper. Everything. The straw, the puzzle, the remaining food. When he was done he tossed on the bloody shirt, then probed the wound. It seemed to have stopped bleeding.

He checked the room one last time, noticing something he'd missed on the mantle – the brown bottle. He emptied the pills on to the mound before dousing it all with what was left of the kerosene. Without hesitating, he scraped alight one of the matches from the Hot Chili Bordello and tossed it on the pile. There was a deep sound like something passing, fast and unseen. Their things were fully involved in seconds. The pills were the last to catch. They bubbled and spurted multicolored flames.

David retreated as far as the street. The fire moved through the house like a living creature, as if it possessed cunning and will of its own. A few times it looked set to blow itself out, only to blaze back to life, having found a second wind. After several minutes a car passed. The driver stopped, backed up, rolled down his window. He was an old man with sad, seen-it-all eyes.

'Your house?'

'No.'

'You call somebody?'

'Not yet,' David said.

'That's some cut you got yourself there, my friend.'

'It's worse than it looks.'

The man stared at him in confusion.

'Not as bad, I mean,' David corrected himself. 'Not as bad as it looks.'

'Well, guess I better go give the fire boys a holler,' the old man said, putting his car in gear and driving quickly away.

The fire burned on. David watched it until he heard a siren. Then he got in the Honda and drove the few miles to WBRR. One end of the 'Ten Days of Giving' sign had fallen over the doorway. He brushed it aside and stepped into the lobby. The clock said eleven forty-five. There was somebody on the desk he didn't know, a temp who looked warily at his blood-streaked face and disheveled clothes. Everyone else would be inside, frantically working the phones. Not just taking calls now but making them as well. Imploring. He took out the money he'd received for the stolen watch.

'What's this?' the temp asked when he handed it to her.

'A contribution.'

'Who's it from?'

'Nobody.'

She looked like she wanted to ask him something else but he was gone. He started to drive home but then caught a glimpse of his gashed face in the mirror. Though no longer bleeding, the wound was still open, its edges red and swollen, like a painted laughing mouth. It would need stitches, maybe more than a couple. So he detoured to County, hoping that Rowdy would be there, hoping he could get this taken care of quietly. He drove quickly, the Honda's new carburetor firing smoothly. The mechanic had done a good job. Mary Beth came on as he pulled into the parking lot, announcing that although a large anonymous donation had just been received they were still far short of their goal. The ten days of giving were over. There would be an announcement about the station's future later in the week, she said. As David closed down the motor her rasping voice died away, that word rattling through his mind, as if it were the only one she'd said. Anonymous. Anonymous. Anonymous.

EPILOGUE

The marker lay face down in the scorched grass. He locked his car and walked over to check if it was broken. But it was fine. Some vandal had torn it up, that was all. He wiped off the bits of dead grass covering his name, then used the sharp point to forge a new hole. The summer earth was baked solid, but he finally managed to bury it to the hilt. He gave the wood a brief shake, then stepped back and looked. It was even.

The building was quiet when he entered. He went straight to his office, keeping the lights off, intent on savoring the few moments of silence. But then he noticed the flashing light on his phone. Voice mail. There were two messages. The first was his wife. She must have called in the few minutes since he'd left home that morning. As he listened he absently ran a finger along the smooth, bone-white scar beside his right eye.

'Listen, hon, I forgot to tell you, they moved Lamaze to five tonight. Something about a meeting the midwife has to go to. So be sure you're there on time, all right? The other thing is about that gazebo. I think I want that Edwardian deal after all. Now, the guy said that if we . . .'

He hit the fast forward button, scrolling the tape to the end of the message, her voice garbled like the call of a flightless bird. Some salesmen had arrived, he could hear them ribbing one another by the coffee machine. He released the button to let the second message play. It was someone inquiring about Smoke Rise. He wrote down the details. When the message ended he checked his watch, then buzzed the sales director. The guy picked up on the first ring.

'Mark? It's me. Let's meet at ten. Tell the others, would you?'

'Could we make it eleven?' the salesman asked. 'I've got a lot on my plate.'

'Tell you what,' he said quietly. 'What do you say we go ahead and make it ten.'

On the way out to get his ritual cappuccino he stopped by the conference room, just to make sure everything was set for the meeting. Redwine was on his boat – this was going to be the first sales conference he ran solo. Everything was in place: the overhead projector, the charts, the stack of three-by-fives filled with leads that he would distribute among the salesmen like a bishop passing out dispensations. The model of Smoke Rise rested in the middle of the big oak table. He shot his cuffs as he stared down at it, his eyes following its familiar contours, its projected streets and buildings. Although there had been considerable shock that the city had decided to reopen Nowheresville so soon, no one was surprised when Redwine won the bidding to develop it. And though he would still maintain a vague overall control of the project, he'd wanted someone to oversee the nuts and bolts of its transformation into a private community. There was no doubt after the Elk Run publicity triumph who was his man. Who would come up with the name, hire the planners and architects, design the ad campaign that was now attracting so much attention. Oversubscription loomed. It was going to be a big success.

Satisfied that everything was set for the meeting, he headed across the street to the Bottomless Cup. It was a hot midsummer day, the air sultry and unmoving – for a moment he thought about skipping the cappuccino. But habits were habits. He moved quickly, anxious to get back to the office's air-conditioned cocoon. He'd taken several steps past the *Record*'s vending machine before the picture on its front page settled in his mind. He stopped abruptly, standing perfectly still on the sidewalk for a few seconds before walking back and feeding two quarters into the machine's pursed mouth. The paper was hot from the morning sun, as if it had been pulled fresh from an oven. He stared for a long time at the lead photo. It was a poor reproduction, the colors bled into each other and the figures were out of focus. And yet it still managed to look every bit as strange and beautiful as the first time he'd seen it. The multitude of trudging pilgrims, the serene mother and child, the wise men with their adoring stares. The fool off in the corner, oblivious to the miracle going on behind his back.

Cathy's story was short and simple. Will June's estate had finally been settled, carved up, sold off at a big auction in New York. And although many important items had changed hands, there was little doubt what the star of the show had been. Before a crowd of hundreds of dealers and experts and collectors, *The Adoration on the Shacktown Road*, by Thomas Apostle, by Sara, by whatever her name might really have been, had been sold for the highest price ever paid for an American Primitive.

The marker lay face down in the scorched grass. He locked his car and walked over to check if it was broken. But it was fine. Some vandal had torn it up, that was all. He wiped off the bits of dead grass covering his name, then used the sharp point to forge a new hole. The summer earth was baked solid, but he finally managed to bury it to the hilt. He gave the wood a brief shake, then stepped back and looked. It was even.

The building was quiet when he entered. He went straight to his office, keeping the lights off, intent on savoring the few moments of silence. But then he noticed the flashing light on his phone. Voice mail. There were two messages. The first was his wife. She must have called in the few minutes since he'd left home that morning. As he listened he absently ran a finger along the smooth, bone-white scar beside his right eye.

'Listen, hon, I forgot to tell you, they moved Lamaze to five tonight. Something about a meeting the midwife has to go to. So be sure you're there on time, all right? The other thing is about that gazebo. I think I want that Edwardian deal after all. Now, the guy said that if we . . . '

He hit the fast forward button, scrolling the tape to the end of the message, her voice garbled like the call of a flightless bird. Some salesmen had arrived, he could hear them ribbing one another by the coffee machine. He released the button to let the second message play. It was someone inquiring about Smoke Rise. He wrote down the details. When the message ended he checked his watch, then buzzed the sales director. The guy picked up on the first ring.

'Mark? It's me. Let's meet at ten. Tell the others, would you?'

'Could we make it eleven?' the salesman asked. 'I've got a lot on my plate.'

'Tell you what,' he said quietly. 'What do you say and make it ten.'

On the way out to get his ritual cappuccino he sto

conference room, just to make sure everything was set for the meeting. Redwine was on his boat – this was going to be the first sales conference he ran solo. Everything was in place: the overhead projector, the charts, the stack of three-by-fives filled with leads that he would distribute among the salesmen like a bishop passing out dispensations. The model of Smoke Rise rested in the middle of the big oak table. He shot his cuffs as he stared down at it, his eyes following its familiar contours, its projected streets and buildings. Although there had been considerable shock that the city had decided to reopen Nowheresville so soon, no one was surprised when Redwine won the bidding to develop it. And though he would still maintain a vague overall control of the project, he'd wanted someone to oversee the nuts and bolts of its transformation into a private community. There was no doubt after the Elk Run publicity triumph who was his man. Who would come up with the name, hire the planners and architects, design the ad campaign that was now attracting so much attention. Oversubscription loomed. It was going to be a big success.

Satisfied that everything was set for the meeting, he headed across the street to the Bottomless Cup. It was a hot midsummer day, the air sultry and unmoving – for a moment he thought about skipping the cappuccino. But habits were habits. He moved quickly, anxious to get back to the office's air-conditioned cocoon. He'd taken several steps past the *Record*'s vending machine before the picture on its front page settled in his mind. He stopped abruptly, standing perfectly still on the sidewalk for a few seconds before walking back and feeding two quarters into the machine's pursed mouth. The paper was hot from the morning sun, as if it had been pulled fresh from an oven. He stared for a long time at the lead photo. It was a poor reproduction, the colors bled into each other and the figures were out of focus. And yet it still managed to look every bit as strange and beautiful as the first time he'd seen it. The multitude of trudging pilgrims, the serene mother and child, the wise men with their adoring stares. The fool off in the corner, oblivious to the miracle going on behind his back.

Cathy's story was short and simple. Will June's estate had finally been settled, carved up, sold off at a big auction in New York. And although many important items had changed hands, there was little